Connection. The watch came alive. Maira couldn't help but breathe a sigh of relief. Not everyone could have done this. She had access to elements of the Network again.

A query scrolled onto the tablet screen: Authenticate Identity.

Maira held the watch up to her mouth. She was careful just to whisper: "Agent Maira Kanhai."

Processing, it said. Identity Verified.

The orange light went out. Maira froze. When the watch came back on, the glow had changed. Ruby red light washed across her face. There was no mistaking what it meant, but the text scrolled on anyway.

Agent Maira Kanhai, the tablet reported with a machine's lack of mercy. Status: Rogue.

It was too much. She was on her own, and she had no one to blame but herself.

TOM CLANCY'S THE DIVISION®

HUNTED

THOMAS PARROTT

First published by Aconyte Books in 2024
ISBN 978 1 83908 274 0
Ebook ISBN 978 1 83908 273 3

Cover art by René Aigner

Distributed in North America by Simon & Schuster Inc, New York, USA
Printed in the United States of America
9 8 7 6 5 4 3 2 1

ACONYTE BOOKS

An imprint of Asmodee Entertainment Ltd

Mercury House, Shipstones Business Centre

North Gate, Nottingham NG7 7FN, UK

aconytebooks.com // twitter.com/aconyteless

*For Gwen and Lauren, the best literary
midwives a book could ask for.*

CHAPTER 1
July 17

Maira Kanhai ran for her life.

The slap of her sneakers against the street seemed absurdly loud in the quiet night. She swerved and cut across a lawn. It had long since gone to weed. Her breath rasped in her chest. Each intake burned like fire. The dark silhouette of a fence rose ahead. She vaulted it without thinking.

Halfway over, her abdomen blared agony. The pain hit like a bolt of lightning. Maira's whole body seized up. She hit the ground on the other side in a heap. The world went white. She wheezed brokenly, fingers digging into tall grass and dirt. Only sheer force of will kept her from screaming in pain.

Get up, Maira, she told herself. Get up and move or die.

She put a shaking hand to her midsection. It came away dry. No red in the moonlight. Her gunshot wounds, only tenuously healed, had not torn open again. Small favors. Maira wiped snot from her face and forced herself up to her hands and knees. From there it was a wobbling lunge back to her feet.

She spotted a house close by. Maira limped over to it and rested her hand against the siding as she kept walking. She glanced over her shoulder. The smoke column from where the aircraft had come down was still visible, a darker black against the night sky. It blotted out stars as it rose. She felt like she'd been running forever, but the crash site was still so close.

She paused in the shadow of the house to try to catch her breath. She strained to hear anything nearby. There were only crickets. No sign of her pursuer. That was less comforting than it might have been. Maira hadn't seen it coming before the first attack either. That image was going to stay with her: the bulky shape looming out of the darkness, ax in hand. There was no humanity there. The mask saw to that.

Maira needed shelter, a chance to recover and make a plan. She was in no condition for a sustained chase. She slipped around to the front of the house as quietly as she could. A larger building sat across the dusty street. "Street" was actually a bit aspirational for this one. It was unpaved, and the collapse of civilization had not been kind to it. It was more of a rut through tall grass these days.

She paused at the front of the house and tried the door. Locked. There was no rusted remnant of a car in the driveway. Maira wondered what had happened to the people who lived here. Had they fled, seeking safety somewhere over the horizon? Had they found it? She shook her head to dash away the thoughts. She would never know, and right now it didn't matter.

A rock through a window would get her inside. It would also bring her pursuer hot on her trail. Despite the fact that she was a trained Division agent, she was up against odds she'd never faced before. She had confronted threats in the past two years that had terrified her at the time, but had always overcome them with quick thinking and capable allies. This time felt different. Regretfully, she turned away from the house. She crossed the old dirt road, low and fast. There was a letterboard out in front of the larger structure. MARYNEAL CHURCH OF CHRIST, the permanent text read. Below that were words missing letters, like a gap-toothed smile.

MA G D AVE ME CY ON U ALL

Maira touched gentle fingertips to the words as she walked past. During the horrors of the Green Poison pandemic, they had been on the lips of billions. She had been raised in a different faith entirely, and she didn't know what she believed anymore. She knew the heartfelt desperation behind that silent cry, though. Different words, perhaps, but always the same terror and sorrow.

Maira paused at the double doors leading into the building and glanced over her shoulder again. A slight breeze rustled the grasses. That was all there was, she told herself. No cold eyes watching her. The skin between her shoulder blades itched in anticipation of a sniper's bullet. These doors gave way at a push, with only a squeak of unhappy hinges. She glanced back one last time and hurried inside.

It was dark within, the air stale and hot. What little light eked in through the stained-glass windows picked out the silhouette of pews. The rows marched up to the front of the church and the podium there, a door on either side leading into the back of the building. Dust lay in heavy layers on every surface. Maira pulled a bandana from her backpack and tied it over her nose and mouth. A cough at the wrong time was the last thing she needed.

A skeleton lay sideways in the front pew, arms still wrapped about itself. It was surrounded by the stains of decay's byproducts, marking the wood and floor alike. Such sights were commonplace. There had been no one to clean up the "mess" the plague had created. Victims rotted where they fell. The small favor was that now it had been so long the most distressing sights and smells were in the past.

Maira walked past the remains to the door on the left. It was locked, the knob rattling in her hand. She bit back a curse and hurried to try its counterpart on the right. That one turned, and she pushed the door open. Beyond lay pitch black. There were no windows in the room to let in even the pale light of the moon.

"ISAC–" Maira started.

She snorted at herself. ISAC wasn't there. She hadn't been connected to the SHD Network for months now. Exhaustion was making her fall back on old habits. There was no supertech at her disposal right now. She was going to have to solve this herself, with the limited resources that she had at hand.

First things first. She glanced at the stained-glass

windows again. Striking up any kind of light in here was going to be a dead giveaway for those trying to find her. She had to find someplace safe to hide fast. Her body was battered to the brink, and adrenaline had carried her this far but would soon give out. Reluctantly, she stepped blindly through the doorway into the darkness beyond. She shut the door behind her, plunging herself into absolute darkness.

Maira took a few seconds to acclimate. There's nothing dangerous here, she told herself. You're fine. You're going to be OK. Her breathing slowed, steadied. She made a mental list of the items that she had with her. It wasn't much. This wasn't exactly an adventure she had planned and prepared for.

Her handheld. Had she left it behind or – no. It was there in her pocket, a solid weight. She pulled it out carefully. Dropping it and losing it in the darkness would be a) disastrous and b) entirely within her idiom. Better to just stay calm and move smoothly. Once it was in her hand, she thumbed the power switch.

The screen lit up. It was still set to the game she'd been playing the day before. The intro music, a cheerful jingle, started up. Maira's heart lurched into her throat. Fumblingly, she turned the sound down as fast as she could. Silence reigned again. She froze, listening intently. Nothing. There was nothing. No one had heard that. It was OK.

Maira turned the glowing screen to the room she was in. Metal and white linoleum. It took her a few seconds to parse what she was seeing in the minimal light. This was a kitchen. The only windows had been boarded over. She could imagine the kind of functions it had once hosted. Bake sales, weddings, all those little country church functions. There was another door to the back of the room. To judge by the glint at the bottom, it led directly outside.

She walked over and made sure it was locked, then sat down with her back against the kitchen counter. She set the handheld down beside her so that the light shone upward. Weariness surged up in her, all-encompassing. All Maira wanted to do was stretch out on the cold tile and let sleep claim her. She shoved it away by force of will. There was one more thing she had to do before she could rest.

Maira pulled the watch out of her vest pocket. It was broken, to all appearances. A crack ran up the face, and blood stained the wristband. She had snatched it off the harness the masked killer had been wearing. It hadn't been the only one there; there must have been half a dozen, some still glowing in shades of red and orange. Some kind of sick trophy display.

The watch presented a challenge. Maira didn't have a brick or contact, of course, but the watch had certain minimal onboard functions of its own. She had a multitool with her. That was just who she was. Maira never went anywhere without something of the sort. She had her thumb drive – it was on the necklace she wore, same as always. Crucially, she also had her tablet in her backpack. The question was, would all of that be enough?

Maira set to work. Prying open a top secret government-issue watch was daunting for some people, but she had been born with the urge to fidget. During her time with the Division, she had taken the time to familiarize herself with the inner workings of their gear in a way that few agents bothered with. Luckily, it wasn't really destroyed. These things had been made to survive a lot. Parts had come loose inside, but they just needed to be reconnected properly.

It came back to life with a gleam of orange light. Dull – it wasn't properly connecting to the Network – but it was there. It was enough. She stuck her tongue out in concentration as she interfaced the watch with the tablet. It wasn't a perfect replacement, but with just the right amount of know-how it could substitute for a brick. And as close as they were to the Core, there should be…

Connection. The dull light brightened. The watch came alive. Maira couldn't help but breathe a sigh of relief. She took a moment to pat herself on the back. Not everyone could have done this. She had access to elements of the Network again. It was a big step up from a few minutes ago.

A query scrolled onto the tablet screen: Authenticate Identity.

Maira held the watch up to her mouth. She was careful just to whisper: "Agent Maira Kanhai."

Processing, it said.

Identity Verified.

The orange light went out. Maira froze. When the watch came back on, the glow had changed. Ruby red light washed across her face. There was no mistaking what it meant, but the text scrolled on anyway.

Agent Maira Kanhai, the tablet reported with a machine's lack of mercy. Status: Rogue.

It was too much. It was exactly what she had feared. Maira pressed a hand to her mouth to stifle the sound of an unwilling sob. There really was no one else to turn to. She was on her own, and she had no one to blame but herself.

She lowered her forehead to rest against her knees and struggled not to cry in the ruddy light of the cracked watch.

CHAPTER 2
August 2

Agent Brenda Wells crouched in the lee of a burned-out building. This was the tiny unincorporated town that lay nearest the Core. The Kansas sun burned hot overhead, and the summer heat had her sweating like crazy. She cradled her Honey Badger in one arm while she pulled out her canteen with the other hand and took a long swig of water. She indulged herself by drizzling a few drops onto her face before returning the container to its cradle.

"I see them," Agent Miller said over the comms. He was up on top of one of the other buildings nearby, acting as their spotter.

"How far out?" Brenda asked.

"Maybe two klicks. They're coming in fast," Miller observed.

"Is it what we expected?" Brenda asked.

There was a pause. "More. I'm counting three upgunned semis and five technicals."

"Well, that's great," Brenda said wearily. "They got reinforcements."

"Change of plans?" asked Teresa from across the road.

Brenda wiped sweat from her face and debated internally. She had six agents. For the Division, that was a tremendous presence. Three cells had contributed members to this action. For that very reason, however, they were a resource to be shepherded. The Division had already taken too many losses over the past few years. They were being bled dry, and she couldn't afford to waste any lives today.

They could fall back. In theory, the emplaced defenses closer to the Core would provide much-needed support and shelter. Unfortunately, those same defenses were still being repaired from a similar attack the week before. If they let the enemy get that far, the fortifications might suffer damage that they couldn't fix.

Then there would be nothing to stop the next group to decide to come and kill or be killed in a Kansas cornfield.

Brenda ran through all of this in a matter of seconds. Her jaw ached from clenched tension. "We stick to the original plan. Just make sure you all bring your A game for this. This is not the time for dumb antics or being heroes. We hit them hard and fast, and we go home. Got it?"

A chorus of assent came back on the comms. Brenda checked the load on her Honey Badger one last time. The magazine was seated firmly, one round in the chamber. She glanced down at her feet. One ended in a combat boot, the other a sprinting blade. Her left leg was a prosthetic from the knee down. If people knew she checked that her shoes were tied and her leg was still attached before every firefight, they'd probably think she was silly. One time she'd watched a man run right out of his untied shoes, trip, and get shot three times before he could get back up. So now she always made sure, just in case.

"Fifteen seconds out," Miller said.

"ISAC, silent count it out for me," Brenda said.

A fifteen second timer helpfully popped up in the corner of her vision and began to tick down. Brenda fished a cell phone out of her pocket. It was the very definition of "nothing fancy" – in fact, it was a flip phone. For today, however, she didn't need fancy. She flipped it open. There was a single number programmed in.

Brenda could hear the roar of the oncoming trucks now. Sticking her head out would be a great way to ruin the ambush, but she didn't need to. It was easy to picture them. The weaponized semitrucks of the Roamers were twenty tons of steel and rubber, covered in jury-rigged armor and guns. As the would-be trucker warlords of the northern routes, these vehicles were their signature equipment. They had a way of staying in your memory. She focused on breathing calmly, steadily.

The countdown hit zero. Brenda hit the call button.

The rippling thunderclaps of sequential high explosive detonations washed over the area. Hard on its heels came clouds of dust flooding down the street. Brenda's call had set off bombs planted all along the sides of the road the

Roamers were coming down. No fancy SHD tech this time – that was becoming increasingly scarce, too precious to waste when plastique and a pipe full of nails would do the trick.

Brenda pulled her mask up over her mouth and nose. "Move! Hit them now!" she barked into the comms.

Brenda came around the corner with her rifle held ready. The blasts had turned the world into a gray nightmare of swirling grit and burning vehicles. Chunks of the walls all around had been gouged by the payload of the pipe bombs. A flaming semi careened off the road and smashed into a ruined building. Blood painted the inside of the perforated cabin.

The door came open, and a man staggered out clutching a pistol. Brenda put a controlled burst of three rounds into his chest before his feet touched the ground. He flopped to the ground in a boneless heap. A flash of orange at the corner of her eye – ISAC warning her of another figure stumbling through the murk. She cut him down with a sweep of fire. He fell, screaming. A quick blast to the head silenced him.

To their foes, the world must have gone insane in an instant. A wave of hot iron had shredded them from both sides, tearing flesh and peeling metal. Within seconds more of them were dead to a barrage of precise gunfire. In the gray fog and chaos, how could they even start to fight back? They couldn't even see the Division agents to try to return fire.

It was the product of layered advantages. An ambush allowed the agents to choose and shape their battlefield.

Overhead, Miller watched with a sniper rifle and an infrared camera. It picked out the warm bodies of the Roamer gunmen from the chaos. That information was fed into ISAC, and ISAC triangulated each target and fed telemetry to every other agent involved in the battle.

The Roamers couldn't see Brenda and her allies. It didn't matter if Brenda couldn't see them either – ISAC told her exactly where to shoot, carving humanoid shapes from the fog with glowing orange pixels. The Roamers were firing in a panic now, shooting in all directions blindly. Brenda ducked into the shadow of a shattered truck for cover.

"Threat detected," ISAC commented in his monotone way. "Hostile vehicular mounted weapon."

There was a .50 machine gun mounted on the back of one of the technicals. One of the Roamers climbed up behind it. They swung it into action, screaming in terror and rage. The rolling thunder of the weapon pounded the air. Blind-fired rounds hissed through the murk like angry hornets. One of the gunman's allies was in the wrong place at the wrong time. She came apart in a spray of blood, chewed to pieces by friendly fire. The gunner didn't even notice, continuing to sweep the battlefield with death.

"Agent down," ISAC said. "Immediate medical assistance needed."

Brenda cursed sharply. She pulled a grenade from her harness and eyeballed the distance to the .50 with a practiced glance. The pin came loose with a flick of her thumb, and she stood up and lobbed the device in a single motion. In a blink she was back down again with her back to the cover, coiled tight. The grenade sailed in a lazy arc and slapped the Roamer in the chest. He had the presence of mind to look down and freeze.

The bed of the technical dissolved into a fireball, and both gun and gunner ceased to exist. Silence settled over the battlefield. Her ears were still ringing. She shook her head with a frown. She was going to be deaf by fifty at this rate. Brenda came to her feet unsteadily, her rifle still tucked into her shoulder. There was nothing. All remaining hostiles had been eliminated.

ISAC marked the fallen agent on her vision. She jogged in that direction, her breathing loud in the confines of the mask. The blade of her prosthetic clicked against the ground as she went. Two of the others had reached him by the time she got there. It was Lloyd. One of those blind .50 rounds had caught him right in the midsection. It had blown through his body armor like it wasn't there. He was lying in a spreading pool of his own blood.

Teresa was desperately trying to bandage the front wound, while Constantin had his hands clamped to the exit. Blood pulsed between his fingers despite the pressure. Brenda dropped to her knees next to Lloyd. He reached out and caught her hand. His grip was wet with his own blood. Brenda held tight anyway.

Teresa was on the comms. "We need medevac now, we have an agent down!"

Lloyd was trying to say something. It was coming out choked with blood, spattering the inside of his mask. Brenda pulled it away with a free hand, wiped his lips. It didn't do any good, just smeared the gore across his skin. She leaned in closer, trying to make out what he was saying. His hand tightened on hers, his nails digging into the skin on the back of her hand.

"I've got you, Lloyd. Hold on. You're OK, you're—" Brenda said.

The grip relaxed.

"Agent vital signs zero," ISAC said. "Agent deceased."

Brenda scrubbed her hands furiously. Red sluiced down the sink drain. It came away in flaky layers. Steam rose in billowing clouds. She had turned it hot – that was the only way to really get blood off in her experience. Maybe it was too hot. The heat felt like it was cooking her hands. She pulled them from the stream of water and gripped the sides of the sink. The mirror in front of her had fogged up. It turned her face to a misty silhouette.

They had brought Lloyd's body back to the Core. He'd be buried at some point.

"Small favors," she said to her obscured reflection. "There's no next of kin to have to write a letter to. Thanks, Green Poison."

Her voice seemed loud in the confines of the bathroom. For a moment, she wondered if anyone could have heard her. Brenda couldn't really bring herself to care. It might not have been the most appropriate sentiment, but who was really going to take her to task for that? Dark humor was a painfully common coping mechanism here at civilization's wake.

One agent's life in exchange for the complete destruction of a hostile convoy. It was a victory by any measure. A stinging rebuke of the Roamers for thinking they could take down the Kansas Core on their own. It was nice to imagine that it would stop there. It wouldn't.

For one thing, the Roamers weren't the only ones who had tried. The Division had no shortage of enemies. Militias, raiders, and petty warlords from sea to shining sea wanted to see them brought down. Stripped of their advantage of secrecy by the actions of the rogue agent Rowan O'Shea, those foes finally had a clear target. They seemed eager to line up for their shot at making the Division bleed.

And they were bleeding. Weapons, technology, and warm bodies to use both. The Division was a lot of things, but it had never been intended as an army. It had never been meant to fight a sustained war. The various hostile factions arrayed against them might have wanted the dramatic victory of wresting the Core away from its protectors, but the attrition was what was really hurting them.

Sooner or later, something was going to have to give.

"Communication request received," ISAC said in her ear.

Brenda raised an eyebrow. That was unusual. If any of the local agents had wanted to talk to her, she would have expected them to come and find her face-to-face. She shut off the water in the sink, absently surprised she had let it run while her thoughts got away from her. That was wasteful. Clean water was a resource more precious than most.

"Patch it through, ISAC," Brenda said.

"Brenda! Can you hear me?"

The voice was a woman's, marred by some static. That wasn't surprising. Infrastructure across the country continued to decay via neglect, and communications was no exception. It took Brenda a few seconds to place it. When she did, a genuine smile touched her lips.

"Agent Heather Ward, as I live and breathe. I'm reading you loud and clear. It's good to hear from you."

"Likewise!" The other woman sounded relieved. "Word is you've been hard pressed at the Kansas Core lately."

Brenda's smile died. "It hasn't been a cakewalk, I'll tell you that much. I don't suppose you want to come and help out? Or maybe take over completely? You know if the Cores fall, that's the end of all that fancy SHD tech we all love to use, right?"

"I wish I could," Heather said. There was a pause. "No, that was a lie. I don't want anything to do with that mess. But I do wish I could help you. I'm afraid that's not why I'm contacting you though."

"I'm going to guess this isn't a social call either," Brenda said wryly. "Where are you at these days? What's the situation?"

"In all honesty? Not that different from yours. I'm down at the Core in Texas. Did you hear about the attack we suffered two weeks ago?"

Brenda frowned. "I did. I'd hoped the other two Cores would be able to preserve their own secrecy for longer, but I guess that was foolish. Too many rogues, too many leaks. I don't know how I can help, though. We're stretched thin."

Heather didn't respond. There were a few seconds of uncomfortable silence.

"You didn't call me for help either, did you?" Brenda said.

"No," Heather admitted. "Look, Brenda. I have some information for you. You're not going to like it."

Brenda narrowed her eyes. "Information about what?" The silence stretched even longer this time. "Spit it out, Heather. I recruited you. I know your background. Don't tell me you've forgotten how to communicate now."

Heather gave a mirthless laugh. "No. This just isn't easy. I want you to understand, I only went along with not telling you in the first place because I thought it was what was best for you."

Brenda did not bother to hide the chill creeping into her voice. "I've always considered myself the best judge of what is good for me."

"You're probably right," Heather said regretfully. "And regardless, the situation has spun out of control. You need to be in the loop. That's why I'm talking to you here and now."

"So tell me, then."

"All right." Heather took a deep breath. "It's about Maira Kanhai."

Autumn. Alexandria, VA

Brenda pulled up to the house at the end of the street. She checked the address. Yes, this was the right place. She got out and removed her sunglasses, tucking them into her shirt pocket. Some of the recruiters liked to wear full suits when they were out in the world, claiming it put forward a professional air, but Brenda found that tactic stifling. The people they were after were nonconformists by nature, so why would they be impressed by a three piece? She satisfied the bare minimum of professionalism with a blouse and some elegant khakis.

The house was nice. Middle class cozy. The kind of place for people who were comfortable but not rich. Brenda preferred this kind of life anyway. McMansions were garish to her eyes. A nice little place, tucked away from prying eyes. That was where it was at.

A minivan was parked in the driveway, a nice silver color, recently washed. It wasn't new but it wasn't rundown either. Walking on by it, she briefly took a look inside and saw a booster seat in the back. It wasn't hard to put the facts together with the tricycle in the yard: these people had a kid. Brenda tucked that knowledge away. Sometimes it helped the pitch, sometimes it hurt it. It depended on a dozen other factors, really.

She took the stairs in three bounds and knocked on the front door, a quick rapping of knuckles. The mat out front said "Beware of Guard Cat." Brenda smiled and made sure to wipe her feet.

The door opened to reveal a woman in her early thirties. She had her red hair plaited into a thick braid, and brilliant green eyes. She wore overalls and a green short-sleeved shirt. She was short, easily a head shorter than Brenda herself, but Brenda could see the cords of muscle on her arms. This was not someone who simply "stayed fit." This was someone who maintained peak physical condition as a carefully cultivated habit.

"Can I help you?" the woman asked brightly.

"I hope so," Brenda said with her best winning grin. "I'm Brenda Wells. We spoke on the phone?"

The woman cuffed herself on the forehead. "Of course! Ms Wells! I'm so sorry, I'm on kid-wrangling duty today, so my brain is scrambled like an egg."

"No problem at all. I could come back another day if you like?"

"No, no, that won't be necessary at all! Please, come in."

Brenda followed the woman into her house. The insides lined up perfectly with the exterior. Nice furniture, but not fancy. Not new, but well-kept. Some pieces that looked like antiques, no doubt passed down from other family members. This family took time to take care of their belongings, either from financial necessity or from intentional practice.

"That's a lovely clock," Brenda said, motioning to a grandfather piece that sat at the end of the hallway.

"Oh, thank you! I restored it myself," the woman said. "Someone sold it for so cheap at a yard sale, and it was in bad shape, but it's amazing what you can do with a little hands-on time."

Handy, Brenda noted mentally. That was good.

The woman led her into the living room. She sat down on the couch and motioned Brenda to a recliner across from her.

"Can I get you something to drink?"

"Oh, no," Brenda said. "That won't be necessary. Thank you, though."

"No problem. If you change your mind, just let me know." The red-haired woman smiled. "So, I'm Rowan. Rowan O'Shea. Same gal you spoke on the phone with. I suppose you already know that, though."

Brenda smiled. "I do, though a little confirmation never hurts. I'd actually love to run through the high notes of your background, too, if you don't mind."

"Certainly," Rowan said. "I guess you have to start with the Army. I enlisted when I was eighteen, and I did two four-year contracts."

"One of those you were accepted into the Green Berets, is that correct?"

Rowan nodded with a chuckle. "You did your homework. Yes, I went to Q Course when I was twenty-one. That's when I signed my re-enlistment to meet the time requirements."

"What did you think of your time with Special Operations?" asked Brenda.

Rowan hmmed. "I can't talk about a lot of it, of course…"

"Of course," Brenda agreed, solemn.

"But I found it rewarding in the sense that it was incredibly challenging. It forced me to grow and learn. All the same, it wasn't where I wanted to spend the rest of my life. I exited the service after that, and I went to school. Well, I had started taking classes while I was in the service, but I resolved to pursue a doctorate."

"And completed that by the age of thirty-two? That's quite the accomplishment."

Rowan smiled. "That's correct. I graduated just last year. I was very proud of that."

"As you should be," Brenda said. "A degree in epidemiology, from the prestigious John Hopkins University, no less. You've led an accomplished life, Ms O'Shea."

"Rowan, please." She shrugged and sat back a bit. "I'm not given to false modesty. I am pleased with what I've done with my time. But I see it as the beginning, not the end."

"Mama!" a young voice called.

"In here, honey! I'm meeting with someone," Rowan called.

A little girl, probably around five if Brenda was any gauge, came running in. She saw Brenda and immediately attached herself to her mother's leg with a bashful look.

"This is Anara," Rowan said. The love in her voice was clear as she caressed her daughter's head. "Can you say hello to Ms Wells?"

"Hello," mumbled the kid.

Brenda grinned. "Nice to meet you, Anara."

"All right, honey, go to your room and play for a bit, OK? We'll have lunch after," Rowan said.

The child toddled off, pausing briefly for another glance at Brenda before disappearing into another room.

Rowan raised her eyes back to Brenda's. "So, you're here to sell me on signing up all over again, right?"

Brenda laughed. "Something like that. I'm not here to get you back into the service, if that's what you assumed."

"Well, that's some comfort," Rowan said dryly. "But I'm not eager to leave my family for any opportunity, so you may end up disappointed, regardless."

"That's the beauty of the offer, Rowan," Brenda said. "The group I represent aren't deploying to the other side of the world for months at a time. In fact, if you leave home at all, at most it will be for a week or so to pursue a training opportunity. And even then, that will be at your discretion."

"Training at my discretion?" asked Rowan with a raised eyebrow.

"We have the luxury of recruiting the best. You already come with an impressive skillset. I'm not going to waste your time demanding you gild the lily."

"OK, so I can train only when I want, and I won't be going to the other side of the world for months at a time. So what do I have to do?" asked Rowan, the skepticism clear in her voice.

"Odds are? Nothing. This group will only be activated under the most extreme circumstances. The most likely outcome is you will spend your whole life doing whatever you see fit, and never be called upon at all."

"Interesting," Rowan mused. "What are the criteria for being activated?"

"Nothing less than a threat to life as we know it," Brenda said. "We are a group dedicated to the preservation of society in the face of the unthinkable."

Rowan tilted her head. "That sounds like it would be a bad time to be called away for work." She looked toward the hallway where her daughter had gone.

"I suppose that's one way to look at it," Brenda allowed. "The other is, if it really comes down to it? If the call really does go out? Then that's a threat that no one will be able to ignore. Do you really want to leave it up to other people to deal with that kind of danger, or do you want to be out there, saving the day and making sure the problem never reaches your family in the first place?"

"Hm," Rowan said thoughtfully. She pulled at her lip a few times with her free hand. "That's a very interesting pitch. And this all does sound… challenging. What is this organization of yours called, Brenda?"

Brenda smiled. "Most of the time, we just call it the Division."

Brenda stormed into the command center at the bottom level of the Kansas Core. The air was always uncomfortably warm down here, the product of too many computers in a space that wasn't ventilated quite well enough. Screens shone all around her, manned by the technicians doing their best to keep the information technology underpinning the Division up and running. Heads turned in her direction as she entered. She wasn't surprised. She knew she was carrying a storm cloud as she went.

"Can we help you, Agent Wells?" one of the technicians asked uneasily. It was the senior analyst on post. He was known for a comfortingly monotone voice, a relief to hear on the radio in high stakes situations.

"I want a communications link established with Agent Thaddeus Greene. Immediately. Highest priority."

The technician blinked. "That could be difficult to do. A number of agents operate outside of easy comms reach these days. It's a matter of–"

"He's near the Texas Core. It should be doable," Brenda cut off the explanation sharply.

The technician cleared his throat. "Ah. Well. Yes, that could help. It may still take some time. If you'd like, I could send you–"

"I'll wait," Brenda said tightly.

This room was not a place of happy memories. This was where the final confrontation with Rowan O'Shea had taken place. It had come down to just Brenda and Maira against the rogue agent, with the security of the whole Division on the line. That showdown had cost Brenda the lower half of her left leg, but Maira had seen the matter through and earned her watch that day.

News of Maira's death down in Texas had hit Brenda hard. She had been fond of the younger woman. Brenda had never taken the time to make a family of her own. In some ways, connections with people like Maira had made up for that. She had been Brenda's trial run in a way to save the Division in the long term, to recruit outsiders into their ranks and keep the good fight going. But by the end, Maira had meant more to her than that. She had been family.

To find out now she had not been dead after all had not put a smile on Brenda's face. Primarily because she was finding out two weeks too late.

"Ah, Agent Wells?" asked the technician.

"Yes?"

"We have Agent Greene, as you requested."

"Very well," Brenda said. "Patch him through to me."

"This is Agent Greene," came a steady bass voice.

"How dare you, you son of a bitch?" Brenda demanded.

Silence hung. Technicians did their best to look anywhere except in Brenda's direction.

"Ah. Agent Brenda Wells. I take it that someone couldn't keep their mouth shut."

"You had no right to ask them to," Brenda retorted sharply. "I should have been alerted the moment that you realized Maira was present during the attack."

"Why?"

The question came simple and cold. Brenda narrowed her eyes. She was not a person given to explosions of temper, but she could feel the heat of anger with every pounding beat of her heart. She reached up and touched her temple, then took a deep breath. Calm. Controlled. She controlled her emotions, they did not control her.

"Because I trained her. I brought her into the Division. For God's sake, Greene, I thought she was dead. Obviously, her status is of concern to me," Brenda said.

"Yes, we all knew it would 'concern' you. What I want to know is, what would bringing this to you have accomplished?"

Brenda frowned. "Perhaps if I had been able to speak to her–"

"No one spoke to her," Greene interrupted. "At least, no one left alive. Maira was present for an assault on a Division Core. I want to be clear – she was on the wrong side and may have played a role in sabotaging its defenses."

"If she really has turned on the Division, then someone needs to bring her in," Brenda said.

"Two agents made contact with Maira following the assault being repulsed. Neither survived the encounter," Greene said flatly.

"You're suggesting Maira killed them?" Brenda asked disbelievingly.

"Is that so hard to imagine? She's fully capable of taking lives, is she not?" Greene asked.

"There are no pacifists in the Division," Brenda retorted sharply. "That doesn't make her a murderer or a traitor."

"No. But it is a familiar pattern, isn't it, Agent Wells? One of your prized pupils going rogue, cutting down the agents sent to bring them in, disappearing off the radar. It's not the first time we've seen that, is it?"

Some ungodly mixture of shame and anger burned Brenda's cheeks. "Maira is not Rowan. The situation is not the same."

"She hasn't come back in from the cold, has she? She could turn herself in at any time, and we could sort all of this out. Instead, she has gone fully on the run."

Not everyone who runs is guilty, Brenda wanted to say. Sometimes they're just scared they won't get a fair shake. And it was the kind of people who said "if you haven't done anything wrong, you have nothing to be afraid of" that you had to avoid the most carefully. None of that was tactful, though. She had to try to remain diplomatic.

"All right," Brenda said. "So, what's your plan to bring her in then?"

"There isn't one," Greene replied dismissively. "Perhaps you have forgotten, Agent Wells, but the world is on fire. The Division has a hundred problems screaming for attention, and one rogue agent doesn't even make the list."

"What?" Brenda asked.

"Like I said, she's gone on the run. Our tracking reports show her headed west. That means she's not an immediate threat. That's enough for now," Greene said.

"Someone has to go after her," Brenda said.

"Why? Because she is important to you? That's not a good enough reason, Wells, and it's exactly the reason we withheld the information from you. You're too close to this matter."

He wasn't wrong. That was the worst part. Brenda knew that he had a point, and she resented that tremendously. Her hands had tightened into fists. She glanced down and forced them to relax. She made herself take another deep breath.

"If no one else can do it, or wants to do it, then I'm going after her," Brenda said.

"There are more important things going on, Wells. Are you going to give up defending the Kansas Core to go on a wild goose chase?"

"That's not up to you, Agent Greene, and I don't owe you any answers. Division agents choose their own missions." Brenda waited just long enough for him to start to speak again, then sharply cut him off. "That being said, you've under-prioritized Agent Kanhai. You realize she is one of the foremost living experts on the SHD Network?"

There was a pause. "I'm aware of certain assessments to that effect. It was brought up in trying to decide how the Core's defenses were sabotaged during the attack."

"And you consider it wise to let someone who can compromise the defenses of an entire SHD Core run free in the world? While we know two of said Cores are hostile targets?"

Rather than answer this directly, Greene replied, "It's wasteful for you to go. You're a valuable asset to the Division. She's already killed two of us, Wells."

"I don't plan to go alone," Brenda replied flatly.

"You can't leave the Kansas Core defenseless."

"I couldn't make anyone come with me in the first place, Greene. For the same reason you can't order me around." Brenda crossed her arms. "Don't worry, though. I know exactly who I need to come with me, and they're not in Kansas."

"Who–"

"Cut the link," Brenda said to the technicians. There was a certain petty satisfaction to it, she had to admit.

"Communications link severed," the tech said uneasily. "Is there anything else, agent?"

"Yeah." Brenda favored them with her most winning smile. "I need transportation to Houston, Texas."

CHAPTER 3
June 3

The exercise mat under Maira smelled like a new car. It was an inane thought, but she held on to it, nonetheless. It was vastly preferable, after all, to focusing on the fact that her torso was currently a howling wellspring of pain. Sweat beaded up on her forehead and streaked down her face. She had her hands placed just above her hips, fingers against her stomach. She could feel her abdominal muscles struggling, twitching.

"And release," Keith said.

Maira let the tummy tuck go with a whimper.

"That must have been what, an hour?" she whispered hoarsely.

"Close!" Keith said encouragingly. "Six seconds, actually."

Maira gave him a flat look. "Six seconds is not close to an hour, and you know it."

"You did ten whole reps, Maira. That's good work no

matter how you slice it. Didn't you ever learn your Einstein? Everything is relative."

Her whole body shook from the effort, too. It was wild to think that little movements like this could demand so much from her. Before the mission to the Gulf Coast, Maira had been in the best physical condition of her life. A couple bullets to the abdomen had taken that away from her in the blink of an eye. It was frustrating. She knew she was lucky to be alive, but that didn't make it easy.

"I'm relatively exhausted, I know that much. What's next on the agenda, Keith?" Maira asked.

He picked up her chart. "Flex," he corrected absently.

Keith was the physical therapist who had been handling her recovery. Everyone around here actually called him "Flex," but Maira couldn't bring herself to. Certainly, he had the physique to make sense of it. The man looked like he could lift a Buick if he wanted to. He had obvious muscles Maira hadn't even known existed before she met him. So, no question where he'd gotten the name.

It was the insistence that people use it that was odd to her. It wasn't just him. Everyone here insisted on going by their nickname for some reason. Different strokes for different folks, she guessed, but it just seemed silly to her. It felt a little cult-y to Maira if she was honest. Like these people had their old identities taken away from them. They were all perfectly nice to her, though. It seemed rude to make too big an issue of it.

"All right, we've got ten pelvic tilts to get through before I let you go for lunch. Same thing as before, we're going to shoot for six seconds apiece, OK? But I need you to tell me if you reach your limit…"

Maira felt like a wrung-out washcloth by the time it was all said and done. Keith gently helped her into her wheelchair. She accepted the return to the conveyance with grim irritation. It was an inescapable part of her recovery process, but that didn't mean she had to like it. She felt so limited. They told her she had every chance to make a full recovery, but there were times when that seemed impossible.

"I'll see you back here after lunch," Keith said. "We'll get through the rest of these exercises."

"I get it," Maira noted abruptly.

"Oh? What do you get?" Keith asked.

"See, all this time I thought they call you Flex because you are swole with the gains of the iron," Maira said.

Keith tilted his head wryly. "I see. And you no longer believe that?"

"Not a bit. I've realized it's because you're morally flexible. You're willing to torture poor little agents who have never done you any wrong."

"It's not much but it's a living," Keith replied dryly. "I'll see you after lunch, Agent Kanhai."

Maira sighed. "Yeah, after lunch, you incorrigible monster."

She wheeled herself toward the door. The physical therapy area was fully equipped. Treadmills, support beams, exercise balls, the works. She had never seen anyone else using any of it, though. Their sessions were always completely solo. That was probably a blessing. Maira didn't necessarily want an audience for her miserable huffing and puffing. It was still oddly lonely though.

To her surprise, however, today someone was waiting in the doorway. Maira had no idea how long they'd been there. It was a woman in a white suit. It took Maira a moment to realize that she was, for lack of a better word, utterly gorgeous. Blonde hair perfectly coiffed into a bob cut. Blue-gray eyes. The kind of makeup that people mistook for no makeup, the "natural look" that was anything but. Even her outfit was immaculate, spotless, and perfectly tailored to her trim form.

Maira, covered in cooling sweat, had never felt quite so plain in her entire life. She had the sudden urge to try to hide her burn scars. She shoved the thought away. It was silly, and worse, there was no point. Her accruing collection of scars was only becoming more impossible to hide as time went by.

The woman smiled then, displaying perfect white teeth. "You were really putting in the hard work out there."

Maira flushed and shrugged. "Oh yeah, really knocking the 'bare minimum of human movement' out of the park." There was something familiar about her voice, but Maira couldn't place it.

"Don't sell yourself short, Agent Kanhai. I've seen my fair share of people get hurt. A lot of people don't give their recovery half the effort I saw out of you today."

"Well, thank you," Maira managed. "You seem to have me at something of a disadvantage, Ms…?"

"Of course, where are my manners? Sokolova. Natalya Sokolova. Please forgive me, I've been waiting for some time now to get to meet you. It's easy to forget that it's been one-sided."

Maira furrowed her brow. That name. She knew that name. "Wait, *the* Natalya Sokolova? The one from all the broadcasts? Aren't you a politician or something?"

"A politician?" Natalya laughed at that. "Oh, don't damn me so quickly. I'm a businesswoman, Agent Kanhai."

"What sort of—"

Natalya held up a perfectly manicured hand, cutting her off. "I want to talk to you, but why don't you save your questions for somewhere a little more comfortable than this doorway? It's your lunchtime, right?"

Maira nodded. "I was just about to head to the cafeteria."

"What do you think of the food?" asked Natalya curiously.

"It's not bad," Maira said. "Actually, if I'm being honest, it's the best I've eaten since the Poison. I have no idea where you folks get all the good stuff from."

"Oh, here and there," Natalya said breezily. "The benefits of foresight, you might say. Part of it is the supply lines, but the other is making sure you have the right people to use what you've put together. Good ingredients are wasted without a proper chef. Then of course, there's what an excellent chef could do. Why don't I show you? Come have lunch with me today instead."

Maira blinked. Lunch? With this gorgeous woman? "That's a very kind offer, and ordinarily I would love to take you up on it, but …" She glanced back at Keith. "I only have so long for lunch."

"Oh, that won't be a problem, will it, Flex?" Natalya asked smoothly.

The physical therapist had stepped aside to let them talk, focusing on putting away some equipment that was no longer needed. Hearing his name, however, he stepped back over. His attitude was carefully deferential.

"Of course not, Ms Sokolova. Take as much time as you like," Keith responded.

"Right," Maira said. She was irritated with herself that the word came out as something of a squeak. "Well, lead the way then, please."

"May I help you?" Natalya asked, putting her hand on the wheelchair, as if intending to push Maira. "I understand you must be in terrible pain."

Warmth spread throughout Maira's chest. "Thanks, but I've got it."

They set off through the complex, with Maira wheeling along in Natalya's wake. The click of the other woman's heels was loud on the metal flooring. The entire base here was very pragmatic, lots of concrete and steel. It made Natalya's flawlessness seem almost surreal. It wasn't that she was a throwback to a time before the Poison – it went beyond that. She was a connection to a time that had never existed outside of glossy magazines and red carpets.

"So where do you stay here?" Maira ventured. "I haven't seen you around before this."

Wherever "here" is, Maira thought. *So far all she'd seen* were boring corridors and windowless rooms. She wasn't even sure what part of the country they'd moved her to. There was a time when it seemed like that should have bothered her, but it didn't seem worth getting worked up about now. They likely had their own security concerns, after all.

"Hm." Natalya seemed amused by that. "I don't stay anywhere exactly. Always traveling, always trying to figure out the next move. No rest for the wicked, as they say."

"Fair enough. Where are you from originally, then?" Maira asked.

"Russia," Natalya allowed.

Maira blinked. "I would never have guessed. You don't have a hint of an accent. You grew up there?"

"I was born there," Natalya said. "My crisp diction is the result of a great deal of money spent by my father. Only the best schooling for his children, you understand."

Maira thought of her own modest childhood, her education paid for through military service. It didn't seem worth bringing up. "Sure, spare no expense, right? The children are the future and all that."

Natalya glanced over at her shoulder at that, the corner of her mouth quirking into a smirk. "Something like that."

They arrived at the elevator and Natalya led her inside. The woman in white tapped in a code, and the elevator hummed into motion. This close, Maira could smell her perfume, some faint and elegant scent. Maira watched the dial over the door. They were currently on floor -3. It scrolled up and passed zero as she watched. She couldn't restrain a soft noise of surprise.

"What is it?" Natalya asked.

"I just haven't actually been above ground since I arrived here. Since I woke up from the surgery, that is. Spent a couple of weeks down in the dark now."

Natalya studied her briefly. "Sounds like this little jaunt is more than overdue, then. Here, let me warm up your day."

She tapped a new code into the elevator controls, and the armored panels on the sides slid away. Maira blinked in surprise. She hadn't even been aware that was possible. There were now glass windows looking out from the sides of the elevator. Warm sunlight spilled in, yellow and inviting. Maira closed her eyes as it touched her face.

When she opened them again, they were rising past the tops of surrounding buildings. Whatever base this was, it was obviously more than just an underground complex. There was a tower, too, rising above a city. Maira would have been lying if she said she recognized it. Her breath caught in her throat, nonetheless. It was like getting to see civilization again after so long.

In the humid climates of DC and the Gulf Coast, cities had grown over quickly. They had succumbed to vines and ivy. Tall grass had punched up through roads, and mildew and mold had claimed the corners. Everything that people had built had fallen away with indecent speed.

This place seemed more intact. It must have been a drier climate, further out west. She could see mountains and dusty plains out beyond the city limits. The view only improved as the elevator scaled the tower. It must have been the tallest building within the city, easily, and they seemed to be headed for the very top.

"Albuquerque, New Mexico," Natalya provided. "Not exactly our top-of-the-line facility, but I'm told you were in a serious condition when we found you. Had to go with what was close."

Maira tore her gaze from the windows to look at the other woman. "What, this place isn't your headquarters?"

The woman in white laughed at that. "Not hardly, Maira. Just one of many sites from which we'll reclaim the world when the time is right."

Maira raised an eyebrow. "And when is that exactly?"

"When the bell rings, obviously," Natalya said lightly.

On cue, the elevator chimed and the doors opened. The suite that was revealed was sumptuous, for lack of a better word. Tiled floors led out from the elevator and into a living room fully laid out with leather furniture. Floor to ceiling windows revealed more vistas of the city and the land beyond. Maira wheeled herself into a window alcove, warm sunlight prickling at her skin. She could see solar panels laid out in the courtyards below, doubtless helping to power all of this.

The click of Natalya's heels behind her brought Maira back to reality. The woman in white stepped up beside her and rested a hand on the back of Maira's wheelchair. Her blue gaze swept the horizon, though her face was difficult to read. Maira supposed Natalya must be used to such views. Maybe this was how she lived all the time.

"It's like a dream," Maira offered.

"Just a remnant of the days we've left behind," Natalya said. "And we're going to have them again, Maira. I can promise you that. Especially now that you're here to help me."

Maira couldn't deny a small blush. She was very conscious of how close Natalya's hand was to her back.

She cleared her throat. "That's the second time you've said something like that. You make it sound like your people came to Houston just to get me."

Natalya tilted her head. "We did."

Maira shrugged uneasily. "I assumed you were there to save my cell as a whole."

Her voice caught. It was still so hard to think of her friends. To really believe that she was never going to see any of them again. They had known they were in for a desperate fight when they confronted the rogue cell on the moored battleship *Texas*. Maira had never imagined, though, that she would be the only one to survive. It didn't seem fair. It wasn't fair, plain and simple.

"You're special, Maira. Don't get me wrong, I wish we'd been able to save your whole cell. If there's one thing I can't abide, it's waste. To see so many talented individuals lose their lives – it's a tragedy is what it is. But if I'm to be completely honest, you were our top priority."

Maira shook her head. "That doesn't make sense. I'm just another agent, and the newest one at that."

"I see," Natalya said softly. "So you still don't understand the part you could play in all this. Well, luckily, you're here now, and so am I. You may not see your potential, but I do. I can assure you that I will make the most of it."

"Make the most of it, how? No one's mentioned anything about any of this to me," Maira said in confusion.

"Of course not. I shouldn't have either, truthfully," Natalya said. "Do you know why not?"

Maira shook her head.

"Because right now your top priority is to heal and get well. That's your job, and as I said down below, you're doing an excellent job of it. I can't wait to see you back in top form."

"You still haven't explained what it is about me, specifically, that you need," Maira pointed out.

"There's plenty of time and no rush. For now, like I said, the most important thing is that we get you back on your feet. And you'll need good food to do that, won't you? I did invite you up here for lunch, after all."

Natalya didn't give any signal that Maira picked up on. Nevertheless, a small group of people entered the room that instant. One of them was pushing a card laden with silver dishes. They brought it over to one of the tables in the suite and began to unload it with easy efficiency. The only thing that kept it from being a snapshot of the lost days of fine dining was that the people were wearing pragmatic coveralls.

That was a relief, to be honest. If they'd all been dressed to the nines in tuxedos, Maira would have started to question if she had hit her head. Even so, the meal they were laying out smelled impossibly divine. Her mouth instantly began to water. She was wheeling in that direction before she thought twice. Only then did she pause and look back, embarrassed at her eagerness.

Natalya chuckled and waved her on. "Please, I'm glad

you're excited. Don't hold back on my account. Help yourself."

Maira nodded and wheeled herself over to the table. It was laid out with a few dishes. Nothing was incredibly elaborate, but that didn't stop it from being the best food Maira had seen since society collapsed. Before that, in all honesty – she hadn't exactly been living the high life even before the pandemic.

She took it all in longingly. Fresh-baked bread, steaming as it was cut. A long, lean cut of meat. The meat was soaked in some kind of gravy, utensils provided in case things got messy. Bowls full of fruit. Nectarines, peaches, plums. Maira's disbelief told her they had to be wax at first. A light touch of her fingers told her otherwise.

"Fresh fruit," she muttered.

"Picked today, unless I'm mistaken," Natalya said.

The woman in white walked over to the other side of the table. One of her attendants slid her chair out for her. Natalya hardly seemed to notice them as she eased into it. The pearls around her neck gleamed in the warm sunlight pouring in through the windows.

"If you'd like, we could get a few peaches cut up, perhaps drizzled with a little sugar?"

Maira gave an incredulous laugh. "I think I would expire on the spot."

Natalya smiled faintly. "Is that good or bad?"

"Good, but unnecessary all the same. At this point I'm pretty sure I could eat my weight in peaches fresh from the..." Maira frowned. "Tree? Vine? ISAC..."

She lowered her gaze and cleared her throat with embarrassment. Nothing like trying to ask your imaginary friend a question in the middle of a conversation. It was funny, the watch and the voice that came with it could be so annoying. Then it was gone, and she found herself missing it dearly. That, and her friends, and the whole life she had lost that night in Texas.

"Tree," Natalya said gently. "It is an odd thing, isn't it? Even without your advanced AI companion, so many people have had to go through something like information withdrawal. As a society, we had become very used to having all human knowledge at our fingertips. And then it was gone."

"Yeah, I guess even before I always had my smartphone in my– Wait, you know about ISAC?" Maira asked with surprise.

Natalya chuckled. "I could tell you that I found out after the collapse brought on by the Green Poison, but that would be a lie. I'm afraid I've always had friends in high places, and known more than I was supposed to."

"I suppose that comes in very handy toward that foresight you were talking about," Maira said wryly.

"It definitely doesn't hurt," Natalya replied. "What is this cut, by the by?"

Her gaze hadn't moved from Maira, but one of the attendants answered. "Elk tenderloin, ma'am. Sourced locally and dry aged for the usual thirty days, of course."

"Elk," Maira said. She spooned some onto her plate. "I think this will be the first time I've had elk."

"I try to stay with what's locally available," Natalya said. "The fruits are seasonal, the elk native to New Mexico's big game."

"Trying to keep your carbon footprint down? I know people that might save your life with," Maira noted. The Reborn took things like that very seriously, she thought drily.

"Once upon a time, maybe. I'm in the business of saving the world. There was a time when climate change was one of the great dangers. Things are different now, of course, but the causes are just as important. Just as urgent." Natalya smiled. "Now it's just a good idea to live sustainably."

"Right. Can't argue with that," Maira said.

She took her first bite of the elk. It wasn't worlds different from beef, of course. It had been cooked to perfection, which didn't hurt at all. The flavor was clean with just a hint of sweetness. Maira swiftly discovered she was famished. For a few minutes the only sound was the clink of utensils as Maira went about the work of polishing her plate.

"You're hungry! Good," Natalya said.

Maira blushed and hastily dabbed at her mouth with a provided napkin. "It's amazing how those little exercises can really work up an appetite."

"We're just machines, really," Natalya observed. "You're repairing some serious damage, so it makes good sense that your body needs the raw materials."

Maira touched a hand to her abdomen. It ached dully even now. There hadn't been any getting away from that since the surgery.

"It sounds like I owe you some personal thanks for having me saved," Maira said. "So, you know, thanks."

"My pleasure," Natalya said. She leaned forward, expression serious. "I saw the video where they fished you out of that water and brought you in. It was touch and go for you. I'm told the cold of the water may be the only thing that kept you alive until we got there. Well, for a certain value of alive."

Maira was in the middle of peeling a peach, but she paused at that. "I beg your pardon?"

"Did they not tell you? Your heart had stopped when you were retrieved. We were able to get it going again, obviously."

"Obviously," Maira repeated wanly. "No, I hadn't heard that part."

"What do you remember?" Natalya asked.

Maira frowned. Happy memories they were not. "I found something in the belly of that ship. Something dangerous."

"Oh?" Natalya asked casually. "Like what?"

Maira paused. "I can't remember exactly. A lot of what happened there at the end is kind of blurry." She dropped her gaze to focus on the peach as she spoke.

It was a lie. Maira remembered perfectly well. There had been bioweapon canisters down there, enough to kill everyone left alive on the planet and then some. The Eclipse virus, it was called, and supposedly it was even worse than the Green Poison. Maira had no love of secrets, but even she knew some things should be left to die and be forgotten.

If Natalya knew she was lying, she gave no sign. She only nodded. "For the best, perhaps. Trauma can take a lot from you. Perhaps it will come back as you regain your strength."

"And then, yeah, I was here," Maira said brightly to move the subject on. "A few shaky moments in and out as they worked, and then back to life like Frankenstein's kid."

Natalya furrowed her brow. Her stunning lack of wrinkles suggested that was not common. "Don't you mean Frankenstein's monster?"

"Hey, no, not a bit. You give something life, that's your kid. If anyone was a monster in that story, it was the deadbeat dad who tried to ditch his freaky science child."

Natalya laughed mid-bite. It seemed to catch her off guard as much as Maira. She hastily covered her mouth, blue eyes wide. "Excuse me."

Maira grinned at her. "Ha! Score one for me. Next I have to try to make you spew."

Both of Natalya's eyebrows went up. "Spew? I don't think…"

"Oh, c'mon! No, it's fine. It was something my brother and I used to do. You say something really funny right when the other person is mid-drink. If you make them laugh at exactly the right moment, it comes out of their nose."

Natalya stared at her. "Please don't."

Maira coughed and looked down. "Yeah, of course not. I wouldn't really. I was just…"

She took a bite of her peach. It melted into her mouth like liquid heaven. For a moment her mind was blessedly clear of all thoughts. That perfect sweetness – when was the last time she'd had anything quite this good? The rhubarb the Reborn had grown was delicious, no doubt, but it didn't hold a candle to this.

Natalya cleared her throat. "You were luckier than you realize, perhaps. Not only are there few enough surgeons left in the world qualified to have handled your injuries, but we had treatments available that would have been cutting edge even in the old world."

Maira didn't have to pretend to be interested here. New technology had always been a fascination of hers. "Tell me about it?"

Natalya fluttered her hand dismissively. "I'm not an engineer so I couldn't tell you all the details. The general idea, however, is that you were given nanite therapy to address some of the worst of your injuries."

Maira looked down at her stomach. "Nanites? Tiny robots?"

Natalya chuckled. "Exactly. They wove the torn tissues back together with a precision that would simply be impossible for human hands, and applied structural reinforcement as well to help avoid re-tearing."

Maira looked up with genuine astonishment. "That's amazing."

Natalya seemed obscurely pleased. "It took a great deal of backing and finagling to see that project become a reality. I'm pleased to see it provide such obvious dividends. If the previous tests are borne out, you will heal faster and more thoroughly than traditional methods could have accomplished."

"I had honestly wondered," Maira admitted. "Don't get me wrong, it still hurts. It's still hard. But I had expected to be even worse off. I guess it's not just my imagination."

"The most important part in your recovery will still be you, Maira. Nanites aside, the outcome will be in your hands."

"Of course," Maira said. She grinned lopsidedly. "Don't worry, Keith gives me that speech once or twice a day. Maybe three times if he's feeling frisky."

"Keith? Ah, yes. Flex. Of course. I hope he's providing you with good care? He's supposed to be the best at what he does."

"He's great," Maira said swiftly. She glanced at a nearby clock. "Speaking of, I really should get back to him sooner rather than later. Like you said, it's on me to make sure I do this right. I hate to miss out on the bread, but I also don't want to go down there swollen like a tick."

Natalya chuckled. "Take it with you! Eat it when you like. And don't talk like this is your last opportunity. I plan this to be the first of many get-togethers."

"How will I… Ah."

One of the attendants was already wrapping the bread for Maira to take with her. She accepted it gratefully. It would make a wonderful snack after the hard work of the second set of exercises. Especially if she could steal a little spread from the cafeteria to go with it.

Maira turned her gaze back to Natalya. She found it hard to lock eyes directly with the other woman. She kept slipping to her forehead. Her cheeks. Her lips.

"So," Maira tried to say lightly. "Not even going to give me a hint what your grand plan for me involves?"

"Hmm," Natalya mulled. A small smile touched her lips. "You wanted to be a coder at one point, right?"

"Wow," Maira said with a wry laugh. "You have done your research. I did. Why?"

"Then here's your hint: I'm going to get your life back on track, Maira Kanhai. And in return, you're going to help me save the world."

CHAPTER 4

Spring. Washington DC

"Twelve hostiles, two groups," Leo said. "One group gathered at the doorway. The others are still inside. Infrared from the drone indicates they're removing the civilians from the building by hand."

"Fight was over before we got here," Eric rumbled.

"They're not soldiers," Brenda said softly. "The world has changed, and everyone is running to catch up."

Brenda crept up the alleyway toward the avenue. She was close enough now that she could hear some of what was happening at the target location. Someone was begging. Cruel laughter sounded. Someone screamed, a high and wavering wail. It cut off sharply. Brenda flinched.

"Bastards," Rowan growled. "Screw this. Let's go."

"We go when we're in position," Brenda said firmly. "Stay cool. Getting ourselves killed will not help these people."

She could feel the younger agent seething. Rowan wasn't angry at her, she knew. Not really. She just had a hyper developed sense of injustice. She took every horror and atrocity of the post–Green Poison world personally. That simmering rage was as much strength as weakness. It made her reckless, but it also gave her purpose.

Brenda reached the end of the alley. There was a concrete barricade there. It blocked her from walking out into the street beyond. It had been set up during the initial chaos of the winter, to judge by the weathering on it. Something to help enforce curfews and traffic control. Now just a relic.

Brenda knelt against it and glanced out. It was much as Leo's drone pass had shown. A gathering of people in front of a ruined shopfront. Maybe ten on their knees, bags over their heads. Half a dozen standing and carrying weapons. They wore a mishmash of ragged civilian garb and crude tactical gear. Their weapons were a similarly eclectic mix of whatever they could find. Splashes of vivid green on their clothes sealed the ID.

"Hyenas," spat Rowan on the radio.

"Yep," Brenda said unhappily.

The other Division agents weren't in plain sight, but ISAC highlighted their locations for her. Eric was one alley up from her own location. Rowan and Leo were coming in from the sides, flanking the target. Everyone was where they were supposed to be.

"All right," Brenda said quietly. "We do this by the book. Hit them hard and fast. If they break, let them go. Priority is the civilians."

"Rog," Leo said.

"On your mark," Eric said.

"Let's go," Rowan said impatiently.

"Leo, Rowan, go!" Brenda said.

"Flashbangs out!" Leo called.

The stun grenades hurtled through the air, thrown by both flanking agents. The side windows of the store were already broken by old riots, so they sailed right in. Brilliant light strobed, internal lightning and artificial thunder. A chorus of screams and shouts erupted. The Hyenas gathered out front whirled in surprise.

"Eric, now!" Brenda said.

"Moving!" he replied.

Brenda moved, too. She backed up six feet and surged toward the concrete. She hit with her shoulder low, and let her momentum carry her up and over. Her boots came down on debris on the other side, broken glass and gravel crunching underfoot. Her M16 was up in a flash.

The Hyenas were still focused on what was happening inside the building. No one keeping watch behind them. Sometimes you only get to make a mistake once in your life. Brenda put a three-round burst into the first one's back. They toppled with a scream, gun falling from nerveless hands. The gunman next to them startled and turned. That got them a serving of bullets to the chest instead, tracking down center mass in a spray of blood.

Gunshots echoed from the building, and Brenda heard the roar of Eric's M60 to her right. His handiwork was right in front of her. Hyenas were scythed from their feet. Most of them died without realizing there was a fight going on. The last one standing near Brenda had figured it out. Screaming a war cry, he raised a submachine gun one-handed and sprayed fire in her direction.

Brenda dropped to one knee as bullets pinged and hissed all around her. She squeezed the trigger, and her M16 shuddered in her grasp. The burst walked up the Hyena, from navel to chest to throat. It killed his howl with a choking gurgle. Blood washed down his chest in a crimson wave. He kept squeezing the trigger for a few more seconds, clicking on an empty magazine. His eyes were empty when he fell.

Brenda cued her radio, but all that came out was a cough. The street stank of cordite and blood. She cleared her throat and tried again.

This time she managed words. "Street clear!"

"Street clear," Eric affirmed.

"Left clear," Leo responded like clockwork.

Silence.

"Rowan?" called Eric in alarm.

Brenda sprinted toward the building, her breath loud in her ears. She hit the door boot first. It smashed open to reveal the old business lobby. This place had been converted into a home for several folks – sleeping bags and little cooking pots and the other random detritus of life, and then it had been torn apart by the Hyenas. She disregarded all those layers and pushed toward the back. Leo came around the corner low and fast, ready to watch her back.

The back door on the right took them into Rowan's target.

They came through tactically, ready for a fight. Instead, there was a silence broken only by whimpers. Rowan stood in the center of the chamber. A Hyena stood against the wall opposite her. They had their hands raised. Rowan's shotgun was aimed directly between their eyes. They were the source of the whimpering, eyes wide with terror.

The rest of the room was a charnel house. Two Hyenas lay where they'd fallen, torn open by buckshot. A civilian lay on a table nearby. What was left of one, anyway. Someone had taken a knife to them. Whatever they'd been doing, it hadn't been quick or clean. Another one was nearby. Throat cut, still-spreading blood all around them. Recent.

The whimpering Hyena's hands were red with blood, up to the elbows. A knife lay at their feet, covered in gore.

Brenda absorbed all of this quickly. She took a slow step forward. "Rowan."

"We should have moved faster," Rowan said dully.

"It's OK, Rowan," Brenda said softly. "This isn't your fault."

"They were going to take his daughter, and he dared to try to stop them." Rowan was monotone. "So they cut him up. Some kind of lesson, I guess. They made her watch, and she started screaming. And her throat, they…"

"Rowan." Brenda tried to keep her voice firm but gentle. "The fight's over. We'll take him back to the White House, and the JTF will handle things from there."

"Two minutes," Rowan said. "Two minutes faster, and she'd still be alive."

"Rowan, please, you don't want this in your head. Just lower the weapon, and we'll go back. It's over."

"No," Rowan said softly.

The shotgun spoke. The whimpering stopped. The Hyena's now-faceless body slid to the ground, trailing red down the wall as it went.

"Now it's over," Rowan said.

She strode from the room without another word, the shotgun at her side trailing smoke from the barrel. Leo stepped aside to let her pass.

"Rowan," Brenda called.

She started after her. Leo caught her by the shoulder and shook his head.

"Let her go," he said softly. "Let her walk it off. We've all had those days."

"No," Brenda said quietly, but she let herself be stopped. She glanced back at the bodies, contorted by violence. "It's not the same. She takes it personal."

August 4

"Rowan," mumbled Brenda as she came awake with a start.

The truck rumbled under Brenda as it made its way along the dusty Texas road. She blinked and scrubbed at her face, taking a moment to get her bearings. They must have left the main highway while she was asleep. Now they were trekking across something that deserved a different name entirely. "Rutted trail," perhaps. All Brenda knew was that her teeth were fit to rattle out of her skull if this went on for much longer.

"Are you sure this is where they're located?" she called over the sound of the rattling rocks and the engine.

The roughneck who had offered to drive her out this way gave her a cheerful nod. "Oh yes, ma'am! You'll see real soon."

He didn't seem perturbed by any of it. The remnants of that old, sad memory still clung to her from her dreams. They made Brenda want to headbutt him. Just once, she thought. One solid impact to ruin his zen. Then they could both be miserable and continue on their way. As it was, it seemed like a poor way to reward him for his help, so she restrained the impulse.

"How have things been down this way the past few months? I've been too preoccupied to follow up," Brenda asked instead to distract herself.

"What, you mean with the war and all?" the driver asked.

Brenda couldn't help a smile. "Yeah, with the war and all."

"Well, I'll tell you, it's been touch and go a couple times after that. On the one hand, some of the Molossi and the Reborn seemed like they never wanted to fight in the first place. On the other, some of them feel like they never got the chance to properly settle their differences. Things get tense, it doesn't help to have a chunk of folks agitating to pick up the fighting again."

"Yeah, I can see how that wouldn't be helpful. What causes the tension?"

"Any number of little things. Somebody wanders where they shouldn't. Says something they shouldn't. Next thing you know, hands are on guns and everyone's looking sweaty."

"But it hasn't broken out into open fighting again?" Brenda asked.

"Not yet," he said, and knocked on the faux wood grain of the dashboard. "The folks you're looking for, they've been a big help as that goes."

"That explains it, then," Brenda said thoughtfully.

"Ma'am?" The driver gave her a quizzical look.

"I was wondering why the cell hadn't moved on already. Now I know. They're keeping the peace."

"Oh yeah, that does make sense," he agreed. "Of course, the one little lady, her leg was broken, too."

Brenda's eyebrows went up. "Broken? Is she all right?"

"Oh, she's fine. She's fine. They had her in a cast for a while, limping around with that gun that's damn near as big as she is. But it came off… must've been two or three weeks back? And ever since then I reckon she's been as spry as a jackrabbit."

That part was good news. Comms difficulties made it hard to get a full picture of events across the sweep of the nation. America was huge, at the end of the day, and the infrastructure got worse every day. As often as not, the Division had to depend on word of mouth these days, whenever a Freighty stopped by who had traveled through a region. Brenda had not even heard that Yeong-Ja was hurt, but it was good to know she had recovered.

The other news wasn't as good. If this place was still teetering on the edge of total war, the cell might very well feel they couldn't leave. As Brenda had made sharply clear to Greene, no one could give anyone orders on these matters. She sighed and rubbed her thigh where it met the prosthetic. At the end of the day, all she could do was make her case and hope they agreed to help her.

"All right, we're getting close now. It's all off road from here, but it ain't far so we might as well walk the rest," the driver said.

"Oh, now it's off road? God above, yes, let's walk, please," Brenda said hastily.

He pulled off to the side of the road, tall grass rattling against the door as he did. Brenda opened it and stepped out to the ground below. The morning sun was bright in the sky, and the heat was just beginning to come on. Brenda shielded her eyes and took a look around. There wasn't much to recommend this place. It seemed more like the edge of wilderness than anything else.

She walked around to the back of the truck to retrieve her kit from the bed. The bag settled onto her shoulders, an old familiar weight. It took her back to the cross-country trek Maira, Leo, and she had endured to make contact with the Freighties. They had saved a lot of lives from famine on that mission – and stumbled onto Rowan O'Shea's machinations in the process.

Brenda still wasn't sure how she felt about how all of that had fallen out in the end. It wasn't so much that she questioned the results: Rowan had to be stopped. That much had been painfully clear. Brenda was grateful that Maira had been there to finish the job when she'd been taken out of action.

No, it was reconciling the things that had come before that still bothered her. Maybe for some people, Rowan was never going to be anything but a murderer and a bogeyman. To Brenda, she had been a friend first. Brenda had trained her. They had fought together in the madness of infected DC. There had been a time, even, when Brenda would have said that Rowan was one of the best of them.

Certainly, better than Brenda herself.

Then everything had gone wrong, and there was no one to blame but Brenda herself. She had lied to Rowan about how her family died. There were no two ways to look at that. Maybe the truth up front would still have twisted Rowan into what she became, but then again maybe not. There was no time machine to go back and find out. All Brenda could do was live with it as best she could.

"You all right, miss?"

The driver was coming back around from the other side of the truck. His words shook her from her dark thoughts. She mustered a winning smile for him and picked up her Honey Badger, letting it rest across her arms. There was no sentiment to that, at least. A weapon was a weapon. She carried one because she had to.

"I'm fine, just letting the weight settle. So, which way do we need to go?"

The driver pointed off through the trees. "Right on this way. Won't be more than a couple of minutes' walk."

They set off together through the tall grass. It rustled around Brenda as she walked, leaving little seedlings all over her clothes. She kept her eyes on the ground. A gopher hole in the wrong place would do a pretty good job of twisting her prosthetic in a most unpleasant way. Better to just avoid that altogether if possible.

They were about halfway to the tree line when a metallic peal rang out. Brenda dropped to one knee. Shouting sounded in the distance. Her gun was at her shoulder and ready to fire as she scanned the horizon.

"Take cover!" she barked at the driver.

It was only a second later she realized he was looking at her like she was crazy. He hadn't even dropped to a crouch. One possibility, of course, was that he had no idea how to handle danger. Not many people were left in the world who could say that, though. The other possibility, which seemed far more likely, was that he knew something she didn't.

"You can get up, ma'am," he said with a grin.

"Are you sure?" she asked.

"Oh yes, ma'am. Can't fault your reflexes, though. You moved like a startled cat."

That wasn't quite the formidable image that Brenda hoped to project. She shook her head and laughed, rising back to her full height.

"All right, let me in on the joke," she said. "What am I missing?"

The driver clapped her on the shoulder. "Baseball, ma'am. All you're missing is baseball."

Another metallic clang, another round of shouting. Also, Brenda realized now, cheering. The truth of the man's words sank in. That was the sound of a base hit, unless she was mistaken. There was a time when she had gone all-state in softball. That might as well have been a lifetime ago.

They continued on through the tree line, only to find it soon opened into a new clearing. The awaited baseball field was there just beyond. It was not a stadium to rival the greats, obviously. It was more of a rough diamond carved out of nowhere. But they had gone to the trouble of cutting the grass and laying the bases. They had even, to her surprise, brought some metal folding bleachers out here so that people could watch the game.

No one was wearing anything approaching a matching uniform, either. It was the same spectrum of hard-wearing clothes that filled out most wardrobes these days: jeans, shirts, boots. All the same, it quickly became clear there were teams. The offense was all wearing green armbands, while the defense was wearing black. Someone was chasing a ball in the outfield as they approached, another sprinting the bases.

A home run in the making, unless Brenda missed her practiced guess. She paused to watch with a smile on her face, resting a hand against the trunk of a tree. It was easy to forget, in a life filled with danger and crisis, how much she missed the simple things. The runner rounded third base, loose ends of their armband fluttering behind them. The ball came hurtling back. It all came down to a split second's difference. The runner slid, kicking up dirt, and–

"You're out!" shouted the umpire.

"Ah, damn," Brenda said with a laugh. "Can we get that on playback?"

Arguments erupted in the stands along the same lines. Brenda watched curiously. Unless she missed her guess, the two teams must belong to the Reborn and the Molossi. That seemed risky. It wasn't as if sports disagreements had never boiled over into violence in human history before. Sure enough, some of the arguments were heated. People were getting red-faced. But nobody was going for their gun.

"Huh," Brenda said.

"What?" asked the driver.

"Nobody's carrying," she realized out loud. There wasn't a firearm to be seen among those gathered.

"Oh yeah. That was one of the first rules put into place. If you want to watch or play, you leave the gun at home."

"And people actually went along with it?" Brenda asked.

The driver shrugged. "I think it reminds people of the way the world used to be. Makes us remember how to be civilized. Doesn't work on everyone, of course, but it helps." He flashed her a wry grin.

The umpire had noticed them across the field. "Time out! Everyone, take a breather, get some water. Hydration is key!"

They rose to their feet, a full height that uncoiled like a lanky ladder. That was enough for Brenda to put together with the voice. She approached with a smile on her face and her hand raised in greeting.

"Colin!"

The medic pulled the umpire mask away to reveal a smile that matched her own. "Brenda! This is an unexpected delight. If I'd known you were coming, I'd have met you on the way in."

They bumped elbows in greeting – for most people, shaking hands had died out during the reign of the Green Poison. The danger of the virus had passed for the most part, but the caution remained. No one wanted to relive those terrible days if they could help it. Something so small likely wouldn't have changed the outcome, but it was something they could control. So people held on to it tightly.

"Comms into the area are spotty at best. I didn't have any good way to send word ahead. Sorry about that," Brenda said.

"Not at all, you're always a welcome sight," Colin said.

"You might not feel that way once I've told you why I'm here," Brenda said quietly.

Colin's eyebrows went up and his smile died. "What happened?"

Two more people approached from the stands. Brenda recognized them both. One was a small East Asian woman with her medium-length hair pulled into a tight braid. There was a gleam in her eyes, a certain unspoken mischief. That was Yeong-Ja Cha, a remarkably skilled sniper who had once worked with the FBI's elite Hostage Rescue Team. The other was a dark-skinned man no taller than Brenda herself, his head shaved and his expression perpetually serious. This was none other than Leo Fourte, once a member of Brenda's own cell and one of her closest comrades.

Brenda couldn't help her smile returning to see the both of them. "You all look so well. Yeong-Ja, I heard you were hurt! I'm glad to see you walking around with no trouble."

Yeong-Ja offered a nod and a faint smile. "Lucky me, I had a sasquatch that fancies itself a medic around to look after me. He kept me from making it worse, and time took care of the rest."

"Brenda," Leo said calmly. "You're out in the field again."

"Leo," Brenda returned in the same even tone. "You've truly mastered stating the obvious in our time apart."

Leo snorted, but there was no heat to it. For all his humorless mien, he was a good-natured person. He was also one of the most reliable agents Brenda had ever known. If she needed someone to watch her back, Leo would always be her first choice. He would grind himself to dust before he gave up on something he considered his duty.

There was something in his eyes now, though. A darkness and a pain she hadn't seen there before. He started to say something and shook his head, looking away.

"Leo?" she asked softly.

"I lost her, Brenda. I couldn't save her. I'm..." His jaw worked soundlessly. "I'm sorry."

There was no questioning who he meant. Maira Kanhai, the fourth agent who had gone to Texas with this group. Brenda saw in that instant how much losing her must have wounded the man. For all the exasperation her quick tongue brought him, Maira had been special to both of them. It hadn't been his fault, but he must have blamed himself all the same.

At least she could comfort him about that. How comforting the rest of what she had to say would be...

Brenda glanced around. There was no one standing near the quartet of Division agents. Her driver had walked off to join the people in the stands, some of whom were still arguing about the last call. Brenda kept her voice low, nonetheless. These days there was no such thing as too careful when it came to sensitive information.

"You didn't lose her, Leo."

That caught all their attention. Leo stepped closer, his frown deepening.

"What does that mean?"

Brenda reached out and gripped his shoulder tightly. "Maira is alive. Let's find somewhere to talk privately, and I'll explain as much as I know."

The processing plant that the cell took Brenda back to was like an odd flashback to life before the Green Poison. From what she had read, this had once been one of the largest such facilities in the United States. Now it was one of the few that functioned at all. The roughnecks had gathered the vast majority of their surviving number here to keep it going. There was a quiet hustle and bustle of people going about their business that was oddly comforting.

So much of the world had been left empty by the pandemic that just being surrounded by the buzz of gathered humanity was a comfort. People in rugged work clothes and hardhats worked all around them, making sure there was enough fuel to keep the Freighties in business – and in turn keep dangerous supply shortages at bay just a while longer. Food flowed in from farms to the west, scavenged consumer goods came from the great cities of the east, and everyone survived one more day.

The conference room they settled into was a simple affair. A table surrounded by chairs, a projector screen up on the wall. For now, the other three sat on the opposite side from Brenda and listened as she filled them in on the basics of the situation. When she was finished, an uneasy silence hung over the room.

Colin was the one to break it. "She was alive, and we left her behind."

Yeong-Ja sipped a cup of coffee she'd picked up on the way in. Her eyes were dark. "ISAC said she was dead. I heard it. You all did."

Colin scrubbed a hand over his face in clear misery. "That's what I get for listening to a piece of shit wristwatch."

"Couldn't have done anything differently," Leo said firmly. "The entire ship was going down. If you had gone below-decks after her, chances are you'd never have come back out."

"And yet somehow she survived," Colin said. He looked at Brenda in an unspoken question.

All she could do was spread her hands helplessly. "There's a lot of gaps in what I know even now. How Maira survived, where she has been, what she's been doing… Your guess is as good as mine. All I can tell you is she showed back up at the Texas Core, among the Black Tusk forces attacking."

"Black Tusk," said Leo softly. "Haven't heard much about them since we left DC. We get the occasional long-range propaganda broadcast out here, but they're not what you'd call a looming presence."

"I don't know much about them myself," Colin agreed. "They showed up in New York and took over what was left of the Last Man Battalion, but I never got a good feel for what made them tick."

"Never dealt with them at all," Yeong-Ja said. "What are they? Some kind of PMC? Rogue JTF? Rogue agents? Warlords?"

"Yes," Brenda said wryly. "I'm not an expert, but I can tell you they're what keeps the brainy analysts at the Core awake at night. I've heard people describe them as the anti-Division."

"I thought the Division was the anti-Division," Colin joked wearily.

"The point is they're all of the above and more," Brenda said. "They have tech that matches, or even surpasses, what's available to us. They operate an entire fleet of hovercrafts and use mil-spec combat drones like they're going out of style."

"If they're such ultimate badasses," Yeong-Ja started, "then why don't we hear more about them?"

"Because they've limited their direct operations to the cities of the East Coast. Don't let that fool you, though, they've got their fingers in the pie all over the country. They just like to operate through local forces and patsies where possible." Brenda motioned to Colin. "The LMB, as you noted, in New York. But also the Hyenas, and True Sons in DC, and we've found evidence of links to the Roamers."

"Well," Yeong-Ja replied. "On the bright side, I think we can safely say they're not behind any of the local unpleasantness."

"Only because it was Keener's rogues pulling the strings instead," Leo said grimly.

"We don't have a shortage of enemies," Brenda said. "That much is definitely true."

There was a conversational lull as the four of them sat and processed the information in front of them. It was Leo who leaned forward first, his eyes dark.

"So Maira has gone rogue then. Just like Rowan."

Brenda looked down with a grimace. "I don't feel like that's certain yet. As all of you noted, Black Tusk hasn't been at the forefront of your worries. Maira may not have even been aware who she'd fallen in with until it was too late."

"But you did say she killed two agents who encountered her," Yeong-Ja said softly.

Brenda winced. "That is how it appears, yes."

"Maira's not the first agent who has gone bad," Colin said unhappily. "We all have experience with that. Even beyond our personal woes, we were just talking about Keener and his group. A Division watch isn't some unbreakable bond."

"Maira, though," Leo muttered. "Not a traitor. Not the type. She was the one who wanted the high ground."

"Life doesn't come in black and white," Yeong-Ja said. "Sometimes that's the part that breaks people, discovering there's not always a right answer."

"We could speculate all day," Brenda said. "The point is, we won't get answers until we find her. Until we bring her in."

"And that's what it comes down to, right?" Colin asked. "You want us to go with you to bring her back."

There was no point in mincing words about it. Brenda nodded. "That's what I'm hoping for, yes."

"I will go," Leo said immediately.

Colin raised an eyebrow. "And what about the situation here? We're the closest thing to a neutral party between the Reborn and the Molossi. If we up and leave, what will they do?"

"Play baseball?" Brenda asked hopefully.

Colin laughed at that and rubbed his face again. "It seemed like a good idea at the time."

Yeong-Ja touched him on the shoulder with a slight smile. "Do not let Colin sell himself short. It was his idea, and it has helped. It has given them a focus for their rivalry that does not involve warfare in the streets."

"But is it enough?" Colin asked. "There are still hot-heads on both sides, and every week it seems like we have to talk someone out of lighting the fire. If this spirals out of control again, we could be looking at casualties in the thousands."

"We can't stay here forever," Yeong-Ja said. "Sooner or later these people will have to maintain a peace without us. Both Raffiel and the colonel seem committed to it these days. Perhaps we should give them a chance."

Brenda recalled the latest intel reports on the situation in this region: Raffiel and Colonel Marcus Georgio were the leaders of the Reborn and the Molossi, respectively.

"Meanwhile, our friend probably thinks we abandoned her to die," Colin said quietly.

"For what it's worth," Brenda interjected. "Beyond the

personal concerns, I think securing Maira could be a matter of serious security implications for the Division."

They all blinked at her.

Leo tilted his head curiously. "Same Maira?"

Brenda snorted. "Yes. Look, I know she doesn't present as the most dangerous person in the world. She's not bad in a fight, but there are plenty of people who are better. That's not the issue. It's what she knows."

Leo shook his head with a grunt.

Colin frowned. "As we've noted, she's not the first Division agent to go rogue. What could she know that none of the rest of them did?"

Yeong-Ja tapped a finger against the table. "No. She's right. I see it. Think about it, when Brenda's tip sent us to the weapons cache, what happened?"

Colin shrugged. "The colonel shut us down. He killed the mobile server and, in the process, deactivated all of our new weapons."

Brenda kept quiet and listened. This part of the story was new to her. She had indeed sent them the coordinates, of course, and hoped it would prove helpful. When word had come that they had managed to defeat the rogue cell, she had felt deep relief. Everything that happened in the middle, however, was a big question mark.

Yeong-Ja nodded. "And?"

"Maira rewired it," Leo said softly. There was a dawning in his eyes now. "Not only plugged us into the rogue network we'd just discovered, but she got the weapons back online in the process."

"Well." Colin hesitated. "That was impressive, I'll admit."

Brenda spoke up now. "It's not an isolated incident. When Leo, Maira, and I stumbled onto Rowan's plan, Rowan had a way of hijacking our SHD tech and turning it against us. It even worked on the defenses of the Kansas Core."

"Right, but that's Rowan, not Maira," Colin said.

"Maira stopped her," Brenda said. "Within a matter of a day or two she figured out how to shut down the hijacking program. In the end, that countermeasure was the only reason Rowan didn't win before we ever reached her."

"The Texas Core attack... I heard rumors," Leo said. "Said the defenses shut off in the middle of the fight."

"Maira again?" Colin said uneasily. "But that doesn't make sense. If she turned the defenses off, why didn't the Core fall?"

"Hostiles fell back at the same time." Leo shrugged. "Not clear."

"Point being, we're talking about someone who can theoretically neutralize our technology whenever she puts her mind to it," Yeong-Ja said.

Brenda nodded. "I've seen after-action reports analyzing Maira's abilities. Not only is she on a rarefied list of people who can pull off stuff like this, there's not many people who could stop her. At this point? She's one of the world's leading experts on ISAC, the Network, and SHD tech in general."

"OK," Colin said. He took a deep breath. "That does paint a very convincing picture of why we shouldn't let her run around loose. Second question for me is, how do we stop her? We don't know where she is?"

"Well," Brenda said with a wry smile. "That part, thankfully, is simpler than you'd think."

"Don't keep us in suspense," Yeong-Ja said lightly.

"Shortly after her re-appearance at the Texas Core, Maira activated a new watch. We can use it to track her. Comms aren't what they were, so our reception of the signal is spotty, but we do have an idea where she is, and if we get close enough, we should be able to lock on and go straight to her," Brenda said.

"Hmm," Leo said thoughtfully.

"Spill it," Brenda said.

"Odd decision. We just talked about how she's the expert on these things – why make it so easy to track her?" he asked.

"Could be she's getting some other use from the watch that makes it worth it," Brenda said with a shrug.

"Could be she wants us to find her," Yeong-Ja said.

Brenda smiled sadly. "That would be nice. But then why not just come back herself? I can tell you she's headed in the wrong direction for that. Tracking has her moving toward New Mexico."

"We'll just have to ask her ourselves when we catch up to her, won't we?" said Colin.

"Now that sounds like a man convinced," Brenda said with a grin.

"Yeah. I'm on board. Let's find Maira and get to the bottom of this, one way or another," Colin said.

"Let's bring her home," Yeong-Ja said hopefully.

"Better us than anyone else," was all Leo said.

Brenda saw the pain in his eyes, though, and knew it all too well. There was the fear in her that it was, in fact, happening all over again. The memory of Rowan laid out with empty eyes, a bullet hole in her forehead, would stay with her forever. She didn't want to add an image of Maira like that to her memories. The thought alone made her throat tighten.

"Good. I hoped that you all… I'm just glad that you're going to go with me. No matter what, it'll be better than facing it alone," Brenda said.

"So you said she's headed to New Mexico, right?" Colin said.

Brenda nodded. "She's not moving terribly fast, either. It might be that she's hurt, or she's just being very careful."

"Then we get a ride up to Dallas – that part should be easy, the Molossi run things that way and are constantly coming and going. From there we might have to take it on foot, but if we hurry, we can cut her off before she ever reaches the state border," Colin said.

Brenda nodded and stood. The others rose as well.

"Grab your gear," Brenda said. "We'll set out as soon as possible."

Just hold on, Maira, Brenda thought. We're coming.

CHAPTER 5

June 14

Hot water splashed against the top of Maira's head. She rested a hand against the shower wall as nigh-scalding rivulets ran down her body. It was only this week that her wounds had been pronounced sufficiently healed that she could stop sponge bathing and take up showers again. That was exciting enough by itself, of course, but then she discovered that the underground facility had hot water. Oodles of it, as a matter of fact, and she was encouraged to make the most of it.

Far be it from Maira Kanhai to look a gift horse in the mouth.

It was tempting to just stay in here forever, but even now there were tasks to be handled. She finished rinsing the soap from her skin and turned the handle until the water shut off. The contrast was sharp; even ordinary air felt ice cold now. Maira hastened to snatch up the nearest towel and dry off. Once she felt the danger of dripping all over the floor was past, she wrapped the towel around herself and stepped out into the restroom.

A few of the other stalls were in use. Steam puffed out of them in little clouds and left a light haze on everything. A couple of other personnel were getting dressed to go on duty. Maira smiled at a few and nodded at others, but the truth was she still scarcely felt like she knew anyone around here. Most of her time was occupied: physical therapy, her projects, food, of course. Glorious food.

And every now and then a chat – or a walk – or maybe dinner with Natalya.

Maira felt her cheeks flush. She glanced around, but nobody seemed to notice her sudden blushing. If they did, they probably wrote it off to the heat from the shower. Maira cleared her throat and hurried over to a sink. The mirror was useless, fogged over. Maira drew a smiley face in it with quick dabs, before wiping it down with a nearby cloth.

Her face was revealed in the cloth's wake. Maira studied her own face for a few seconds. Sharp features, just like her parents. That was never going to go away completely, but unless she was mistaken, they'd softened a little in the past weeks. In truth, she'd looked downright drawn in the recent past. Pushed to the limit, both by herself and by her situation. Kinder living was doing her good.

She could see the tracery of the burn scars even from this angle. It came around the sides of her neck and touched her shoulders. Maira reached to the scars and pressed on them. Her skin paled under the pressure, and she released it, letting the color fill back in. The scars still hurt sometimes. She'd move in just the wrong way or roll over in her sleep, and it would be like someone had stuck her with a live wire.

They weren't the only marks she had on her body. Tiny nicks and scratches. Dozens of little scars, from desperate escapades and raging gun battles. The largest, of course, tracked across her lower stomach: three bullet holes, earned belowdecks in *The Texas*. Maira had never fancied herself a violent person, but increasingly it seemed like her body told a different story. Even then, she had been lucky. The unfortunate ones didn't get to tally their wounds when the fight was over.

This place, though. Maira hadn't even picked up a gun since she'd gotten here. She hadn't added to the blood on her hands. Was it too much to hope that she could turn over a new leaf? They saw value in her here for her mind, for the person she had always wanted to be. Was that such a bad thing to want?

Dizzy.

Maira braced her hands on either side of the sink to keep from falling. She shook her head, to no avail. Then it was gone, the spell dissipating as swiftly as it had come. There had been moments like that lately. It seemed like something that should worry her, but somehow it didn't. It was another part of the impossible life here. A dream she was afraid she was going to wake up from.

"Back to work, Maira," she mouthed to her reflection.

The puzzle waited for her.

•••

Fully dressed and back in her quarters, Maira slid into the chair at her desk and opened up the laptop. It powered up instantly. That alone still hadn't stopped feeling like a tiny miracle. She knew the facility operated a number of solar panel banks, possibly supplemented by other power sources. However they did it, there was always plenty of juice to go around.

Maira tapped in her personal security code and scanned her thumb and eye both. The login screen fell away, and she was plunged instantly back into what she'd been working on before. The special project that Natalya had entrusted to her. She'd told Maira point blank that not only did she not trust anyone else with this job, she didn't think anyone else was up to it in the first place.

That felt good, Maira couldn't lie.

The problem was straightforward on the surface of it. The code that Natalya's organization used to control and interface with their technological infrastructure was compromised. Maira didn't use that term lightly. This was a flaw that ran down into the very heart of the program design. It allowed opposing forces to access the information on the servers without ever passing through the primary access credentials.

Maira frowned and sipped a thermos of coffee. The warmth and taste pulled her briefly from the realm of questionable encryption procedures. Even here she was reduced to instant coffee, but it was nice to have something again. The real stuff was going to have to wait until global trade became a thing again. Who knew when that was going to be? It had been all the Division could do to breathe life into local trade networks.

Back to the code. Why would someone have built it this way? That was one of the big questions Maira had. It felt like understanding the reason could be the key to the method to fix it. Maybe it was a matter of perspective? Until now, Maira had considered the way in which Natalya's organization used the "correct" one. Was that an illusion caused by it being the first method she had encountered?

Translate it into real world terms. There is a warehouse full of top-secret files. Access is supposed to be tightly controlled. So why have multiple entrances operating completely independently of each other? The different access points – the different interface programs – were so separated that one could be used without ever realizing the others existed in the first place.

It felt like a trick. The question was, on who? Maira drummed her fingers next to the laptop, the tip of her tongue sticking out of the corner of her mouth in concentration. Option one, this was some kind of programmer's back door. That was certainly believable; tons of techies left themselves a sly way back into their own creations that avoided security protocols.

This was too involved for that, though. If Maira was putting a back door into this system, she would have tucked it into one access hierarchy, not created multiple complete interfaces. To strain her earlier metaphor, she'd have just put herself on the VIP access list, not create a whole new door with its own security team. Either someone had a complexity addiction, or this was about more than–

A wave of dizziness hit Maira mid-thought. Nausea followed fast on its heels. She braced a hand against her desk to stay steady as her head swam. The scent of the coffee in her thermos was suddenly repulsive. Maira pressed fingertips to her lips in a struggle to keep her gorge from rising. She turned away, breathing hard, saliva flooding her mouth.

Slowly her stomach stopped churning. The queasiness retreated. The spike of fear that came with the nausea didn't help how she felt, but it was hard to get rid of. She had seen her father die to cancer. Weird issues with her body always made her wonder. Maira breathed slowly, eyes squeezed shut. She didn't want any input that would bring the unpleasantness rushing back in. She just stayed sitting very still, even after her body was back to feeling largely normal.

Maira startled at a knock on the door.

"Who is it?" she called.

"I'll give you exactly one guess."

It was Natalya's voice. Maira instantly sat up straighter. "Nat! Please, come in."

The woman in white opened the door and stepped inside. She was as impeccably put together as always. If someone had told Maira that every day the old Natalya got thrown away so a new one could be unwrapped from plastic, she'd almost have believed them. The other woman paused in the doorway with a slight frown as she looked Maira over.

"Are you all right?"

Maira mustered a smile. "I'm OK. Just feeling a little under the weather."

"Shall I fetch one of the doctors?" Natalya asked. "We can't have you getting ill, Maira. I've told you, you're too important."

Maira flushed and looked down. "I'm fine, I promise. Probably just pushing myself too hard too quickly. Need to make more time to rest."

Natalya stepped forward to within arm's reach, and Maira's heart sped up of its own accord. "Then don't talk about doing it: do it. Listen to your body and give yourself what you need. I need you at your best, do you understand?"

The blonde woman gently brushed a few strands of Maira's hair out of her face, smoothed it over to the side. Maira's hair had only recently begun to grow back long enough for stray locks to even be an issue. She looked up into Natalya's eyes for a split second, swallowed hard, and looked away again.

"Of course," Maira said. Was her voice squeaky? It sounded squeaky in her ears.

Natalya slipped past her to sit on her bed, crossing her legs. "So, speaking of that little puzzle I gave you, have you made any progress?"

Maira blew out a sharp breath with some relief. Work was a safe topic. She could handle work. "It's a mess, if I'm being honest. I can't even piece together why someone would design a system this way. It's a security issue fundamental to the entire structure, not something you can just patch out."

Natalya studied her with piercing eyes. "Does that mean you can't fix it?"

Maira gave a lopsided grin. "Hey, I didn't say that. I just want you to understand how amazing I am when I pull this off. If I make it look too easy, nobody will appreciate me."

The woman in white smiled slightly. "Don't worry about that. I promise you, fix this problem, and your name will go down in history."

Maira shrugged abashedly and changed the subject quickly. "What I'm surprised by is how you realized this was a problem in the first place. The traffic you're concerned about never even interacts with your system. It bypasses it completely."

"It would be a funny story, if real lives weren't on the line," Natalya said. "We attempted to shut down an enemy system, only to discover we'd crashed our own in the process. They were one and the same."

Maira shook her head wonderingly. "That's wild. Talk about being hoisted by your own petard."

There was something brittle and cold in Natalya's smile now. "Yes. I felt quite foolish at the time. Not a feeling I appreciate, or one I intend to suffer again."

Something about her demeanor unsettled Maira, but it was hard to grasp why. Her worries felt slippery, like they couldn't latch on to anything. The concerns slipped from her mind as soon as they'd started to make themselves known.

"Well, I'm sure we can figure something out to make this work the way it should," Maira said placatingly.

Natalya arched a sculpted eyebrow. "Do you have any thoughts on how you'll do that yet?"

Maira frowned and scratched her chin. "Well, trying to work outside-in is hitting them where they're strong. Any other access point is going to have its security outward-facing, after all. So I think we use the problem to fix itself, so to speak."

"The fact that we're accessing the same resources," Natalya said.

"Exactly," Maira said. "We have our way in, and these rebels of yours have theirs. The key isn't to take theirs away, it's to make it useless to them. That's the general approach. I'm still working on the specifics. But I have hope that there will be results sooner than you would think."

"What about next month?" asked Natalya with a certain dry smirk.

"Uh," Maira said intelligently.

She turned and stared at her computer, scrunching up her face. To say that was faster than she'd planned for was to give her the undue credit of having made a timeline yet. Still, it wasn't impossible, necessarily. She worried at her lip for a moment.

"I don't want to promise you something only to disappoint you. I mean, I don't know what strategic concerns you're managing here," Maira admitted.

Natalya reached out and lightly touched her shoulder. "I know I'm asking a lot. We're all under a lot of pressure, and I hate to put it on your shoulders. I appreciate the urge to manage my expectations. But I also don't want you to hold back for fear. Be ambitious. Let me worry about the big picture."

"OK," Maira said. "Well, the next step is really to dive into the coding proper. If that goes well, it could be a matter of weeks. If I run into more trouble than I expect? It could take a lot longer than that."

"Is there anything I can do to help you along?" asked Natalya.

"No. Well…" Maira hesitated. "There is one thing. I had a necklace before you all saved me in the river. I was wondering if that was retrieved along with me? It's important to me."

"A necklace?" Natalya paused. "I do seem to recall something of the sort in the report. There was a thumb drive on it, correct? It was put through a routine security check, and all they found on it was pictures."

That was odd. Maira hid the frown that wanted to surface. They'd gone through her personal belongings? It was true that most people would only find pictures on the drive. Family photos, especially ones of her and Kazi, her brother. The fact there were also weapons-grade programs carefully concealed on the drive was another matter. She suddenly felt reluctant to admit to that part of things.

"We can't risk anything," Natalya said with a small smile. "I'm sure you understand."

"Sentimental value," Maira reiterated in response. "It'll give me some peace of mind, help me focus on the work, especially to have my family close. Is there really a problem with that?"

Natalya's brow furrowed briefly before smoothing into placidity. "I see. If such things are important to you, I will of course ensure it's made available to you again. Then, I tell you what, in two weeks I'll have what you need to conduct the first practice run. We'll see how it goes, and we'll adjust our expectations from there. How does that sound?"

Natalya stood as she spoke, her hand slipping from Maira's shoulder to the back of her neck. "We can trust each other, Maira. Let me prove that to you. I'll do my best to secure the thumb drive. And in return…"

Maira looked up at her and swallowed hard. It was hard to concentrate with that warm touch on her skin. The other woman was actively touching her burn scars. Maira didn't want to care. She didn't want to be alert for any sign of disgust. She just couldn't help it.

To her surprise, there was nothing. Natalya didn't so much as flinch.

"I'll do everything I can do to make your request happen for you," Maira said firmly.

Natalya smiled down at her. "I know you will." She paused. "Ah, that reminds me, I have a little present for you."

"Oh?" Maira managed.

Natalya finally let go of her to reach into her suit jacket and retrieve a package. It was something wrapped in manila paper, about the span of both of Maira's hands. Natalya set it down on the corner of Maira's desk.

"Just something to express my appreciation for all the hard work you've already done," the woman in white said. "I know none of this can be easy for you. You're still recovering from gunshot wounds, and grieving those you've lost besides."

Maira lowered her gaze, a lump in her throat at the reminder of her friends. "It's actually for the best. Better to have something to work on than wallow in my fears and sorrows."

Natalya smiled. "We're the same that way. It's a good thing you've found your way to us, Maira Kanhai. This is a place for people who know that drive, who find relief in pushing ahead. You belong here. I can see it. I hope you can, too."

"I do like it here," Maira said quietly.

"Good. Well, it sounds like you have your work cut out for you. I'll let you get back to it. But I'll see you soon, all right? Take good care of yourself until then."

As quickly as that, Natalya was gone. The scent of her perfume lingered in her wake. Maira took a deep breath and closed her eyes. She needed perfume of her own. Competing with Natalya at being perfect was a losing game, obviously, but that didn't mean she couldn't rise to the challenge just a little, right? How long had it been since she'd tried to take care of herself that way?

Maira sighed and looked at the package the other woman had left. She picked it up curiously and weighed it in one hand. It wasn't heavy. She shook it very gently and nothing rattled. She couldn't help but laugh at herself; a kid testing a present before Christmas morning. With a shrug she unwrapped it.

She knew what the plastic shape was before it was half revealed. A handheld console. Maira stared at the device resting in her hand. One of these had been her constant companion before the Green Poison. So many happy memories of games played. She ran her fingers along the plastic casing. The power button was here and...

Beep. The device came alive in her hands.

"Holy shit, it works," Maira said.

She sat up and goggled as the screen lit up and showed the game currently loaded on the machine. A puzzle game – not her all-time favorite, but a fun time waster. Maira couldn't keep a broad smile from her face. To have one of these again, to have it working and the means to play it...

"Kazi would..."

Maira shut her eyes tightly. Her brother would have gone nuts. They'd had one of these back at Athena, and kept it going as best they could. As power died and everything started to fall apart. Stolen moments of happiness, flashing colors and smiles lit by screenlight. She'd played it less after he'd been killed, and finally given it up when she'd left to follow Brenda into the world of the Division.

Now one had found its way back to her. Like the promise of a life she'd given up on.

Maira looked at her laptop, screen still open to the beginnings of code. She turned off the handheld with a click and a warm smile. It would be there tonight after she had finished putting in her time. She needed to earn this gift, and everything it meant.

Maira flexed her hands, popped her knuckles, and went to work.

CHAPTER 6
August 5

"You're trying to tell me there is not a single vehicle in your entire pool that can be spared," Brenda said through gritted teeth.

The Molossi quartermaster slouched back behind his desk with a cold smile. "I'm afraid all Molossi equipment is currently dedicated to the mission of keeping the peace in this region."

It was the end of the day, and the sun was setting. Red-orange light slanted through the window blinds. It was unpleasantly warm in the little office. It really wasn't big enough for the three of them: Brenda, Colin, and this representative of the local paramilitary force. They were all sweating. The Molossus would occasionally mop the drops from his brow with a towelette. Brenda could feel her shirt sticking to her. It was just one more aggravation on top of everything else about this situation.

Brenda took a deep breath and mustered her best winning smile. "Look, I understand you folks are on the front lines protecting the people around here. It's impressive what you've accomplished, and I'm sure we're all grateful for it."

Brenda could see Colin's mouth twist across the room. He was standing off to the side of both Brenda and the Molossi official. Brenda sighed internally. He was a good person, heart of gold. Never had a poker face worth a damn, though.

"This thing my cell is doing, though, could have far reaching consequences," Brenda forged on. "This is a chance to get out ahead of a problem before it becomes a crisis."

"That's always the excuse with Division agents. 'Oh, this time it's a crisis, this time it's the end of the world, and if you don't do what we tell you, you'll be sorry.' Well, guess what, agent, the end of the world came and went, and you and yours didn't even slow it down." He pulled at his collar and glowered at her. "Now it's up to us to fix your mess."

Colin spoke up. "That's what she's trying to tell you. We're trying to prevent another mess from happening. We're trying to be proactive here, and if you help us, we'll all be glad of it in the long run."

The man gave him a dirty look. "If it was that important, it wouldn't be the Division handling it, now, would it? Who do you work for again, exactly? What operational authority do you have?"

It was everything Brenda could do for a second to

not snatch this smug little jackass across his desk. She wondered, briefly, how many headbutts it would take to knock all his teeth loose. Three, she figured. Like the licks getting to the center of a Tootsie Pop.

She closed her eyes for a second and re-established her calm. There were times when people brought the marine out in her. That wasn't going to help anyone today, though. Even if they could, in theory, punch this man out and steal a vehicle, that would be disastrous for the whole Gulf Coast.

"Look," Brenda said. "Couldn't you just run it up the chain and make sure your superiors agree with you on this matter? I understand there has been tension between our organizations in the past, but strides have been made. Nothing stays the same forever, right?"

Colin was making a face again. Something like someone had shoved a whole lemon in his mouth and made him bite down. He made eye contact with Brenda and made a visible effort to get his expression under control. It was partially effective.

"If it will get you out of my office, I will radio in to command. I can assure you, though, you're wasting your time. We're not in the business of enabling vigilantes."

There was a deep irony in that statement. Pointing it out wouldn't help. Brenda just smiled again. "Thank you. We'll wait outside."

She caught Colin by the arm and pulled him through the door out onto the asphalt outside. It was still too hot, but at least out here it wasn't stifling. There was even a breeze blowing through. It tugged at her hair and clothes, a welcome if negligible cooling. The door shut behind them with a jingle.

The Molossi vehicle pool was laid out next to the office, behind a chain link fence surmounted by razorwire. It laid to instant ruin the idea that there was nothing to be spared. Nearly twenty black Humvees waited beyond, each one geared for a combat zone. Other vehicles loomed besides: Strykers and Bradleys for the most part, along with a few MRVs.

"Good thing the Roamers don't have any of those," Brenda muttered.

A Mine-Resistant Vehicle would have blown right through that ambush she'd set in Kansas. Bad enough that the northern trucker-warlords had gotten their hands on so much armament for their semis. With proper military equipment and the know-how to use it and keep it running, they'd have been ten times the problem they already were.

The other two agents waited beside the fence. Brenda paused to marvel again at the sight of Yeong-Ja carrying her TAC-50. The specialist rifle was nearly as tall as the woman herself. It felt like some kind of absurd mecha reference to Brenda. She'd always loved those shows, the crazier the better. The power of friendship, and a hundred tons of hot steel.

"Any luck?" Yeong-Ja asked as they approached.

"Not yet," Brenda said wearily.

"It's too bad the Freighties don't have any convoys headed out west for the next several days. We could always wait..." Yeong-Ja said.

Brenda shook her head. "My instincts tell me that if we take too long on this, we're going to lose our chance to catch her at all." In truth, she was itching to be on the road even now. Bandying words with this paramilitary bureaucrat had strained her patience. "I requested he take it up with his superiors. We have to hope that will get some traction."

Colin winced. "Yeah, that's why I made the face there, sorry. I mean, it's not impossible, but there's no love lost with the upper echelons. Most of them are old pals of Colonel Georgio, and they've internalized his vendetta."

"I thought you said we'd made progress on that?" asked Brenda.

Colin shrugged uncomfortably.

"We gave him his son back alive," Leo said flatly. "It was a start. Didn't make us meilleurs amis overnight."

"Look at you with the Frenglish," Brenda teased lightly. "Used to have to get you five shots in before that came out."

"He's been lively with it since he found his brother," Colin observed.

That was another piece of information that Brenda was still absorbing. Leo's hope of someday finding his brother had been a fundamental part of him since they were activated. They had even discussed, once upon a time, taking a "sabbatical" to go searching for him after they'd resolved the food crisis. Of course, one thing had turned into another, and nothing went according to plan. For him to have stumbled onto his brother anyway by pure chance… It was astonishing.

Of course, it had been touch and go at first – Raffiel's

allegiance to the Reborn had placed him as a threat to the Division. Since he had taken the faction over, however, he had become their best chance at forging lasting peaceful ties.

Leo gave them both a dry look. "Doing my best to bring the tiniest bit of actual culture into both of your lives."

Brenda huffed at that. "Have you even tried any of the manga I suggested to you? Because I'm telling you, if you just give them a chance…"

"I'm still puzzled," Leo cut her off. "As to where you think I'm going to get these comic books from."

"Comic books? Comic books!" Brenda said, aghast. "Look, I have some with me in my bag. Next time we stop for the night, you're reading at least one."

Leo scrunched his face up in the manner of a child confronted by a plate heaped with broccoli. His eyes darted over Brenda's shoulder, and the expression vanished into granite smoothness in an instant. That was all the warning Brenda needed. She turned to face the Molossi quartermaster with her arms crossed over her chest.

"That was faster than I expected," Brenda admitted.

"We pride ourselves on efficiency," the black-uniformed man replied.

There was a certain sullen cast to him that gave Brenda hope. Whatever word he'd gotten back from his superiors, he wasn't completely on board with it. And given his general attitude up until this point, that could only be good news for them. There was no point in aggravating matters, though, so she just waited patiently for him to spit it out.

"It is the opinion of my superiors that you should be provided with a level of assistance," he finally said begrudgingly.

"Thank you for taking the time to check with them," Brenda offered with her best winning smile.

His own expression stayed sour. "I am on record as protesting this waste of resources. If it will get you out of my hair and far away from here, however, perhaps they have a point."

"It will," promised Brenda. "As soon as you provide us with a vehicle, we'll be on our way. Heck, if you're lucky, you'll never hear from us again."

"Do not get my hopes up too much," he said flatly.

"Right." Brenda cleared her throat. "So, that vehicle?"

The man's lip twisted. He turned to head for the gate into the motor pool and motioned for them to follow. He unlocked the opening as the agents trailed behind and led them inside. They passed Humvees and Bradleys and continued on into the far end of the lot. He stopped there toward the very end and turned, keys in hand.

"Your ride."

There was a certain smug satisfaction to him now. Brenda immediately realized why. The last vehicle out of the entire gathering had clearly seen better days. It was a 4x4 pickup truck, and while it was definitely of military design it was also obviously from a completely different era. They hadn't even bothered to repaint it; it was still done up in faded army green. The back was an open bed, and while the front was spacious someone was going to have to ride in the rear.

"Where did you even find this?" Brenda asked defeatedly.

"The M37 is a storied design," the Molossus said with feigned offense. "Perhaps it's a bit long in the tooth, but it has served ably for decades. You can't ask for a more reliable transport."

"Sure, if we were going to the Korean War," Brenda said. "This cannot be what your superiors had in mind."

"Selection of vehicle was left to my discretion, depending on our needs and availability. This is what I have determined we can spare." He closed his hand around the keys with a shrug. "If you do not want it, however, you are welcome to depart immediately. On foot."

"No," Brenda stopped him. She took a deep breath. "Leo, check it out if you would be so kind."

The other agent nodded impassively and went to investigate. He spent a few minutes kicking tires, peering through the windows, and checking the engine. He even crawled under the vehicle for a minute, emerging and clambering to his feet. He dusted himself off and only then did he give her a nod.

"It works."

"Of course it does," said the Molossi logistician. He genuinely seemed somewhat affronted now. "Say what you will, I wouldn't give you a broken truck."

"I can't imagine where I'd get the idea you might," Brenda said dryly.

She held out her hands for the keys, and the man dropped them into her palm.

"I believe that sees through any possible business

we could have," the Molossus said. "Good luck on your journey."

He turned smartly on his heel and departed. Brenda watched him go with an urge to throw a brick at the back of his head. With a sigh, instead she turned back to the truck. The damn thing was older than she was.

"All right, Leo, you take the wheel. I'll ride shotgun." Brenda turned her gaze to the other two agents. "You two OK with posting up in the bed for now?"

Yeong-Ja nodded. "That won't be a problem."

"No complaints about feeling the wind for a while," Colin agreed. "Though we might want to find something to weigh Yeong-Ja down with. Otherwise, if Leo hits too big of a pothole, she could go flying right over the side."

Yeong-Ja smirked and gave the medic a jab in the side that made him wince before laughing. They piled into the back, and Brenda and Leo added their go bags. Brenda kept all her weapons with her, the Honey Badger propped between her knees. Leo ditched everything except his sidearm for now.

Brenda climbed into the passenger side as Leo clambered into the driver's seat. She tossed him the keys across the gap between them. She set about getting herself as comfortable as possible.

"ISAC, show me a route," Leo said. He nodded at whatever the AI showed him. "Looks like we're going to be riding I-20 for hours."

Brenda glanced at the setting sun. "All right. I'll get some shut eye. If you find yourself nodding, wake me up and I'll take over driving. I don't want to stop if we can avoid it."

Leo nodded and started the truck up with a twist of the keys. The engine rumbled like distant thunder. Subtle it was not, Brenda thought. They would have to hope stealth never became the deciding factor in their mission.

Brenda kicked her boots up on the dashboard and leaned against the door. Her mind felt crowded with concerns, clamoring for attention. She pushed them aside through long practice. Any agent worth their salt learned to sleep when they could. If someone had to wait for ideal conditions, death by exhaustion was going to come first.

The vehicle pulled out from the lot and onto the waiting roads. The truck might not be exactly what she'd had in mind, but it still gave them a massive advantage over Maira's speed on foot. The mission was looking up. That was her last thought as sleep closed over her like a blanket.

Brenda woke to a hand on her shoulder. She started, but it was only Leo. Night had fallen while she slept. The truck rumbled along under a sky full of stars, the moon a Cheshire Cat's smile among them. A glance in the rear window revealed the two other agents had fallen asleep as well. Colin was a gangling, snoring heap, while Yeong-Ja was curled up in a ball against his side.

"Is it time to swap out?" Brenda asked, scrubbing a hand over her face.

"No," Leo said. "It has only been a few hours. But we're passing the scene of the crime."

Brenda raised a questioning eyebrow.

"The place where Maira killed the two agents."

"Allegedly," Brenda corrected.

Leo's only response was a graceful brushing motion with his hand. Brenda wasn't sure if that was tacit agreement, or simply a declaration that it didn't matter.

"Do you want to take a look?" she asked instead of pursuing the matter.

"Could be informative," Leo said.

"How much of a detour is it?"

Leo frowned in thought. "An hour out of the way, perhaps. No more than that."

"All right, let's make it happen," Brenda agreed.

They left the highway for smaller side roads. The drive passed in a comfortable silence. Brenda and Leo had been in the same cell ever since the original outbreak. Shared hardship forged tight bonds, and they were no exception. A passing familiarity in the old world had transmuted into something like family in the time since.

Even without ISAC to guide them, it was clear when they arrived at their destination. It was the scene of no small devastation. An aircraft had crashed here. Its tail was still pointed to the sky like an accusatory finger, a silhouette against the stars. Brenda opened the door of the truck and jumped out, her boots crunching on a layer of ash and fragments. She paced in a slow circle around the crater.

The aircraft had gouged a wound into the ground on impact, and to judge from the scorched surroundings a fire had spread from there. Whatever other evidence there might have been of that night's events was gone. Only the skeleton of the shattered transport remained; scavengers had seen to the rest. That was no surprise. The materials were useful in a dozen ways in a survival-focused world. It could even have been Division elements that had stripped it. With the moon a waning crescent in the sky, they broke out flashlights to help them navigate the crash site.

"So was she on the bird or did she bring it down?" Leo asked as she came back around.

The two in the back had woken up. Leo was staring at the debris as if he could unlock its secrets through concentration alone.

"On it, we think," Brenda said. "The crash was what the two agents were originally sent to investigate. They reported Maira's presence upon arriving at the scene, and then contact was lost. A follow-up investigation found their bodies."

"What was the condition of the bodies?" asked Colin with a medic's interest.

Brenda shrugged. "I didn't see any specifics like that in the report. Not like they had a coroner to send them to and get an autopsy done."

"Just like Maira to get lost at the bottom of a river and turn up in a plane. So let's see it happen," Yeong-Ja said. "ISAC, give us an ECHO of the events involving Agent Kanhai that night."

The system was capable of pulling information from a variety of sources and reconstructing that into a holographic playback projected onto the contact that agents wore.

"No data available," ISAC replied.

Brenda frowned and exchanged surprised looks with the other three cell members. Each of them had seen ECHOs created with far less available information. Especially with two agents and their own ISAC instances present and recording, it should have been an accurate source for their investigation. At the very least it should have provided something.

"ISAC," Brenda said. "We want to see a recording of the events of the night of July 17."

"No data available," the AI repeated.

"That's impossible," Leo said flatly.

"It should be," Brenda agreed uneasily. "I can't think of any reason why the agents' equipment wouldn't have been recording the entire time they were here."

"After they were dead, even," Colin noted grimly. "We saw ECHOs that continued after the wearer was killed."

"Unless someone deleted the information," Leo said.

"That's not possible either," Brenda said. "None of us has the ability to delete or overwrite ISAC data. It defeats the whole purpose of the system if you can't trust the information it provides."

"We couldn't," Leo said pointedly. "Could Maira?"

Brenda's denial died on her lips. She rubbed her eyebrow with a thumb as she thought it over. Maira was acknowledged these days as one of the foremost experts on how ISAC actually worked. She had the background and the hands-on experience to go with it. Hell, she had created a program that could neutralize control of SHD tech almost by accident.

"If anyone could do it, she could," Brenda conceded reluctantly.

"But why?" Colin asked with manifest confusion.

"To hide her guilt?" offered Leo.

"Then she's doing a poor job," Yeong-Ja noted dryly. "She's been declared a murderer and a rogue agent. The only ones even asking these questions are us. If she runs into any other agents, they'll probably shoot her on sight."

"Something strange is going on here, that's for sure," Brenda said. "I already thought something about this whole situation smelled wrong, and this feels like confirmation."

"No answers," mused Leo. "Just more questions."

"Sometimes you have to figure out the right question first," said Yeong-Ja.

"All the more important that we catch up with her, then," Brenda said after a thoughtful silence. "That's where our answers are. Let's get back on the road."

The drive back to the highway was just as quiet as the trip out to the crash site had been. The timbre of it was different this time, though. Brenda's mind ran in circles. There were too many unknowns. Maira had vanished after the events in Houston, presumed dead. Her last acts on the record had been to ensure a deadly threat was neutralized. Where had she gone? Why come back and attack the Division? If she had been on that plane, who had shot it down?

Had she killed those two agents that night?

Brenda had accepted that at face value upon being told. Part of her assurance had been faith in ISAC. The AI system was far from perfect in any number of ways, but all agents counted on it to be objective and reliable. If those assumptions were wrong, it could change a lot of things. Especially depending on who could alter its database.

If ISAC wasn't tamper-proof, how many wrong decisions had she made?

"Unknown transmission detected," ISAC announced.

Brenda straightened with surprise. The mirroring reactions of the other agents assured her the warning hadn't been a figment of her imagination.

"Play the transmission, ISAC," Brenda said.

A burst of noise hit their ears. Brenda winced and involuntarily touched her earpiece, tempted to pull it. She fought the urge and tried to focus. The noise juddered back and forth across the scale. There was something curiously orderly about it, but no meaning that she could discern. It reminded her of nothing so much as–

"Encrypted comms," Leo said.

Brenda nodded. "Been a while since someone went to the effort. ISAC, any hope of cracking the comms?"

"Encryption source unknown. Decryption key required. Decryption failed," ISAC replied.

None of this group had the skillset to change that out in the field. They would have to return a recording to the Core and let the technicians there do their work. Brenda had missed Maira ever since she'd been separated from her younger friend. Now she felt that gap even more deeply. Maira had been the one with the best grasp of information warfare.

The transmission was still squealing and barking in

her ear. Brenda glowered. "Cut that unless it becomes something intelligible, ISAC. Can we pinpoint a source?"

"Three sources detected," ISAC replied promptly. "I-20 northeast traveling west."

"Mobile sources," Yeong-Ja said thoughtfully on the cell comm network. "Are there supposed to be any friendlies out this way?"

"No," Brenda said worriedly. "The Freighties didn't have a convoy taking this route for another few days, or I would have asked for a ride with them. No agents are supposed to be out this way either; the whole point of us going was so no one else had a chance of intercepting Maira."

"Molossi?" asked Colin.

"You would know them better than I would," Brenda said.

"We're already too far west for them," Leo replied.

"Unless they've decided to expand in this direction now that there's something like peace with the Reborn," Yeong-Ja said.

"I think if they were planning a big move, they would have refused to help us at all," Colin said.

An uneasy silence settled as the quartet mulled over what they knew.

"So best guess," Brenda summed up. "Somebody new, or somebody we know is being shady. Either way, they're going our way. How far away are they, ISAC?"

The response came in two parts.

"Unknown radio source location detected within thirty miles," the AI said.

At the same time, they got a projection of a map on their interfaced contacts. It showed the local web of roads in shimmering orange lines. One showed their location; they were even now rejoining the interstate. A blinking dot indicated their mystery source, on the road behind them.

"Going to overtake us," Leo said.

"How sure are you?" Brenda asked.

"Completely," was the dry response from Leo.

Under her own wry look, he shrugged and elaborated. "Same route but they're going faster and they're behind us. At this rate we have maybe an hour and a half before they're right on top of us."

"Time to put the pedal to the metal, huh?" Colin offered.

Leo shook his head. "We're going as fast as this truck can manage, about fifty miles per hour. Whatever they're in, they're outpacing us with no problem."

"Options?" Brenda said.

"Abandon the road until they're past," Leo said. "Or get ready to find out who they are after all."

Brenda took a deep breath. "We don't know they're hostile."

"The Division is not overblessed with friends these days," Yeong-Ja commented wryly.

And one of them is out there in the desert ahead of us, alone and probably hurt, Brenda thought but didn't say. She wanted to, but it felt like so much wishful thinking. What were the odds that Maira was still really their friend? One ISAC glitch didn't prove anything. She still had a lot to answer for.

Instead, Brenda just said, "I don't want to lose the time it would take to give way."

"If this turns into a problem, we could lose a lot more than time," Yeong-Ja noted reasonably.

Brenda nodded. "I know. I say we stay the course. If nothing else, we'll get some answers as to who we're dealing with."

"I hate mysteries," Colin said. "I'm in."

"At least we won't be bored," Yeong-Ja said.

Leo gave a slight nod, as expressive as he was likely to be.

"All right. Let's go into this with eyes open," Brenda said. "I'm not looking for a fight, but if they turn out to want one, I don't want us caught with our pants down."

The energy of the group shifted. None of them were strangers to the desperate firefights of the new age. They set to work prepping their weaponry with practiced ease. There had been a time, Brenda mused, when the idea of a raging gun battle on the roads of the United States would have seemed like so much over the top fiction. Now it would be just another bitter evening's work.

Colin passed Brenda's kit from their packs in the back, leaning around to hand it to her through the window. That would have been a maneuver for the rest of them, but his long frame made it relatively easy. Brenda spent a few minutes making sure her Honey Badger was ready to go. The action was oiled and smooth. Leo was occupied at the wheel, so she took care of his gear as well.

"Back to the MP5?" she commented lightly. "What happened to the minigun from your report?"

"Too noisy," Leo said.

"Like any of us are going to escape tinnitus anyway," Brenda muttered. "All these gunfights are hell on our ears."

"What was that?" Leo asked.

Brenda gave him a raised eyebrow. He graced her with a brief smile that cracked his granite facade.

"A joke," Brenda said wonderingly. "An honest to god funny from the world's original straight man. Your brother must be a good influence."

"He is."

"I'm sorry to have pulled you away from him again," Brenda said.

Leo shook his head. "He understands. This is the world now. He has his own work; trying to change the Reborn is no easy task. They could do good, but they were on a bad path. Changing that is like bringing the *Titanic* about."

For Leo, it was practically a speech. The topic must be near to his heart indeed. For all the seriousness of the words, Brenda couldn't help but smile about it. It was good to see him care so much about something more than the next mission objective.

"Headlights," Yeong-Ja said.

Brenda glanced in the side mirror but didn't see anything. She leaned out of the window. The wind whipped at her clothes. If she strained, she thought she could just barely make out the faintest gleam behind them. If she hadn't been warned, she doubted she would have caught it. The other woman must have eagle eyes.

Brenda pulled back into her seat and rested a hand on

the Honey Badger. Her palms were sweating. Her intuition had been honed by years of bad situations, and something about this felt wrong. Dangerous. *Please let me be wrong*, she thought. *Just this once, I'm OK with being wrong.*

"Can you make out any details?" Brenda asked.

A glance back showed Yeong-Ja had put her rifle on a tripod in the bed. She was laid out now, looking through the scope.

"Trailer trucks. Three of them. Militarized."

"Well, that narrows it down, doesn't it?" Colin said uneasily.

"Why would the Freighties lie to us?" Brenda said. "They've been reliable allies from the moment we made contact with them."

She saw Leo glance in the rearview with a grim expression. "Roamers."

"There's no way," Colin protested. "This far south?"

"Three is a Roamer combat unit," Leo said. "They're hostile."

"I could fire the first shot," Yeong-Ja said with a sniper's calm. "But I do not like the idea of guessing who I'm shooting at. Friendly fire isn't exactly friendly."

"We could try to make contact," Colin said. "If they're Freighties, they'll respond to a radio call."

"If they're Roamers, and we reveal we're Division, they'll respond, too," Brenda said wryly. "We just won't like the form the reply takes."

It was always better in battle to be the one who shot first. That was one of the great tautologies. The moment they lost the initiative, they would be at a disadvantage. We're the only ones Maira can count on, Brenda thought. If we risk this here, we risk–

"We're the good guys," Yeong-Ja said firmly. "It might be a risk, but that's what separates us from the enemy. We do things the right way."

"She's right," Colin said without hesitation. "We should try to contact them."

A surge of frustration rose in Brenda, but it died as quickly as it came. The dynamic was familiar. She couldn't help but smile. Chance might have brought these agents to Maira's cell, but they were the right companions for her. Hadn't it been Maira who held Brenda to a higher standard? Nobody was perfect, but if they gave up trying then what was the point?

"Leo?" she asked.

There was a lot in the look he exchanged with Brenda. Parallel thoughts. Their shared experiences in the DC operational area had made them harsher. Colder. Pragmatic, and perhaps too much so. They were lucky to have people who could still pull them back from the brink.

"Call them," he said.

"All right," Brenda said. "ISAC, put me on a general comm frequency. Prepare for broadcast."

"Acknowledged," ISAC said.

"Unknown vehicles," Brenda said with steel in her voice. "This is Division Agent Brenda Wells. Identify yourselves."

"Unknown transmission has ceased," ISAC said.

A silence stretched. The headlights behind them crept closer, clearly visible now. Leo tapped his fingertips against the wheel, a soft tattoo, the only betrayal of any nerves. Brenda reseated her rifle in her lap. Whatever happened, she told herself, they had done the right thing. Sometimes that had to be enough.

"Unknown transmission has intercep–" ISAC started.

"Incoming!" roared Colin.

Brenda had enough time to look into the rearview mirror. A dark shape hurtled toward them on a tail of smoke and fire. A rocket. Leo swerved with impeccable reflexes. Tires squealed against the asphalt. The missile burned through the place they had been a half second before. It detonated up ahead, a sudden dazzling brilliance.

"Unknown hostile detected," ISAC said blandly.

"There's our answer!" barked Brenda. "Return fire!"

The two in the rear went to work immediately. Brenda could hear the first shots ring out. She put it out of her mind swiftly. She had to trust them to handle their part of things. For herself, her best bet for right now was suppressive fire. She leaned out the window with the Honey Badger planted in her shoulder and opened up. She swept across their foes with controlled bursts. The weapon hammered away, recoil pounding into her shoulder.

Return fire came quickly. The flash and spatter of small arms. Up top, a machine gun's muzzle flash flickered and flared. Most of the shots were wide, lost to the darkness of the night. A few hissed past. A round hit the truck roof near

Brenda's arm. The vehicle was not armored – the round punched right through that and cracked the windshield.

Another rocket-propelled grenade came howling in. Leo swerved again. It impacted on the road to the left of them, washing that side of the vehicle in flame. The sudden movement threatened to launch Brenda out of the vehicle completely. She teetered on the brink of the fall. Asphalt hissed by, eager to skin her like a peach. Colin cried out in pain.

Brenda caught hold of the window frame with her left hand. It was a white-knuckled grip that took skin off her palm. Through main strength she pulled herself back up, teeth gritted the whole way. Her right hand was still holding on to the Honey Badger through long-trained reflex. Two more bullets came through the rear window and went through the windshield, missing bodies by nothing more than luck.

"Yeong-Ja, shut that damn machine gun down!" yelled Brenda. "Colin, are you all right?"

"Yeah," he replied on the radio. His voice was tight with pain. "My right arm got burned."

A thunderclap resounded, and the greater cacophony quietened by a noticeable notch.

"One less machine gun," Yeong-Ja said. On the job, her voice was so flat it barely even conveyed satisfaction.

"This goes on much longer, it's not gonna matter," Leo said shortly. "They'll catch up and just run us right off the damn road."

"I kn–"

"Unknown broadcast detected," ISAC announced.

"What?" Brenda sputtered. "Another one? A new broadcast?"

"Confirmed. New broadcast source detected," said the AI.

"Is this one encrypted?" called Colin.

"Unknown." The system couldn't tell them – that would require a judgment call beyond its capabilities.

"Play it!" snapped Brenda.

In the meantime, she knocked out what was left of the rear window with the butt of her rifle. Scraping the shards out of the way she scrambled through the opening to join the other two in the bed of the truck. A hiss-pop of a near miss made it clear that the destruction of the machine gun nest had not defanged their foes. Brenda kneeled and returned fire. The semis were close enough now that she could see her occasional tracer rounds ricocheting from the heavy armor plating the Roamers had installed.

In her ears there was more juddering static. The new broadcast was indeed also encrypted. Colin was slumped against the side rail of the truck bed, his right arm clutched to his chest. She could see the scorch marks. A little drone hovered near him, administering a spray to his burns. He had his sidearm in his left hand and was plinking away with it gamely.

Yeong-Ja squeezed off another shot. It must have taken one of the drivers, because a pursuing truck veered sharply off the road. Hitting rough terrain shifted its weight too much and it crashed onto its side, toppling off into ruin. That took care of a third of their original problem at least, Brenda thought.

"Good kill," she told the sniper.

"Not enough," was the terse reply.

As if in reply, a bang slammed through their entire truck. Brenda lost her balance and sprawled into Colin. He caught her in both his arms before she was sent tumbling, but she heard the agonized intake of breath as he was forced to use his injured limb. She gave him a grateful nod and struggled back to her knees. The shaking didn't completely stop – the whole vehicle shuddering as it went.

"Leo!"

"We lost a tire," the driver said on the radio. "That is bad, for the record."

This was turning desperate quickly. It was time to use some special assets, limited quantities or not. Brenda kicked her go bag to where Colin sat. He holstered his pistol and gave her a questioning look.

"Seekers!" she called.

Colin nodded, and Brenda turned her attention back to their enemies. They were gaining by the moment now. A silhouette on the top of the nearest was moving. Brenda gauged with practiced eyes. A person carrying something bulky, and her breath caught. Another of the damned RPGs.

She sighted in and fired off a series of bursts, emptying her magazine. The figure jolted upright and then fell away into the night. Their oblong burden went with them. Brenda released her breath. A few more seconds of being alive, purchased.

Something slapped her in the chest. The wind knocked

out of her, Brenda fell back against the window frame leading into the cab. Coughing uncontrollably, she looked down. A crater decorated the front of her vest. She touched disbelieving fingers to it. Everyone who lived this way had a bullet with their name on it. Had hers finally come home?

Colin pushed past her, his arm full of footballs. That was their shape, anyway. Brenda blinked at him and shook her head, trying to catch her breath. Her hand was still pressed to her chest. The pain would pass, thankfully. Without the armor she'd be dead.

"How many?" he called.

"All of them!" Brenda wheezed back. Needs must when the devil drove.

He shrugged and scattered them across the ground behind the tail of the truck. Each one lit up with an orange glow as it hit the ground and spun into action. ISAC fed information directly into Brenda's eye. Colin had done exactly as she asked, and now five seeker mines were racing toward their two remaining pursuers. She allocated them down the middle as much as possible – two and three.

One of them completely didn't notice. The other one must have been more familiar with SHD tech. They veered desperately to try to evade, risking the same fall that had destroyed the first semi. They managed to restabilize their truck before it tipped. Unfortunately for them, the devices weren't called seeker mines for no reason. They followed the movement smoothly.

The one who hadn't deigned to attempt an escape ran

over theirs first. They slipped under the semitruck as it came on, and then there was a brilliant flash as all three detonated at the same time. High explosives lifted the truck clear off its wheels for a split second. When it came crashing down it was done. There was no armor underneath. The vehicle was gutted completely, belching fire through shredded cab and trailer alike.

The second truck was caught sidelong. Because of the vector, the two that had gone after it hit the wheels directly. They exploded in the moment of contact, a heartbeat apart. The angle of the blast kept it from simply annihilating this final truck. Instead, it ripped the wheels away in a geyser of flame. The force of the detonation lifted the vehicle to the side, and all the skillful driving in the world ceased to matter. It toppled onto its side on the road with a tremendous crash. It scraped on for a dozen yards, trailing a rain of sparks as it went.

They hurtled on. The scene of devastation retreated into the night behind them. Unfortunately, their own shuddering craft was not improving. If anything, it was getting worse. They were driving through a cloud, Brenda realized now that the sense-numbing cacophony of battle was gone. She rolled and crouched to peer through the back window. It was steam, leaking from the hood of their truck.

"I have to stop!" Leo called.

"Do it," Brenda replied.

Colin scrambled back to her on his hands and knees.

"You took a hit?" the medic called.

Brenda nodded and motioned to her chest. He leaned closer, and the little drone hovered up next to him. Helpfully it turned on a penlight to show the impact site. Brenda wasn't sure if she couldn't breathe or if she was just scared to try.

Colin straightened and clapped her on the shoulder. "Plate's intact! Stopped it cold, you're good to go."

Brenda's shoulders slumped with relief. "Not today."

"Not today," the medic replied with a slight smile.

Yeong-Ja had moved to a cross-legged position and had her rifle settled across her lap. She offered Brenda a tired smile. "Nice trick with the bombs."

"Nice shooting. Teamwork makes the dream work."

"Any fight you walk away from, right?"

Leo slowed the truck and pulled over onto the shoulder of the road. Something about that put an obscure smile on Brenda's face. An old habit, getting out of the way of oncoming traffic. They'd seen four moving vehicles this entire drive, and they'd blown up three of those. What killed the smile was listening to the way the engine sputtered as they came to a halt.

"Yeah, that's what I'm afraid of," Brenda belatedly replied to Yeong-Ja.

She hopped over the side of the truck. Her prosthetic dug into her leg as she hit the ground. It hurt but she ignored it. Leo opened the driver's side door and got out. His expression told Brenda everything she needed to know, and her heart sank.

"What happened?" Brenda asked.

"Have suspicions," Leo said as he moved around to pop the hood.

It came up with a fresh wave of hot steam that sent him stepping back quickly and waving his hands defensively. It filled the air with the scent of hot metal and dampness. Brenda crossed her arms over her chest and stayed out of the way. She had her skillset, and it didn't include this. Better to help if he asked.

Instead, he just stood there and shook his head. "Damn."

"Lay it on me," Brenda said.

"Tire was bad enough. Don't even have a replacement. But this? Shot went into the engine block. Holed the radiator."

"That sounds bad," Colin offered.

"It's bad," Leo agreed.

"Give me options here," Brenda said. "Can we limp on? Go slow?"

Leo shook his head. "The damage will only worsen if we try to force this."

"OK. Can you fix it?"

Leo gave a mirthless smirk. "With a soldering iron and a replacement tire and time … maybe? As it is …" He gestured to the empty stretch of road before and behind them. The clouds of smoke to their rear marked the desperate battle.

"Between the blown tire and a radiator leak? This is a few tons of scrap metal and rubber now."

"The Roamers were in contact with someone in the middle of all that," Yeong-Ja pointed out. "They could have reinforcements on the way right now."

Brenda winced at the reminder. "ISAC, what was the origin of the second broadcast signal?"

"Approximately four hundred miles to the west," ISAC replied promptly.

"Show me a map," Brenda said with a frown.

The requested image popped up in her vision. The rough indicator of the signal source left little doubt of its origins.

"El Paso," Brenda said. "They were talking to someone in El Paso."

"If those were Roamers – and they sure as heck fought like Roamers – what are they doing with friends in El Paso?" asked Colin.

"That's an excellent question," Brenda said. "And we're going to find out whether we like it or not."

"Why is that?" asked Yeong-Ja.

"ISAC, show them the map, and add the locator beacon we've been tracking."

Each of the agents now saw the same thing: the road to the west, and on it two things. The mystery signal, and the locator beacon of one rogue agent, Maira Kanhai.

"We lost our speed edge," Leo pointed out.

"The greater part of it," admitted Brenda. "But whatever has happened to Maira, she's not moving fast. Maybe half the speed I'd expect of her at her best. I hope y'all are ready to have some fun."

Colin groaned. "I hate it when Marines say stuff like that. It's never actually fun."

Brenda grinned at all of them. "Grab your packs, agents. Lose anything you don't need.

"It's time to step it out. We're on foot from here, and we've still got a ways to go."

CHAPTER 7

June 28

"Fifteen minutes until test initiation," said the lead facility technician.

Maira sat off to the side with her arms crossed over her chest. The room was unpleasantly stuffy and warm. Too many computers in too small a space with too little ventilation. The steady thrum of all those machines soothed her, but she could have done without the waste heat they produced. It had her sweating.

Well, at least, that was one of the reasons she was sweating. The other was that the time to test her code had come upon them all too swiftly. Maira had worked as fast as she could, but she felt far from confident that her creation was ready for implementation. Nerves had been prickling at her all morning, threatening to make her sick. She hadn't even been able to choke down a breakfast of scrambled eggs and venison sausage. It had turned her stomach just to look at the spread.

"Ten minutes," called the technician.

Her nerves made Maira want to fidget. She did her best to ignore them. Even so, every few minutes she'd catch herself plucking at her sleeve or repetitively popping her knuckles and made herself stop. *What are you so scared of?* she demanded internally. *It's the first test. Nobody expects this to be perfect. What do you have to prove?*

More aptly, who did she have to prove it to?

Maira's gaze darted to where the impeccable Natalya Sokolova stood as an involuntary answer. Yes, if she was going to be honest with herself, that – or rather who – was what was weighing on her. She wanted to look good in front of Nat, and the woman had come in person to witness this demonstration. Natalya thought Maira was something special. What if today proved her wrong?

By contrast with Maira, nothing seemed to bother the woman in white. Not the heat, not the constant chatter of various technicians going about their work, and certainly not the pressures of this test. She just watched everything with keen eyes and a faint, pleasant smile. This might as well have been a scrimmage match for the office baseball team for all the worry she displayed.

Maira still wasn't clear who Natalya really was. She had been introduced to this place as a government facility, operating under the onus of the Department of Homeland Security. Natalya wasn't a government employee, though. In the world before the Poison, she had been a Fortune 500 CEO. Yet everyone here answered to her with no hesitation. No one questioned her authority.

"Five minutes."

"So explain the way this test will work to me again?" Natalya asked.

Maira blinked. She'd gotten so wrapped up in her thoughts she hadn't realized the other woman had moved over to stand next to her. She had probably been staring at her vacantly while her mind ran. A flush of embarrassment darkened her cheeks. She cleared her throat.

"Well, your technicians have partitioned off a section of your local servers to act as a simulated hostile server. I'm not a hundred percent on what they did for that part; would be unfair if I had a hand in creating the circumstances of testing my own work, after all." Maira gave a nervous smile.

Natalya returned the smile calmly. "And now we're going to release your new code into that simulated server and see how it performs?"

Maira nodded. "That's the long and short of it. If it works, it should isolate the code structure and leave it vulnerable to a takedown that won't impact any of your other technology. Just like you wanted."

"And if it doesn't work, then we'll try again, won't we? The whole point of doing this today is to figure out what doesn't work so you can improve the next iteration." Nat reached out and squeezed Maira's shoulder. "Relax. We're not at the end game yet."

Maira took a deep breath. "You're right. It's silly to expect it to come out of the gate working perfectly."

But she wanted it to. That was the truth. She wanted to

wow everyone here with how clever she was, especially Natalya. This was her wheelhouse, she was back doing what she enjoyed, and what she was good at. Was it too much to ask that she exceed everyone's expectations in the process?

"Test begin," said the lead technician.

This was not the Hollywood version of hacking, unfortunately. There was no giant screen with a percentage meter to fill up, or a 3D representation of a fantastical battle taking place. In the heat of the humming room, nothing changed. A few technicians leaned closer to their workstations. Maira's stomach muscles clenched. She pressed a hand to her torso, her mouth too full of saliva. She was not going to throw up. She wasn't.

It was just nerves, she told herself as she fought her rising gorge. There was nothing more to it than that. Even so, she'd been nervous a lot in her life. She'd faced deadly catastrophes and life-threatening crises. This extreme nausea was something new and different. She didn't appreciate it at all. Maira pressed the back of her hand to her mouth and tried to think about anything except her roiling stomach.

Natalya was watching her with a raised eyebrow. "Maira? Are you all right?"

Maira nodded. She was afraid that if she tried to talk it was going to come out with projectile puke. She clenched her jaw tighter. Beads of sweat broke out on her forehead. The room felt even hotter, the air oppressively thick. With no conscious thought she stumbled to the door. Out in the hallway it was cooler. She was able to take in a deep breath, and force back the nausea for now.

The door opened again, and Natalya emerged. Concern was written on her face.

Maira held up a forestalling hand. "I'm sorry. I'm just not feeling well."

"Should I send for a doctor?" the other woman asked.

"No, please don't. It's just an upset stomach, I promise. Just my nerves getting the better of me."

Nat studied her. "Something you ate?"

"I don't think so," Maira said. "I didn't even eat breakfast."

An expression Maira couldn't read flashed across Nat's face. "You can't skip meals, Maira. Your body is still healing. You have to provide yourself with the nutrients it needs."

"I know, I know," Maira said. "I just really wanted everything to go right today. I guess I got too wrapped up in my own head about it."

There were muffled cheers on the other side of the door. Maira couldn't help but straighten up on hearing it. There weren't a lot of reasons people would be breaking into celebration in there. Unless…

Natalya smiled slightly. "Come on, it sounds like you're missing your moment of triumph."

Maira breathed and rubbed her stomach. The sick feeling ebbed back. It was still there, but it felt bearable now. And she did want to find out how the test had gone. Getting a report on it later wouldn't be nearly as satisfying as seeing the results with her own eyes.

"All right," Maira said. "Let's go see what's what."

Natalya opened the door and motioned her through. "After you."

Maira's knees hit the bathroom floor and she yanked the toilet seat up. She barely made it in time; the nausea hit her like an oversized ocean wave. Her body convulsed and she curled over the rippling water. A weak sputtering of liquid sprayed from her mouth. It hit the water and dissipated as murky clouds.

There was no chance to pull away. The muscles of her body kept clenching, like she was a washcloth someone was trying to wring out. There was nothing to throw up aside from bile and acid. It burned the back of her throat. Her legs slid against the tiled floor, and she caught hold of the rim of the toilet with desperate hands to hold herself up.

It hurt. Not that vomiting was ever a fun time, but her abdominal muscles still weren't fully healed from her gunshot wounds. They protested each convulsion with a siren of pain that started tears in her eyes and made her want to scream. The fluorescent lights of the bathroom seemed to burn unbearably bright. It was like they were lasers trying to drill into her skull.

Finally, the spasms in her stomach stopped. Maira was left slumped against the toilet, limp and shaking. If someone had been torturing her, she was pretty sure she would have told them whatever they wanted to hear. As it was, she was bewildered as to where this suffering was coming from. She wrapped an arm across her face and tried to focus on breathing in the comforting darkness.

Slowly some of her strength came back to her. She was able to get back to her feet. The toilet flushed automatically as she walked away from it. She washed her hands with mechanical efficiency. The face looking back at her in the mirror was not comforting. She looked exhausted. Used up.

"Come on, Maira," she told herself. "There's work to be done. There's no time for this bullshit, whatever it is."

She walked out of the bathroom and slowly headed back to her personal quarters. It had been almost two hours since the test was complete. It had been a qualified success; not perfect, but more effective than anyone had hoped for the alpha of her code. Better yet, she now had a grasp of what the weaknesses in her design were, and she already had ideas on how to improve the next version.

Unfortunately, her symptoms were only getting worse with time. Something was obviously going wrong. The issue was she had no idea what. Food poisoning, as Nat had conjectured? Something more sinister? There was no telling, and for some reason Maira felt reluctant to turn herself over to the medical department.

She opened the door to her room. The only light came from the screen of her laptop. Even that was unpleasant to look at. It seemed to throb in time with the beat of her heart. She sank into her seat with a sigh and rested her chin on her hand. Lines of code filled the screen. She scrolled through them slowly, making notes here and there as she went. Improvement possibilities, weaknesses to discard.

It was odd: as bad as her body felt, her mind seemed as sharp as a scalpel. If anything, she felt like a fog in her head was clearing up. Fixing the code felt easier than it had since she started. Maira had managed, of course, but it had always felt like it was pushing uphill for some reason. Now it was level ground again, and that was encouraging.

Encouraging and concerning. That clarity brought with it some unwelcome thoughts. For one thing, only now was she starting to realize just why the system structure seemed so familiar. Namely, this wasn't her first time writing a program to infiltrate it. To put it bluntly, whatever system Natalya and her people wanted hacked bore an awful lot of similarities to ISAC.

That was worrisome for obvious reasons. The Division might not have been the ones to save Maira, but that didn't mean she wanted to turn on them. She wished she could have contacted them; long distance communications were growing more difficult with time. And if that wasn't what was happening here, who else could Natalya be planning to target? ANNA, possibly? Certainly, the rogues were a threat someone would have to handle eventually. Maira had had a personal hand in stymieing their plans twice, but they would keep trying.

Then, of course, there was the danger of proliferation. Even if ISAC wasn't the intended target, the program would work on it. Once the code was out there in the world, it could end up in dangerous hands no matter how good the intentions behind it were. There was no putting the genie back in the bottle. And if someone managed to isolate ISAC and bring it crashing down …

The Division would suffer. Stopgap measures would help,

but there would always be those outside their walls. Agents would die, and communities who depended on them for protection would be left painfully vulnerable. Maira wasn't sure she could live with herself if she allowed that to happen.

She still had her own programs, of course, the ones she'd carried in her thumb drive through years of desolation. A talisman that kept coming in handy at the oddest moments. Thank goodness for a waterproof casing, or her trip into the bay in Houston would have put an end to it once and for all. She reached to where she wore it around her neck and fiddled with the strap. She had asked Natalya for it directly, and it had been returned the day after, along with a joke about Maira needing to sign an NDA to keep it. It felt good to have it back.

The door swung open with no warning. Maira's hand fled her necklace like a spider running from a switched on light. It was as instinctive as a flinch, and she cursed herself for it half a heartbeat later. Fiddling with a necklace was not suspicious. Acting like someone had caught her with her hand in the cookie jar was.

Luckily, it wasn't Nat, nor was it security troopers storming in with guns drawn to haul her to the brig. Instead, the bulky shape of her physical therapist pushed into the room pulling a cart behind him.

Maira raised an eyebrow, urging her heart to slow down. "Keith! Good to see you."

"Hello, Maira," the man replied amiably. "Sorry to burst in on you like that, had my hands full with the cart here."

"Yeah, I can see that. You know we already did physical

therapy today, right? I don't have two rounds in me if that's what you're thinking."

Keith rumbled a chuckle. "Not at all, don't worry. Even I'm not that sadistic. Nah, the boss lady asked me to come check on you."

Maira smiled lopsidedly. "She worries too much. I told her I was fine. I'm just a little under the weather."

"I hear you, but she wasn't in a mood to listen. Gave me very clear instructions."

"And these instructions involved a cart?" Maira asked interestedly.

He laughed and opened the side to reveal dishes. "Food, hot from the cafeteria. And before you even start, she didn't leave any wiggle room for you either. You are to eat, no questions asked."

Maira sighed. "But I… all right, fine. Roll them out."

Keith busied himself setting up the food, and Maira watched him. It was a veritable smorgasbord, likely one of everything they'd had on offer. No wiggle room indeed. She was clearly expected to make herself eat something from what was available.

"I have to admit, Maira, getting a look at you, I feel like she had a point. You don't look well."

"Just what every lady likes to hear from a strapping gentleman," Maira said dryly.

"Ha! No offense. But your health is our number one concern, you know that. And while I was less certain about this next part, now that I'm looking at you? I think you do need it."

"Next part?" Maira asked.

Keith reached into the cart again and came out with an IV bag and everything needed to set it up. He waggled it at her and shrugged.

"You can't be serious," Maira said.

"Afraid so. Again, boss's orders. Besides, I can tell you're dehydrated just by looking at you. You have to take better care of yourself, Maira."

Maira drummed her fingers against the arm of her chair. Something about all of this sat really wrong. Maybe it was just that rising paranoia, but didn't this seem overboard? Food, IVs, both carried by someone they knew she trusted? She eyed the bag. It looked like nothing except saline. Would she be able to tell if there was anything else in it?

"Roll up your left sleeve, please," Keith said.

Maira flinched. What was she going to do? The man had his orders. Refuse? Get violent? She didn't want to hurt Keith. She didn't have any good reason to hurt anyone. They were just concerned for her. She was sick and they were trying to take care of her. Why was she being like this? Things had been so easy. She had felt so calm for weeks. Why was she getting so high strung now?

"All right," Maira said finally. She rolled up her sleeve as requested.

She picked at some steamed corn while Keith went about his work. The needle pressed into her arm easily, a flash of cold and a flicker of pain. Nothing terrible. Soon the drip was going. Maira watched those clear drops run slowly through the tube into her body. Just saline, she told herself. Hydration. Hydration is important.

"All right," Keith said. "You appear to be compliant, lucky me."

Maira gave him a tired smile. "Did your orders include beating me up if I wasn't?"

His smile faded briefly. It came back in full strength quickly. "Of course not, Maira. I'd never do anything to hurt you."

"Thanks, Keith. I appreciate you looking after me. I'll tell Nat you did a great job."

"Flex," he corrected in the habitual manner. "You're too kind. I'll get out of your hair. Enjoy your night, OK?"

He left, and the door slid shut behind him. Maira sat there and frowned. Drip, drip, drip went the IV. It was nothing, she insisted to herself. Wild paranoia. She was embarrassing herself thinking this way. These people had taken her in. Saved her life, and given her purpose. Who was she to question them and their motives like this?

Brenda had saved her life and given her purpose, too. But she'd never hesitated to question Brenda.

The thought came unbidden. It made Maira's hands tighten into fists. Brenda… Her cell might have died in Houston, but Brenda would still be out there somewhere, alive. And if this program she was making stripped the Division of its defenses, even if it took down dangerous rogues at the same time, Brenda would be one of the ones to pay the price. Maybe even lose her life.

No. Maira couldn't just close her eyes to that risk. She turned her gaze back to the computer screen. It seemed blurry. She rubbed her eyes on her sleeve and shook her head. What had she been thinking about? The Division? The code? Something. She swallowed hard. The nausea seemed to be receding finally, thankfully.

Brenda.

Maira reached up and touched the necklace with its USB drive again. No, she didn't want to hurt anybody. Not here, and not back in Kansas. But not hurting people wasn't a passive thing. It meant taking responsibility and figuring out how to do the least harm. She took the USB and plugged it in. There was a certain program among her suite of tools that she had in mind. A seeker. It would slither through databases and around defenses, collecting data as it went.

Nat would be angry if she found out, Maira thought. It almost made her take the thumb drive right back out of the computer. Instead, she shook her head fiercely and glowered. Nat wanted what was best for her. If her benefactors here had nothing to hide – and surely they didn't! – then the program simply wouldn't find anything, would it?

Mostly what Maira wanted now was to put her head down and fall asleep. Instead, she started up the program and got it ready to run. Topic? it queried. No searching tool was useful without key words to arrow in on.

Maira thought for a moment, and then tapped keys slowly. M A I R A K A N H A I, she spelled out. There was no harm in that. If there was information here about her, she had a right to know. Right? Right. Maira gave herself a firm nod and set the program to work.

She sat back then. For some reason it seemed really

hard to string thoughts together. The slow drip of the IV in her ear was making her sleepy, she thought. No one could blame her if she took a little nap. After all, one way or another, the program needed time to run.

Maira's eyes slid shut. When they opened, the truth would be waiting, she thought. One way or another.

CHAPTER 8

Spring. Washington DC

"It was intentional," Rowan said.

The younger agent's gaze was distant. Soot stained her face and clothes. The stink of burning plastic, rubber, and wood intermixed clung to her like an invisible cloud. Wood and the tang of chemicals. Worse yet, there was just a hint of the sweet tang of cooking meat. It made Brenda want to step back. She restrained the impulse.

"It might have been," Brenda replied. "We'll investigate to the best of our ability–"

"No," Rowan said coldly. "You don't understand. You weren't there."

Brenda frowned. It was true. She had been called away to the other side of the city when the report of the fire arrived. She'd hurried as fast as she could, but you could only cover terrain so fast on foot. By the time she'd arrived, the building was already a gutted husk of its former self.

"OK," Brenda said. "I missed the action here. Then help me understand."

It was snowing ash. A slow but steady flurry of gray flakes from the sky. Rowan held out a hand and let one land in her palm. She touched it with her thumb, and the fragile flake smeared against her skin. Rowan stared at the mark with eyes that saw everything and nothing.

"The report came in while we were sleeping. Eric was on watch and heard the radio call come in, woke the rest of us up. We set out immediately, grabbed our guns and went. We still took too long. The whole thing was burning by the time we got there."

Brenda looked past her. The fire had mostly burned out by now. The only thing that remained of the tenement building was a smoldering black ruin. There was a small gathering around the devastation. Other Division agents, but also some of the locals. Someone was weeping. Everyone looked grim.

"What did you do?" she asked Rowan.

Rowan shrugged. It was a minimal gesture, a slight shift of her body. "What could we do? There's no fire department to call. Some people had already gathered, folks were trying to throw buckets of water on it. Too little to change the course of things." Her lips pressed into a thin line. "There were people still inside. We could hear them screaming."

Brenda closed her eyes. What could she say to that?

Rowan continued in a dull monotone. "We tried to go in after them. It was probably suicide, but we had to do something, right? We had to try."

"Of course," Brenda said soothingly. She glanced to the side. Leo and Eric were nearby. Both were just as dirty as Rowan, but none of them seemed hurt. "I'm glad none of you were injured."

"That's because we couldn't get in." Rowan laughed. It was a mirthless, hollow sound. "There were chains on the doors."

Brenda winced. "A security measure? It seems reasonable until–"

"No," Rowan cut her off. "The chains were on the outside of the door."

Brenda felt her heart sink. "Are you sure?" That was a stupid question. She felt a surge of irritation with herself. "Why would someone..."

"I've been wondering that all night," Rowan said. She reached up and absently wiped at her face. All she managed to do was smear ash and soot around. "Maybe they pissed off the True Sons or the Hyenas. Maybe it was one person with a grudge. I don't know."

"As if the world isn't dark enough," Brenda said softly.

She stared at the ruined building. A hundred people could have lived here, easily. She had hoped most had gotten out. If the fire had been set intentionally and the doors barred, though, those chances worsened dramatically. The death toll of this one act of arson could run into the dozens.

"We failed them," Rowan said, bitter.

"We're not miracle workers," Brenda replied sadly. "I'm sure you did everything you could."

"Maybe." Rowan shrugged again. "That doesn't change

the outcome. It doesn't bring any of these people back from the dead."

The red-haired woman didn't wait for Brenda to reply. She walked away, shoulders slumped. Brenda watched her go with sorrow. This was the kind of night that stayed with a person. She had to hope Rowan wouldn't let it eat her alive.

"Hey," Eric said at her elbow.

Brenda jumped. She breathed out sharply when she saw who it was, and craned back to look the immense man in the face. "You just took a week off my life. Nobody as big as you should be able to move that quietly."

He gave her a wry smile. "Sorry. Maybe we can put a bell on me sometime." He motioned after Rowan. "How is she?"

Brenda shook her head. "She's taking it hard."

"That's what I figured," Eric said. "We should keep an eye on her."

There was a wariness in his voice that wasn't like him. The entire time Brenda had known Eric, he had been one of the most genial people she'd ever met. The very definition of the gentle giant. If anything, he was usually too trusting.

"Any particular reason you're especially concerned about this one?" Brenda asked.

Eric studied her under heavy lids. "How much did she tell you?"

"It was pretty grim," Brenda said. "You got here too late, the fire had already spread. There was screaming inside, and y'all couldn't get to them because the doors were chained shut from the outside."

"All of that is true," Eric said quietly. "She left out one thing, though."

Brenda frowned. "What?"

"There was a guy already here when we arrived. Someone who lived in the building, he said. He'd gone for a walk because he couldn't sleep and came back to the fire."

"Damn," Brenda said. "That's heavy. We should ask him if he saw anything."

"Nothing useful," Eric said. "Go on, ask me why I'm so sure."

Brenda's frown deepened. "Why?"

"Because when Rowan realized those doors were chained shut, she cooked off. She snatched him up by the collar and started screaming. Saying he must have been in on it, to not be inside. That maybe he was the one to lock the doors."

"Oh, God," Brenda said.

She could already imagine how that would look to outsiders, a Division agent screaming at a civilian as a tragedy played out in the background. People wouldn't understand there wasn't always something they could do.

"Yeah," Eric said tiredly. "She was shaking him around. Pressed her shotgun to his head and started yelling that he had better tell her anything. Dude was sobbing, kept insisting he didn't know anything."

"What did she do then?" asked Brenda.

"Said if he wouldn't talk, he was useless." Eric's eyes focused on the middle distance as he remembered. "I stepped forward. I didn't want her to do anything she couldn't make right. She locked eyes with me then, and..."

He shook his head. "Let me tell you. You could see the fire there. Like it had spread to her brain and was burning her up from the inside."

"Did she hurt him?" Brenda asked softly.

"No," Eric said. "She looked at me, then she let him go and told him to get lost. But for a second there, Brenda, I really thought she was about to push that guy right into the fire, too."

They stood in silence. Only the murmur of other people in the crowd talking and the hissing pops still rising from the dying fires broke that stillness.

"All right," Brenda said finally. "We'll keep a close eye on her. Thank you for telling me."

Eric nodded and walked away. Brenda stood silently for a few more minutes. She wasn't technically Rowan's superior – all Division agents ranked equally. But the cell looked to her for guidance, and she wanted to be Rowan's friend. She couldn't stop thinking about what the agents she'd left that night to go consult with had told her. It had been weird, but not a big deal when they'd asked to speak with her alone. She had trekked across the city and arrived at their safehouse. She'd known something was wrong the moment she walked in. It was the expression on their faces.

"Brenda," one of them had said immediately. "Thank you for coming. We have news about the family of one of the members of your cell."

Brenda's eyebrows had gone up. "That's big news. What is it?"

"It's about Rowan," the man had said grimly. "And Brenda? You're not gonna like what I'm about to tell you."

August 18

"Brenda? Brenda, I need you to wake up."

She came up with her sidearm in her hand. Yeong-Ja caught her wrist before she could bring it to bear.

"Easy does it," the sniper said. "We're not in immediate danger."

Brenda took a deep breath and nodded. "OK. What's the situation?"

It had been two weeks since they'd left the site of their battle with the Roamers. They followed the highway west from there, moving fast to close the gap with the intermittent tracking signal that Maira produced. The journey had been tiring but uneventful so far.

The prior evening, they had made camp by the road. Night had fallen while Brenda slept. The sky overhead was full of stars. The surrounding landscape was lit by the glow of a gibbous moon. A rusty duet of snores announced that Leo and Colin were still sleeping in their bedrolls.

"Not sure. There's a group headed toward us on foot. They're coming from the same direction we're going."

Brenda followed her pointing finger. She could just pick out what Yeong-Ja was talking about. They were using flashlights, whoever they were – that was the only reason Brenda was sure they were there at all. Otherwise, it was just a collection of dark shapes in the night. She gave Yeong-Ja a quick nod.

"Good call waking me. Any idea how many of them there are?"

"Maybe fifteen?" the sniper hazarded. "I'm not certain. I couldn't tell if they were armed, either."

"All right," Brenda said. "Wake the others up."

It was still summer, and the hot days made for balmy nights. They hadn't bothered with a fire, there was no need. Brenda was grateful for that now. The light had given these interlopers away, there was no reason to think their own position had been betrayed. Soon the rest of the cell was awake and alert.

"Weapons ready?" asked Leo.

"Better safe than sorry," Brenda confirmed.

They had used up some ammunition during the fight with the Roamers, and especially without the truck there was no way for them to carry arbitrary amounts. Brenda had six magazines if she counted the one currently locked into the Honey Badger. That was one hundred and eighty rounds all told. It sounded like a lot until you actually got into a firefight. If they got into any sustained fighting, it wouldn't take long before she was down to her sidearm and angry words.

Brenda assessed the terrain with a sweeping gaze. It wasn't a great place to get into a fight with superior numbers. There was nothing but scrub brush and the road. There were mountains off in the far distance, but the land was a flat sweep toward them. Minimal concealment, no cover. Fifteen people… if they were armed like the agents, and shooting started, this was going to turn into a bloodbath.

"We could evade them," said Yeong-Ja. The sniper might as well have read her mind.

"I'd like to," Brenda admitted. "But there's two issues. For one, they're coming from our destination, and we could use some answers about where we're headed."

"I like not walking into things blind," opined Colin.

"Me too." Brenda grinned. "The other thing is that if this is a patrol of some kind, and we dodge them here, they'll be behind us instead. If we run into trouble heading into El Paso, we could find ourselves caught between a rock and a hard place."

"OK, that doesn't sound fun, I admit," Yeong-Ja said.

"How are we playing it?" asked Leo.

"Diplomatically if we can," Brenda said. "We have no proof these people have done anything wrong, and I don't want a fight if we can avoid one. Besides, dead people are bad at answering questions."

"One of the great truths of our time," quipped Yeong-Ja.

"Leo and Colin, you'll come with me to approach them. Yeong-Ja, you hang back and keep low. You and your TAC-50 are our ace in the hole if this does get ugly," Brenda said.

Yeong-Ja nodded and turned to walk into the nighttime darkness. The other two formed up loosely on Brenda and they all moved to greet their unexpected guests. Brenda could hear them talking as they got closer, and she understood the dialect to be Spanish. Whoever they were, they weren't even trying to maintain any tactical discipline. A quick glance to the others and a round of shrugs confirmed they were in the same boat she was: no one spoke that language.

"Kids," Leo said quietly as they got close enough to make out more of the people approaching them.

Brenda snapped her gaze back to the oncoming group. He was right. Yeong-Ja's guess on numbers had been about right, but only about ten of them were adults. The others were children, ranging from little ones to teenagers. One was a toddler, held in the arms of a weary-looking man.

They were armed, but it wasn't the arsenal of soldiers. A few hunting pieces, a smattering of handguns. If this was a patrol, Brenda wasn't sure what it was hoping to fend off. The idea of a firefight became even less appealing. Brenda had done her share of fighting since the Green Poison, but the idea of firing a weapon in even the rough direction of children made her feel sick at heart.

Instead, she slung her Honey Badger and stepped forward with her hands raised. "Hello there!" she called.

They panicked and some of them immediately scattered. They'd had no idea the cell was there, and further, they hadn't even been on the lookout for such a threat. Definitely not a military operation of any kind. One of the ones carrying a rifle held his ground, but his eyes were wide with fear. He looked to be in his late fifties, maybe a bit older.

"Who are you?" he called back with a shaky voice.

"Nobody looking to hurt you!" Brenda responded calmingly. "My name is Brenda. I have two friends here, Colin and Leo. We're just travelers heading west."

There was a time when Brenda would have led with the

fact that they were Division agents. She wasn't trying to hide it; the watch and the brick both had their telltale glows for anyone in the know. Even so, since the Division had been ordered to disband, she'd laid that aside for introductions. It was frustrating enough that they'd been sidelined so casually. In the field, it could make for a lot more trouble than it was worth these days.

The spokesman seemed to relax if only marginally. "My name is Diego. Hello to you and your friends, Brenda. I hope you are telling the truth about not hurting anyone. We are not looking for any kind of trouble."

"That's the last thing I want, too, Diego," Brenda said.

She headed closer. A few of them shone their flashlights at her. It was dazzling, but she didn't protest. Instead, she put on her warmest smile and held up her hands again.

"What brings you folks onto the road so late at night?" she asked.

"Trouble," he admitted wearily. "I hope you are not headed to El Paso, amiga."

Brenda furrowed her brow. "We're not here for the tourism, if that's what you mean, but our course might take us through the city. Where's the issue?"

"A month ago, I would have told you it was no problem. The city was where my family and I lived, along with many others. Life was not easy, but we have gotten by."

"What changed a month ago?" asked Colin with concern.

Brenda suppressed a sigh. The boy was an irrepressible do-gooder. It was a good quality, just perhaps a bit hazardous to the idea of staying on-mission.

"Los Hermandad del Cuerno de Chivo," he said. The weight he gave the words imbued them with audible capital letters. "The Brotherhood of the Goat Horn."

"I'm going to be very honest with you," Brenda said. "That is not a name that sounds friendly."

"It suits them that way," Diego said. "A month ago, they came up from the south. They are not good neighbors. Bandidos, the kind who live by the gun and try to take whatever they want. They appropriated the food, the homes, anything that caught their eye. Life was already hard, how can one survive when you can't even eat the food you grow?"

"The Goat Horn?" asked Colin.

"I have seen their flag," Diego confirmed. "It is symbolic. The horn, it is the magazine of the AK-47."

"That certainly sounds like the kind of thing that ruins a neighborhood," Brenda agreed. "Why wait a month to leave?"

Diego sighed and shrugged. "We had a life there. It is not an easy thing to just let go of. But it became clear that Los Hermandad, they are here to stay. I cannot risk my family. So, we leave. We are traveling by night to avoid the heat."

"That's probably smarter than what we've been doing," said Colin.

"Couldn't stay and fight?" asked Leo.

"We are not soldiers, and they have come with many guns and men willing to use them," Diego said. "Perhaps, if all the families in the city had banded together, we might have fought. But people are afraid, not just for themselves, but for their children."

The man holding the toddler squeezed the child tighter, eliciting a soft sleepy noise of protest. Leo nodded grimly.

Diego motioned to them. "You look like soldiers. I have heard rumors that there is an army in Dallas. That they will protect people."

"The Molossi?" asked Colin.

"That is the name," Diego said with excitement.

A murmur passed through the group. Brenda couldn't help but be darkly amused. The Molossi were not her idea of saviors. Even so, she had seen worse, and the reports indicated that the conflict with the Reborn had brought out the worst in them. Certainly, Dallas had seemed peaceful enough when they passed through. Better than Washington or New York, if she was forced to make that assessment.

"The Molossi will protect you," Colin said with confidence. "And it's not as though there isn't plenty of room in Dallas."

"Even a cactus bears fruit," said Diego philosophically. "You have given us good news, many thanks. I wish I could have given you better."

"I'd sooner have a bad truth than a pretty lie," said Brenda. "You've given us information we didn't have, thank you for that." She glanced the weary group of refugees over. "If you would like, we could join camps for the night, help keep you secure."

"You are kind," Diego said. "But we must move on if we are to reach Dallas with the food and water we are carrying. I wish you safe travels."

"The same to you, Diego," Brenda replied. "I hope you and your family find a home where you will feel safe."

Diego nodded and turned to regather his group. They set out once more under the moon, headed off into the east. Brenda watched them go for a little while. Finally, she sighed and trudged back to the camp the cell had set up. There was still time for a bit more sleep.

"The Brotherhood of the Goat Horn," Yeong-Ja said. She had gotten back to camp first and was sitting with her rifle across her thighs. "Bandits, he called them. ISAC kept me up to date."

Brenda nodded somberly. "Criminals and would-be warlords. I'm guessing those won't be the only refugees fleeing the area in the near future."

"Birds of a feather with the Roamers," observed Leo.

"I'd bet you a shiny nickel that's who they were in contact with. They must be trying to forge some kind of alliance," Brenda said.

"If they've got as many gunhands as Diego suggested, that could be a dangerous combination," Colin said.

Brenda nodded. "The last thing we need is for every damn Roamer truck to come with a platoon of soldados."

"Can't fix it tonight," said Leo.

Brenda sighed and nodded. "All we can do is get some rest while we can. We'll make El Paso tomorrow."

"We could go around," said Colin.

Brenda thought that over. "ISAC, show me the latest map."

The AI obliged. Brenda stared at the lay of the land, and that blinking dot that represented Maira Kanhai.

"Maira's going around the city, that's clear enough," said Leo.

Brenda nodded. "But that's adding travel time for her, on top of her moving slower. If we can just go through El Paso, we can catch her easily on the other side."

"Assuming we get through without incident," said Leo.

Brenda sighed. "Yeah, assuming. I think it's worth the attempt. If we just keep our heads down, maybe we won't even run into these bandidos."

The sun was hot overhead as they closed the final distance between them and the city. The road had become more and more cluttered with dead, rusting cars as they got closer. By the time they reached the city limits, the highway was packed full of abandoned vehicles. Brenda contemplated that detritus as she put one foot in front of the other and tried not to think about how hot it was.

"People going in, nobody going out," she said.

"They must have been rushing the border," Colin said softly. "Trying to escape the Green Poison as it spread."

It was a grim thing to imagine. Brenda remembered the panic of those days well. By the time anyone knew there was a problem, it had infected people all over the country. News disagreed with itself by the hour. Safe havens at one moment were deadly abattoirs the next. People ran in every direction, and failed to find safety no matter where they went. Of course, some of them would have imagined that Mexico represented sanctuary.

"Quite the reversal of fortunes," Yeong-Ja said darkly.

"In the end, what we all had to learn was that the virus didn't play favorites," Brenda replied.

"Problem," Leo said.

Brenda tensed. "What?"

He pointed, and she followed his finger. They could see the rising buildings of the city, from apartment complexes to towering skyscrapers. One of the tall buildings closest to them stood out for a singular reason: it was sprouting a rising plume of black smoke, vivid against the azure sky.

"Nobody likes a fire," Colin said. "But why is it a problem for us?"

"Not just any fire," Leo said. "Controlled. Smoky. It's a signal fire. Someone knows we're coming. Forward scouts keeping an eye out for anyone approaching, or looking specifically for us."

"That could just be paranoia talking," Yeong-Ja said.

Brenda shook her head. "No. My gut's telling me he's right. We need to–"

Automatic weapon fire swept their position. Glass blew out in nearby cars. Leo fell back like a sack of bricks.

"Agent down," commented ISAC.

Brenda crouched and sprinted for cover. It was pure instinct; her conscious mind hadn't even caught on yet. It was only when she slammed her shoulder into the back of a sedan and dropped to one knee that she had the presence of mind to opine on the situation.

"Shit!"

There was more than one shooter. Her ears told her that, with the chatter of more than one weapon melding into an overlay of sound. Brenda glanced over the top of her makeshift cover, but near impacts drove her back down with a hiss. She looked off to the side. Leo still lay where he fell. For a moment, all she could see was the bodies of Eric and Rowan laid out in death. Terror for her old friend threatened to spike in her chest. The other two had scattered to seek cover just as she had.

ISAC fed her data on Leo's vitals. He wasn't dead, thankfully. Heartbeat was strong. Respiration rate was erratic. He needed help, that much was clear.

"We need to get Leo to cover," Colin said urgently on the comms.

"Agreed," Brenda said. "Can you move him?"

"Say the word," the medic replied firmly.

"Yeong-Ja, you there?" asked Brenda.

"Got you, ma'am," Yeong-Ja replied.

"Good. You and me, we provide covering fire. Colin, get him out of the open. On three."

Three heartbeats. Brenda came up smoothly to her full height and rested the Honey Badger against the top of the car. She opened fire with no concern for picking her targets. Instead, she swept suppressive bursts across anywhere their enemies could have been. Yeong-Ja's rifle thundered a counterpoint. The volume of hostile fire died down appreciably.

Colin sprinted. He crossed the distance between him and their fallen comrade in the blink of an eye. Brenda monitored his progress with her peripheral vision. He skidded in next to Leo with a textbook baseball slide. He was back on his feet, carrying the other man, before she could blink.

A ping and the Honey Badger's action locked. Empty. Brenda discarded that magazine, tossing it to the dusty road. She pulled another from her harness and slapped it home. A figure was sprinting toward them up the road. Brenda zeroed in on him and opened fire. Two bursts and he toppled to the side, painting a nearby car with sudden crimson.

A thunderclap. A headless body toppled into the open a hundred yards away. A .50 round had reduced his cranium to nothing but wet ruin.

"One," Yeong-Ja commented.

"Do you have any idea how many we're dealing with?" Brenda asked her.

"Too many," was the uneasy reply. "I've spotted at least twenty. Looks like more are coming from back in the city."

"Shit," Brenda growled. "Colin, how is Leo?"

"He took three to the chest. Armor stopped those. Another went through his shoulder," Colin reported tersely. "He'll live."

Brenda had taken her fair share of hits to the plates. They did not stop a round from hurting, only from wounding. Leo's chest was going to be pure bruises tomorrow if he survived this. If any of them survived this, she mentally corrected.

Another heavy boom shook the air. One of their assailants had made the mistake of trying to advance through the dead and rusting cars that filled the road. Yeong-Ja rewarded him with a round through center mass. If these fighters – Brotherhood men? – were wearing armor, it didn't do him any good. The sniper round went through him like a hot knife through butter, and he sprawled artlessly into the dust.

"Two," Yeong-Ja said. "This is bad, Brenda. Confirm reinforcements approaching. They'll have the manpower to just overrun us if that's how they want to do it."

"It would cost them," Brenda said sharply.

"Yeah," Yeong-Ja agreed. "Will that bring us back from the dead?"

Brenda glowered. Another rain of fire blew out windows nearby, spattering the dirt with glittering bits of glass. She hunched. Her forehead burned. She reached up to touch it and came away with droplets of blood. A tiny shard must have glanced off her face.

Maira would be right there on the other side of the city. They could have swooped her up tomorrow, put this chase to an end. And besides, to be turned away, to be forced to abandon a whole city to these people...

Brenda cursed and pounded her fist against the side of the car. Thin metal dented under the blow. Her hand ached and she blew out a frustrated sigh.

"Fall back," she radioed. "Fire and movement for me and you, Yeong-Ja. Colin, your top priority is getting Leo out of here. We'll regroup once they stop pursuing, and go around the city."

She glanced back toward the shining city in the distance. Diego and his family had gotten out, but it hadn't seemed easy. Who knew how many more people they were abandoning to an unknown fate?

But that wasn't the mission. Not this time. Brenda

squeezed her eyes shut for a second. Maira was out there, too, and Brenda couldn't just abandon her either. Not after they had come so far to try to bring her home.

"We'll be back," she promised El Paso. "Maybe not tomorrow, but we'll be back."

CHAPTER 9
July 16

The computer chimed. Maira yanked herself awake at the sound and realized she had fallen asleep at her desk. Sticky strands of spit connected her arm to her lips. She wiped them away with a flash of irritation. The emotion receded as quickly as it had risen. Feeling was hard. Thinking was even harder. It took too much energy to do either over such trivialities.

She blinked at the screen. The light hurt her eyes at first, but as they adapted, she realized the screen was giving her a notification. It was a report. She frowned. Why would there be a report coming in? She had finished work for the day. There shouldn't have been anything running.

She reached for the mouse. It took her a few tries. It felt like the device was swimming around on its own. At last, Maira caught hold of it and pulled up the alert. A search of some kind coming back. She recognized the program, vaguely. Wasn't it one of the ones she kept on her…

Wait, yes. Something tried to fire in her brain. She had set a sniffer program to collect whatever information she could, right? Information about her, specifically. It had finished the job, and it had dug things up. She tried to focus on what the screen showed, but the effort made her head ache.

There was another problem. Now that the file was in her work, anyone with access could see it. That was...

Maira paused, her thoughts slipping. It was dangerous, that was what it was. They shouldn't be keeping secrets from her, especially not about her. But if they were, well, no one liked it when she dragged secrets out into the light.

What was she afraid of?

The fear seemed nebulous. Unimportant. Nat wouldn't hurt her. Keith wouldn't hurt her. None of these people wanted anything bad for her. That was obvious. Maybe it was just about her recovery. All doctors kept reports. Maybe it was nothing. She was stressing too much. It would be so much easier to just relax and let the future worry about itself.

Still, it was better to not make them angry, right? Maira didn't want them thinking she was a snoop. She guessed she was a snoop, at that, but they didn't need to know. That wasn't a flattering image, and she wanted Natalya to think well of her. So, what was to be done?

Delete the information?

No, she'd just gotten it. She hadn't even read it yet. That was silly, a waste of time and effort. Better, she decided, to find a place to print it out. Then she could read in peace, and destroy the paper, too. And, she wouldn't have to stare at the screen anymore, which was making her feel a little nauseous.

Maira got her legs underneath her. They were very wobbly. She was like a baby horse, she thought. The image dragged a disoriented laugh from her. Gotta get out of her room and go gambol in the fields where she belonged.

She had stood up too soon, she realized. She hadn't even transferred the file yet. She sat back down with a thud and a sigh. Move the file onto her thumb drive. It would be safe there for now. The transfer complete, she pulled out the drive and put it around her neck. Then, she erased the program from the computer. Nat didn't need to know. Maybe she'd come clean about it later, when she was feeling more herself.

Back up again. The world lurched as she moved. For a deeply unpleasant moment, she felt cognizant of the spinning of the Earth. It was just whirling, and she was stuck to it like a little action figure glued to a bowling ball. And from there, they were spinning around the sun. And the sun was...

Maira closed her eyes. Stop. Don't think about it. Just let it be. Breathe.

The spinning slowed. She walked out of her room carefully. The printer was not far away, she knew that much, in this large room full of servers. It was up one floor and down the hall. There was no reason that should be a difficult journey. Maira set out, one foot in front of the other.

The elevator. She was there. When had she gotten here? She frowned and shook her head. The doors were shut. She just had to push the button to call it. Maira missed on her first two attempts. The third time was the charm, and the button glowed.

She leaned her head against the metal of the wall. It was cold against her flushed skin.

She came to with the ping of the elevator. That wasn't right. Why was she in the middle of the hall like this? She was on her knees, slumped against the wall. She was supposed to be at the printer. There was something important to take care of there.

The irritation died away into meaningless mumbles. She pushed herself up from the wall. The elevator was open. She staggered inside and hit the button for the floor up. Turning away got her legs tangled somehow. By dumb luck, she caught herself against the rail on the far side. There was her reflection, distorted, in the metal of the paneling.

She didn't look well. She wasn't well. Something was wrong, wasn't it? Maira couldn't put her finger on it. But that was the problem, right? She couldn't think. It was like trying to build a pyramid with oil-soaked marbles. Trying to catch an eel with her bare hands. It was…

The door opened. She sighed and set off once more. Down the hallway. Fluorescent lights swept past overhead. She was moving so fast. Too fast. She must have been going ninety miles per hour. The cops would pull her over at this rate. Her mom would not be amused about that.

"You're a bad example to Kazi," her mom had always said. "One black sheep will infect the whole flock."

I'm sorry, Mom, Maira thought. She couldn't save her mom. She couldn't save Kazi. She wasn't even doing a good job of saving herself, currently.

The printer was right in front of her. Maira frowned. This part should be easy. She tried to plug the USB in. Wrong way. She turned it over, tried again. Wrong way again. She frowned at it. There were only two ways. She peered at the end, peered at the socket, and slowly lined them up. Click.

Find the file. There it was. Now print. The printer hummed into motion and papers began to slot out into the holder. Soon she had her handful of pages. A glorious triumph. She could read them in her room.

She ensured she deleted any record that she'd printed something from her workstation. If Nat found out, Maira wasn't sure she could handle the disappointment. But she needed to know what the file said on her. Something was screaming dimly in the back of her mind. The file was probably just a doctor's report, but in a sick way, she wanted to see what had happened to her. That was normal. Right? She wasn't doing anything wrong. She could tell Nat later. It would be OK.

She just had to make it back somewhere safe. She turned around with a weary sigh and set forth.

Maira sat alone in her room. She was sitting on her bed, her legs pulled up against her chest. The light was overhead. She tilted her head back and looked at it. It shimmered under her gaze, the edges flickering with rainbows. Her mouth was very dry. She reached up and scrubbed a hand against her lips. They stuck to her skin like paper.

Paper.

There was a piece of paper. She looked down at where it was tucked into the gap between her legs and her chest. Printer paper, covered with text. More than one, actually. She reached up and touched it slowly. It was important, wasn't it? It was hard to care.

There was a lot of that lately, wasn't there? Every night after dinner. She would finish her work for the day, honing the program. She would eat and come back to her room. Then the world would just fade into meaninglessness.

The light swam. Sparkles fell like rain. She reached up to catch them, but they passed right through her hand and disappeared into the floor. Maira swallowed, and her dry throat constricted for a moment. It didn't want to work. That was worrisome, wasn't it? No, it didn't matter.

She needed to read the paper.

Why? What was so important about some piece of paper? How could it possibly matter?

Maira blinked rapidly, trying to force herself to concentrate. The paper was a printout. It came from a program. Her program. This was the information she had sent it to collect. This was what she had waited for. She needed to read it, and then...

She drifted. She was lying on her side on the bed, her eyelids heavy. She shook her head groggily. Now was not the time for sleep. Slowly, painstakingly, she got her arm under her body and pushed herself back up to sitting. She had to read the paper, and then she had to destroy it before anyone else could read it.

The pages were bunched up in her hand. Maira didn't remember doing that. She gritted her teeth and smoothed them back out. The words on the first page swam in front of her eyes. She closed her eyes tight and rubbed at them. When she took her hands away, it seemed clearer. She could read it now.

It was a collection of information from all throughout the database of her keepers. Information specifically about her. Some of it was just her background, if surprisingly complete. The way her father had died. The way Kazi had died. Tears welled up in Maira's eyes, uncontrollable. She dashed them away and bit her lip until it bled. The pain focused her. Cut through some of the fog.

There was more here than just her dossier. A treatment plan. Some of that was predictable, too. Her retrieval from the depths of the Houston bay. She had actually died, if briefly. Her heart had stopped anyway. They had managed to resuscitate her and stop the bleeding, barely. The surgeries that had followed were listed, along with the plan for her physical therapy. She was in a facility in Albuquerque, apparently. That was a detail that might be important. She tried to memorize it.

There was also a plan to drug her.

She blinked and reread that. It was spelled out very clearly in black and white. Mind-affecting drugs had been steadily supplied through her diet. Microdoses of gamma-hydroxybutyrate laced throughout her food and drink. They didn't flinch from explaining the purpose either. To keep her docile. To lower her inhibitions. To keep her from questioning.

To keep her in this dreamlike state.

They had increased the dosage following the first test. They were concerned that she was getting suspicious and wanted to keep her in line. Let it ease off a little during the day so she could code, and then drown her thoughts out from the evening on. It had been working too, hadn't it?

Maira blinked and stared at the wall. There was drool and blood from her lip on her chin when she came to. She wiped it away with shame. Just knowing about the drugs in her system wasn't going to fix it. The effects were still there. But it did make sense. It cast the recent past in a different light.

She was a prisoner, and they were using her. That was the truth. She dug her fingers into it, clung to it.

The rest of the report was about failed access attempts. There was more information on her, but the program hadn't been able to break through the defenses to access it. No doubt they were monitoring the thumb drive, too, for any signs of foul play. She'd been lucky, but that luck wouldn't hold for long.

This was enough, though, to finally understand one critical fact. These people weren't her friends. She had to get out of here, somehow.

She could stop eating, come off the drugs. Judging from past experience, her mind would clear within hours. Unfortunately, that had taught her another lesson: withdrawal would hit hard and fast. The nausea, vomiting, light sensitivity. How was she supposed to try to escape while debilitated to that extent? They would catch her in a heartbeat, and after that they'd realize she was on to them. They'd tighten security, start administering the drugs directly and forcibly if they had to. She'd never have a chance again.

Despair welled up in her like a black spring. Maira rested her chin on her knees and fought the urge to cry brokenly. She felt so helpless. How was she supposed to do this alone? Her captors – Natalya – they had every advantage. The game was rigged from the start. How was that fair?

She took a deep breath. It didn't matter. Fair didn't enter into it. What mattered was that she had to get out of here, and she had to keep them from misusing her program. If they had been prepared to treat her like this in order to get it created, odds seemed good their plans for it were far from benevolent.

And of course, right now what she needed to do was get rid of this paper. She contemplated the trash chute. In theory it would get taken off to be incinerated, but could she really count on that? There was no evidence they went through her trash, but she couldn't trust that they didn't either.

Instead, she tucked the papers into her pocket and stepped out of her room. The dormitory area was quiet. Maira took a few seconds to contemplate all those sleeping people. The stolen data had suggested this place was, in fact, partly run by the SHD. The idea of a whole government department working with her captors was daunting. They were only part of what was happening here, though. It was some kind of cooperative effort between them and a group called Black Tusk. Maira had heard that name in passing regarding events back east, but it had never been the most important thing on her plate.

Unfortunately, that ignorance was coming back to bite her now. The Division didn't give generalized threat briefings. Everyone was just left to operate as they wished, taking on missions ad hoc. Right now, Maira wanted to curse that approach. Maybe if she'd known more about the threats the organization faced as a whole, she would have recognized the trap she was in sooner.

Maybe.

With a sigh she headed for the bathrooms. Someone was taking a shower, and she could hear them singing to themselves in the next room over. Another person sat in one of the stalls. Maira pretended to look herself over in the mirror. Weary eyes in a drawn face looked back at her. When was the last time she had really felt good? Gotten a proper night's sleep? She couldn't recall. Even earlier, when the puzzle of the code had been fun, the pain of her healing wounds still kept her up at night.

The person in the toilet departed. Maira turned and proceeded into one of the stalls herself, shutting the privacy door behind her. She pulled the paper from her pocket and looked it over one last time. Albuquerque. Even if she got out, it would be a long trek to reach somewhere in the hands of friendly forces.

She shook her head. That was something to worry about

later. She shredded the paper into little bits and let them flutter down into the toilet water, then flushed it. The evidence of her activities vanished, swirling. Maira turned and sat on the toilet. Her eyelids felt as heavy as lead. It was everything she could do to keep them from sliding shut on her here and now. Forcing herself to concentrate through the drugs was taking a toll, exhausting her.

After a few minutes, she sighed and rose back to her feet. She would have to start trying to figure out an escape plan tomorrow. For right now, all she wanted was to rest. She proceeded back to her room and fell into her waiting bed.

A knock on the door wrenched Maira from her sleep. She raised her head blearily. For a second, she had no idea where she was. She was lying on her bed, fully dressed, her pillow soaked with drool. Whoever it was knocked again, insistently. She wiped at her face with a grumble and staggered to her feet.

"If you're here about me missing physical therapy, Keith, then you can kiss my…"

Maira swung the door open and froze. It was not Keith on the other side, but rather the woman in white herself. Natalya Sokolova. She regarded Maira with an arched eyebrow and a quirk at the corner of her mouth.

Maira laughed nervously. "Nat! Forgive me, I had a rough night."

"I can see that." Natalya reached up as if to touch her face. "What happened?"

Maira stepped back and winced as she felt her own

split lip. She'd bitten down hard enough to bleed, she remembered that now.

"I slipped and fell in the shower, bit my lip when I hit the ground," Maira lied.

Nat apparently took her physical retreat as an invitation inside. She stepped past Maira and went to sit on the bed as was her habit. The pearls she wore around her neck gleamed in the fluorescent lighting. She gave a small smile; her teeth were just as perfect and white.

"I'm going to need you to be more careful, Maira. You're very valuable to me." Natalya motioned to Maira's chair. "Please, sit. I have good news to share with you."

Maira settled into her chair uneasily. She felt befuddled looking at the other woman. Part of that was doubtless still the effects of the drugs in her system. It had eased from last night, but she would have to avoid doses somehow to clear her head completely. It wasn't the entirety of her feelings, though. She was also still struggling to reconcile Natalya with the truths she had discovered.

This woman had been kind to her. She had been a friend. She had been... what? More than that, maybe? Maira shied away from the thought. It hurt now. How much of this was illusion and lies? Could she trust anything she had experienced? Anything she had felt?

"You look like you just bit into a lemon," observed Natalya.

Maira winced and forced a smile onto her face. "The rap to the head left me with a headache that hasn't gone away. I'm probably just concussed."

"I certainly hope not," Natalya said dryly. "Especially

considering I'm here to tell you we're ready to take your program to the next operational stage."

"What?" Maira blurted.

"It's time for a field test, and we have the perfect chance to do one. Tomorrow, as a matter of fact. We'll be deploying forces against a heavily defended target, and your program is going to spell the difference."

"That's... uh... That's very exciting," Maira said. "What is this target, exactly?"

"A hostile enemy server site in a remote location," Natalya said smoothly. "I can't say much more than that due to operational security. I'm sure you understand."

"Of course." Maira laughed weakly. "I have serious concerns as to whether the program is ready for that level of implementation, though. To be betting lives on it..."

"The moment was going to come sooner or later, and it has arrived. Don't worry, Maira," Natalya said.

"That's easier said than done. If the program were to fail under field conditions, that would put deaths on my conscience," Maira said.

"It will be on me, not you," Nat said soothingly. "Besides, I am not putting all my eggs in one basket. We will be bringing overwhelming firepower to bear. With your help, what I want is to turn a definite win into a crushing victory. I want to rout them."

"Well, that's good," Maira said. "I'm sure it will be a major triumph for you."

"We'll bring you back word of how the program does the moment we can," Natalya said.

Maira blinked. "You're leaving me here?"

"Of course. You're too valuable to be risking on field operations. The code is designed to be usable without you present, correct?"

"Of course," Maira said. "But… I…"

What if her suspicions were correct? What if the target was the Division? At this point, a working program might be the worst outcome. She could try to sabotage it, of course, but the technicians that worked for this Black Tusk organization weren't fools. They would notice unless she was particularly careful.

"I need to be there," she finished.

Natalya crossed her arms. "Oh? I'm sorry, Maira, I know you want to see if your program works, but that's a nonstarter."

"Right, no, I get where you're coming from," Maira said rapidly. Images welled up in her mind. Her program unleashed. Division agents slaughtered, stripped of their defenses. No. That couldn't come to pass. "But this isn't just about what I want. I'm saying it's important I'm there. Anyone can use the program, yes – but not just anyone can keep it from failing."

"Why do you think being there will let you guarantee success?"

Maira hesitated. "Maybe not guarantee, but definitely improve the chances. Something always goes wrong when the rubber hits the road. If I'm there, I can fix it on the go. I can address unexpected variables. Nobody else can do what I do. That's why you wanted me in the first place, right?"

Natalya frowned. "I don't know—"

"I can give you that crushing victory you want," Maira said.

Natalya drummed her fingers against her upper arm. "You feel very strongly about this."

"I do," agreed Maira. "Sure, you're confident you can pull this off even if the program fails. But why risk it? The less losses you take, the better, right?"

"That's true. Even my resources are not unlimited, and I abhor waste," mused Nat. Her eyes were distant briefly before she sighed. She looked Maira directly in the eyes instead. It made Maira tremble, but she bore it. "Very well. You can go along for the mission. But I want you in a transport near the back, ready to escape the moment anything goes wrong."

There was something in her voice. *Maybe she does feel something for me*, Maira thought. But if Nat did, there was something unpleasantly patronizing about the emotion. It was not the concession one makes to an equal who has convinced you, but an indulgence extended to a subordinate. A pat on the head for a favorite pet.

Maira struggled to keep these thoughts off her face. Instead, she tried to look very grateful. "Thank you, Natalya. You won't regret giving me this opportunity."

"I'm sure I won't," replied the Black Tusk leader. "At any rate, that's all I wanted to tell you. If you are indeed going, you'll need to prepare yourself. And make sure you're well rested. I want you at your best."

"Of course," Maira replied with an uneasy smile. "Don't worry. I'll be at the top of my game."

Natalya left, and Maira turned off the light switch and sat in the darkness of her room thinking. If this target is as remote as she claims, Maira thought, they'll have a harder time keeping me under their thumb. It certainly can't be as carefully guarded as this place is. This could be my one chance to get away before it's too late.

There was one problem with that idea. If she did manage to get away on this mission, they would still have her code. It would be right here on their servers, ready to deploy. Maira narrowed her eyes and opened her laptop. That wouldn't do at all.

She searched through the programs at her disposal and chose the perfect one. High-level encryption. She set it to work and sat back again, watching as the screen flickered through activities. There was a lot of planning to do if she wanted to make the most of this chance.

"All right," the pilot said over the comms headset. "We're nearing the target. Taking up a holding pattern."

The roar of the aircraft's engines would have made normal listening impossible. Luckily, Maira had been provided with the headset so she could keep track of what was going on both here and at the site. She had a little backpack to keep all her gear in, too. Multitool, the gaming handheld, her tablet, a few other knickknacks. Less fortunately, her two handlers were far better equipped. They sat across from her, their faces concealed with black balaclavas. They were dressed in full black combat gear and carrying SCAR MK16s. One of them even had a small aerial drone with him, of a design so similar to SHD tech that it made Maira flinch. Nominally, the two were here for her protection. Maira's head was clear enough to grasp they were here to keep her on a leash.

Aside from the pilot, the three of them were the only ones on this particular Black Tusk aircraft. Maira wasn't sure exactly where Natalya was, only that she hadn't accompanied the strike force on the final approach.

She had laughed when Maira commented. "I'm too valuable to be risked, too."

Natalya had not been lying about how formidable the strike force being deployed was. It must have been a full company's worth of armed soldiers, supported by combat drones and robotic walkers. It would have been a deadly display of firepower even in the old world; post-Green Poison, it was outright overwhelming to imagine in action.

As Maira watched through the window, the transport aircraft carrying all those fighters peeled away to continue on. Hers began to slowly circle the central point of the target. They were up high enough that Maira couldn't make out anything to clarify exactly what they were here to destroy, and the nighttime darkness didn't help. The terrain here was flat and forested. It could have been any number of places she'd visited in her lifetime.

In a way, it was a joy just to be out and away from the facility. Maira had never considered herself a granola girl, at one with nature. But the world had changed, and everyone had had to change with it. Being cooped up inside for weeks at a time felt very strange now.

"Landing forces," reported someone across the comms.

It didn't take long from there for the fireworks to start. Those Maira could see even from where they were. Brilliant detonations that lit the darkness up like strobes. Trailing lines of light as machine guns opened fire and tracers burned through the air. There had been a time when she would have declared herself no one's idea of an operator, but her experiences in the Division had honed Maira. She could well imagine the chaos and cacophony as the battle below unfolded.

"Resistance encountered," was the calm, sanitized report that came on the radio.

"It's time, Maira," said Natalya over comms. "Implement your isolation program."

Maira took a deep breath and set her hands to the keys of the computer in front of her. She liked to strike a dramatic maestro's pose in moments like this. Movies had always made it seem like hacking was won by the fastest fingers. In this case, the success of the program would not depend on how rapidly she could type. Most of the work went into setting it up ahead of time. She deserved a little drama in moments like this, though. Thus, the pose... and she hit the enter key. The program set to work, seeking out the enemy network operating below and beginning its infiltration and attempted deployment.

She paid close attention regardless. The program would do its work independently, but the circumstances encountered could be important. Maira watched as it worked its way through protective firewalls. Her stomach quickly began to sink. This wasn't just some casual similarity in structure.

She cleared her throat, licked her dry lips. "Program is initiated."

Maira looked out the window again. The fight below still raged. An explosion tore several trees down at a go. Elsewhere the licking tongue of a flamethrower lashed out. The fact that the whole forest was not soon ablaze spoke to recent rains here. It was no struggle for her to imagine the nightmare of that weapon. She had seen flamethrowers at work before. For a second, she was back at the farm up in the Virginia mountains. Her hands shook.

She turned her head away and found herself locking eyes with one of her supposed bodyguards. There was a coldness there. They had no reason to be suspicious of her, but these two hadn't been chosen for their personable nature, that much was painfully clear. She had to assume they had been selected for their ruthless efficacy instead. She had no weapons.

Maira looked back to where the program continued its work. It was past all the defenses now, and worming its way into the depths of the enemy code structure. It would infest every corner, and then it would rewrite them. Partition them, so there was no overlap. Only then would it begin its final task of subverting the control functions and bringing that isolated segment of the network crashing down.

Her worst fears were spelled out there. This was no random target. Nor was it just slightly familiar. She knew everything about the way this server was set up. She had worked closely with one that was almost identical. This was an ISAC server, which meant the enemy Black Tusk was here to destroy was the Division. But the familiarity ran even deeper than that, and the growing knowledge cut Maira to the bone. She knew what the target was now.

They were attacking a Division Core.

CHAPTER 10
August 21

The sun rose over the New Mexico desert. It dyed everything in brilliant shades of pink, red, and yellow. The land here smelled earthy and herbal by turns, with occasional sparks of bright floral nights as flowers bloomed. Brenda sat at the edge of the cell's small camp and breathed it all in. The journey had not been an easy one so far, but they came now at last to the end. Brenda had been through hundreds of fights in her life. This time, though, she would not go in blazing. Maira deserved better. And if Maira really had gone bad... well... If this was her last sunrise, she wanted to enjoy it.

What was she expecting? She still wasn't sure. They were within hours of catching up to Maira's signal, but they had no clearer idea of what drove her on this dangerous journey. Brenda couldn't stop thinking about the erased ISAC recording. A fumbling attempt to hide Maira's guilt, or part of a conspiracy to frame her? If Maira didn't want to be found, why not disable her locator beacon? They had known from the beginning that it was within her capabilities, but she'd never done it.

"Heavy thoughts?" asked Leo.

He came walking up behind her, stepping lightly as always. He had an understated grace that was at odds with his granite face and bulldozer personality. A man like that should have moved like a bull in a china shop, but Leo never had. Each step always seemed carefully considered. He chose them as carefully as his words.

"What are we going to do?" Brenda asked. It came out more forlorn than she had intended.

Leo sank down onto his haunches next to her. He scooped up a handful of desert soil and let it run loose through his fingers. He did not look at her, just watched the grains slip away.

"Whatever we have to do," he said.

"That's not an answer," Brenda said. "Are we really going to shoot Maira?"

He frowned distantly. "I don't want to."

A small statement, perhaps, but one freighted with emotion she had seldom heard from him. Leo dusted his hands off and shook his head.

"She helped me find my brother. Chose to spare him when she had every reason not to. Rescued both of us from a fate worse than death."

He looked at Brenda finally, and there was sorrow in his dark eyes.

"She is family."

Brenda nodded. There was a lump in her throat. It made it hard to talk. She took a few deep breaths until the feeling eased, scrubbing a hand across her face.

"We can talk her down. We have to. Once she sees it's us, she'll come with us," she said.

"I hope you're right. If there is a limit to what I can forgive myself for doing, this would be it," Leo said softly.

The crunch of boots on sand announced the approach of the other two Division agents. They made an odd pair walking up, the tall medic and the tiny sniper. Both were already geared up for this final leg of their journey. Pistols in thigh holsters, long guns slung around their bodies.

"So, this is it, huh?" asked Colin quietly.

"Seems that way," Brenda said. "She stopped for an hour a little way up the road, then pressed on for a few more. She hasn't moved since. Either she's run out of steam by coincidence, or she knows someone is catching up to her."

"What was the first stop?" Yeong-Ja asked.

"A Division supply depot," Brenda said with a wry smile. "We'll take a quick detour and check it out for ourselves, but my guess is she's been angling toward it for a while now. Gearing up before her final destination."

"So she could have full access to an arsenal of SHD tech?" asked Colin.

"It would have been mostly depleted when local agents got called up and grabbed gear themselves, but we have to assume she's some degree of armed and ready. We can't be sure what tricks she might have up her sleeve until we find her," Brenda said.

"Be nice if she left some ammo for us," Yeong-Ja said with an effort at lightness. "I can't be the only one who's uncomfortably low."

"She's the thoughtful type, but I wouldn't hold your breath," Brenda replied dryly.

"We can try to find another depot on the way back," Colin said. "Come on. Let's go bring our girl home."

They trekked alongside the road headed north. The cell had roughly arranged itself into a V formation. Brenda took point, with Yeong-Ja and Leo just behind her. Colin brought up the rear, a little way behind Leo. Brenda assumed it was to keep an eye on the injured man. The gunshot wound was staying clean and beginning to heal thanks to the medic's ministration, but that wasn't something Colin would leave up to chance. He wouldn't relax until they were all back somewhere safe and sound. That was just who he was.

The sun was unpleasantly hot already, even though it wasn't yet noon. Brenda took a slug of water from her canteen. The water tasted like the rubber of the container, but in this dry expanse, that did nothing to diminish its appeal. She swished it around her mouth to prolong the sensation before swallowing. They would have to find some way to replenish their water supplies, she knew; there was just no way for them to carry enough for the whole journey in one go.

"Smoke," called Yeong-Ja.

Brenda frowned and followed her gaze. Yes, there was

a faint column rising toward the vivid sky. She pulled up the map and contemplated it. Surely they had left the Brotherhood behind? There couldn't be another ambush, could there?

"That's about where the depot is supposed to be," Brenda said. "I'd bet my ass on it."

"Not taking that bet," Leo said.

"What, you don't want to win Brenda's ass?" asked Yeong-Ja.

The other three agents turned to stare at her.

The sniper shrugged expressively. "It's a nice butt. I'm flat as a board back there. That's all I'm saying."

"I don't want to talk about any of your asses," Colin said plaintively.

"Yeah, Yeong-Ja. That's unprofessional," Brenda said firmly. Then she cracked a grin. "You're making our precious angel uncomfortable."

Leo sighed. "The depot?"

"Right," Brenda said. She swept her eyes back in that direction. "There's no telling, but I don't like what my gut's telling me. We approach tactical, with heads on a swivel."

A round of nods showed everyone was on board with the idea. There was no further chatter as they approached the site. Their formation widened the closer they got, to make it more difficult for any one attack to threaten all their lives at once. The skin on the back of Brenda's neck crawled, and she had learned long ago to listen to her body about these things. Something bad had happened here.

It turned out to be a gas station. That wasn't unusual; they made excellent cover for the various stashes and comms points the Division had prepped across the United States. No one thought twice about strangers stopping through a gas station and leaving with their arms full. Of course, this place had been abandoned for over a year now. Like so many isolated locales, it had not survived the collapse of society.

Worse than neglect had happened to this one, though. The smoke cloud billowed skyward from the rear of the complex. Brenda took the lead and slipped up to the side of the building. She checked inside the station first. There was nothing but dust and shadows. No footprints marred the coating that she could see. There were, however, a few bullet holes in the glass of the front windows. Old or new?

She made her way carefully along the side wall and peeked around to the back. This was where something had happened. The dumpster here had been slid aside on rails. Normally this would have revealed a hatch down into a small bunker where the supplies were kept. This one, however, was spewing smoke toward the sky. The hatch had been blasted completely clear of the opening and lay nearby, bent and twisted.

There was no sign of any hostiles. Brenda stepped forward and clicked her comms to indicate the other agents could move up to join her. She swept her gaze over the area. There were more bullet holes in the back wall of the gas station. Bursts of automatic fire, she judged with an experienced eye. Some sort of gunfight?

The bunker itself was completely inaccessible now. She had guessed as much from the smoke and the battered hatch, but someone had demolished the place with high explosives. Even with a team and proper tools it probably would have taken more than a day to clear the rubble, and that supposed there were deeper areas still intact with anything worth salvaging.

The others had arrived. Each of them examined the area. Brenda was grateful for the additional eyes. Not only did it help to have more than one person looking, but they each brought their own lens of experience to the task. That was one of the many reasons that the Division had considered it wise to pull from diverse backgrounds when recruiting.

"A fight," Leo said. "I'm not sure if the destruction of the depot is what kicked it off or what ended it."

Brenda nodded. "Someone must have jumped Maira."

"Or she jumped someone else," Leo said darkly.

"Didn't you say she quit moving a way up the road, too?" asked Yeong-Ja worriedly. "What if she's severely injured?"

"Or someone just has the watch she was using," said Leo grimly.

"You are full of cheerful possibilities," Yeong-Ja said with some exasperation.

"I don't think so," Colin said. He had just finished a little lap around the area. "If she had taken a bullet or something, there would have been spilled blood. There isn't any. Whatever happened, I think she left here intact for now."

"That means there was nothing from her assailant, either?" asked Brenda.

Colin nodded. "I wouldn't be able to tell the difference just by looking, there's just nothing."

"Inconclusive skirmish," Leo conjectured.

"Maybe." Brenda frowned at the tableau. "We'll find out soon enough. There's nothing here for us. We need to push on and reach Maira as fast as we can."

No one argued. They left the gas station moving faster than they had arrived. Brenda could tell from looking at their faces that this oddity had them all worried. Someone had apparently attacked their friend, and it wasn't clear who that might have been. There was no lack of hostiles in the general area, with the Brotherhood of the Goat Horn taking over El Paso just to the south. It could have been that simple.

But something told Brenda things were only getting more complicated.

Summer. Washington DC

"You wanted to talk?" Rowan asked.

They had taken over a small office building in west DC to act as their temporary camp. Each member of the cell had claimed their own abandoned office for a room. It afforded each of them a degree of privacy, a luxury they weren't always extended these days. Unfortunately, being inside the building was unpleasant in other ways. The power was currently dead. That meant no air conditioning, and it was a hot and muggy day.

All of them had abandoned jackets and vests for the moment. Brenda longed to switch out for a pair of shorts as well, or maybe just to return to nature and be stark naked. On the other hand, you could see the Potomac from the window of the office she'd chosen. The river flowed along with slow inevitability. The banded water snakes that frequented those green waters weren't venomous, but the reptiles had a nasty bite, nonetheless. She had no desire to stumble into one with bare legs.

Brenda sighed and turned from the window to face the other agent. Rowan stood in the middle of the office at the position of attention. Old habit or mockery? Brenda could only wonder. The smaller woman was sweating. She had stripped down to jeans and a sports bra. Brenda contemplated the scars that marked Rowan's pale skin. No one came through these times unscathed.

"I hoped we could talk, yeah?" Brenda said. "Informally, person to person."

Rowan relaxed, but only as far as parade rest. It was too clean, Brenda thought. There was definitely some element of mockery there.

"I'm at your disposal," Rowan said.

Brenda's brown eyes met Rowan's green. There was something unstable in Rowan's gaze. It made Brenda feel uneasy. It was like watching someone walk a rail at the edge of a cliff. All she could do was wonder what push was going to make the other person fall.

It didn't help that she was about to do some pushing.

"Tell me about your family, Rowan."

Rowan's eyebrows went up. She hadn't been expecting that.

"Which part? I haven't spoken to my mother in more than ten years. My father lived in Montana, but I haven't heard from him since the pandemic began. As for my husband and my daughter..." Rowan's cheek twitched. Some repressed emotion.

"They lived nearby, right?" asked Brenda.

Rowan nodded. "In Alexandria." Her gaze was piercing. "Why are you asking me this?"

Brenda crossed her arms over her chest and leaned against the office desk. "We've been working together for months now. You never talk about them."

Rowan bit her lip. "I had to leave them."

Brenda raised an eyebrow and waited.

"When we were activated," the other woman finally continued. "The Division sounds like a great idea right until your watch lights up and it's time to go. Then it means leaving your family while the world is falling apart."

"That must have been hard," Brenda said.

"Do you have any kids?" asked Rowan.

Brenda shook her head. "It never felt like the right choice for me."

"Then you can't understand," Rowan said quietly. "It was the hardest thing I've ever done. I think about them every day."

I can't do this, Brenda thought. This is too much. I'm going to be the one to kick her into the abyss. She fidgeted with items on the desk. An old stapler, some papers gone yellow. A family photo sat at the corner. She picked it up and wiped away the dust, then sighed and set it back down.

"What is it?" Rowan demanded. There was real fear in her now. "What are you not telling me?'

"This isn't easy," Brenda started. She frowned and shook her head. "No... I mean... I can't imagine..."

"Brenda?" Rowan took a step closer to her. "Did something happen to my family?"

Brenda winced. "I received word," she said unhappily. "I'm afraid your family was found during the cataloging of a high casualty event."

"What?" Rowan asked. Her eyes were wide. "Where?"

"Roosevelt Island," Brenda said. "There was a battle."

"What?" Rowan repeated. She shook her head rapidly. "No, that doesn't make sense. I told you, they're in Richmond."

Brenda cleared her throat. "I don't have all the answers, I'm afraid. It's possible they were caught trying to head north. Or maybe they were sent here during a quarantine sweep down that way."

"A quarantine sweep?" Rowan wavered. "What? Why were... Roosevelt was a quarantine site. Why would they be taken to the island?"

"It must have been believed that they were infected." Brenda felt at a loss. How was she supposed to say these things? What were the right words? Nothing could be correct in the face of this.

"Believed." Rowan sat down slowly in the middle of the room, right on the floor. Her face was blank. "What do you mean believed? Did the virus kill them?"

Brenda crouched in front of her but couldn't bring herself to look her in the face. "No. As best the catalog team could tell upon examination, they were clean of the Green Poison at the time of their death."

"Then why are they dead?" Rowan demanded. Her hand whipped forward and caught hold of Brenda's wrist. There was a startling strength in her grip. It hurt immediately, small bones grinding together in Brenda's arm. "What happened? You called it a high casualty event."

Brenda licked her lips nervously. She wanted to take her arm back, but that seemed absurd in the face of the other woman's loss. "There was a battle. A force attacked Roosevelt Island, and was engaged by the hostile faction known as the Outcasts. Your family were caught in the crossfire."

"No," Rowan said flatly. "No, that doesn't make sense. You said they were healthy. They shouldn't even have been there. Why would they be there? Who would hurt them? You're not making sense."

Brenda pulled at her arm a little, but Rowan's iron grip didn't budge. "I'm sorry, Rowan. I don't know. All I can tell you is somehow they ended up in the quarantine, and things went wrong from there."

Rowan's face had gone gray. There was something in her eyes. Brenda couldn't help but think about what Eric had said that one night. The fire in Rowan's head, ready to burn down everything.

"Who?" Rowan rasped. Her grip only tightened. The pain spiked. "Who did this? Who attacked the island?"

There it was. The question Brenda had dreaded. It didn't leave any room for omission or evasion. She knew the answer. It was the Division. They had launched the assault and kicked off a bloodbath.

The Division had made Rowan leave her family, and then it had gotten them killed.

But what would Rowan do with that knowledge? Brenda was afraid to find out. Afraid to set that fire against the organization she believed in. Rowan was a capable fighter and a brilliant mind, an epidemiologist in an age of pandemic. The Division needed her. But even more importantly, Brenda needed the Division.

"The True Sons," Brenda said. It came out soft. Had she really meant to say that? It was in the air now, done. "They launched the attack."

"The True Sons," breathed Rowan.

Slowly, her grip on Brenda's arm relaxed. She let go and sat back. Her eyes were wide, luminous. That fire was in them all right. It burned bright now, flaring into an out-of-control blaze. There was no telling how much it would consume before it guttered out.

But it wasn't aimed at the Division, Brenda told herself. This will be OK. We can make this OK.

"The True Sons," Rowan repeated. And she smiled. A wide smile, bright and ghastly. "Good to know. Thank you for telling me."

"Signal is right up ahead," Leo said.

His voice brought Brenda back to the present. Her heart ached at the old memories. Not again, Brenda thought. Not this time. She'd be damned if she let it happen again. One star left in her care had fallen and burned to ash, crumbled in her hands. This one she was going to save, and set it back where it belonged in the heavens. Come hell or high water, she would not fail Maira the way she had failed Rowan.

It was almost noon now. The sun beat down like a physical force. Wind blew in brief gusts, but it didn't carry much relief. It was dry and hot, and carried sandy grit. It cast everything in stark light. There was no safe place to look, everything was too bright and made her squint. Her hand beat a brief tattoo against the stock of the Honey Badger.

The signal was coming from a little shopping center on the side of the road. A gas station, a few fast-food eateries, a couple of little outlet shops. Nothing impressive or unusual. This place had nothing flagged in their ISAC databases. Brenda swept her gaze over the buildings but couldn't see anything unusual.

"Yeong-Ja? Do you see her?"

The sniper lowered her rifle and shook her head. "I don't see anything."

"Well, the watch is here, if nothing else. Let's find it," Brenda said. "Move out."

They closed in on the cluster of structures slowly. It was hard to tell what they'd all been originally. Signs had fallen, windows had grimed over. Just another dead stop in a mortally wounded nation. Another tombstone on a way of life that seemed gone forever.

"Rogue agent detected," announced ISAC.

Movement caught the corner of Brenda's eye. She whirled. Something was rising behind the murky window of one of the buildings. She just had time to take in the shape.

"Turret! Cover!" Brenda yelled.

She dove. The turret opened fire with a roar, blowing out the glass of the window in a tinkling rain. Fire swept the place Brenda had been standing. It hissed past over her head, a narrow miss. The other agents were scattering, trying to present a confusing target. The roboticized weapon did not hesitate. It tracked one and continued to spray fire.

Brenda pulled an EMP grenade from her harness. Sometimes, it astounded her what life experiences came in handy, and again she thanked her lucky stars for softball. Some things stayed with you, and she'd had a killer throw ever since her all-state days. She hurled the explosive charge toward the window. There was a brilliant flash and the turret froze. Brenda stared at it, breathing hard. It was still. The EMP burst had burned its control system away.

"Status report!" she called.

"Yeong-Ja and I are good," Colin said breathlessly.

"I'm OK," Leo gritted. "I bashed my arm on a wall getting to cover. I think it's bleeding again."

"Shit," Colin said. "I'm on my way."

He set off at a run across the open ground. Brenda raised her head, eyes going wide. "Wait, Colin!"

The medic tore right through a tripwire without ever seeing it. It sent him into an uncontrolled tumble. He went down in a tangle of limbs, yelping on the way. With a ping, a dusty bin the tripwire had connected to tipped over and spilled a trio of football shapes. Each was marked by glowing red rings. They were painfully familiar.

"Seeker mines!" barked Brenda.

They came whirling on, tracking straight toward their fallen friend. Brenda lunged to one knee, gun blazing as it came up. The vast majority of her wild fire went wide, accomplishing nothing. By dumb luck she caught one of the explosives with a bullet, and it cooked off into an immediate explosion. The wash of fire swept over a second, and that one detonated as well in a secondary hammer blow. They were close enough that the force tossed her back onto her butt, driving her teeth together with a painful click.

She could see the third one, intact and closing on Colin. There was no way she was going to bring the Honey Badger to bear in time. He threw up a hand desperately as if to stop the thing by sheer force of will. It exploded and the shock wave sent him rolling away, yelling and desperately trying to curl up to protect himself.

Brenda blinked. The smoke was clearing. Yeong-Ja stood with her sidearm in hand, fear written on her face. Yeong-Ja only relaxed when she saw Colin in one piece rather than shredded across the field.

"Nobody move," Brenda rasped into the comms. Her ears were ringing. "She has rigged this place to hell and back. Just check yourselves and slowly get to your feet."

Brenda staggered to her own feet. Her nose was bleeding, probably from the overpressure. She spat red to the side where it speckled the dusty pavement. She felt certain that her body was going to hurt like the devil as soon as adrenaline wore off, but if that was the total of the butcher's bill, she counted herself lucky.

"I'm all right," Leo said.

"Me too," Yeong-Ja said.

"Damn wire cut my leg," growled Colin. "Got a nasty gash on me. But… thanks, Yeong-Ja. It could have been way worse."

"You know I've got you covered," the sniper replied.

Brenda swept her gaze over the shopping center again. She still didn't see anything out of the ordinary. That did nothing to comfort her. They hadn't spotted the first two traps either. She felt certain that if they set off farther among the buildings there would be some other deadly display waiting for them.

Instead, she took a deep breath. "Maira!"

Brenda's voice rang out across the center. It was only greeted by silence. She took the chance to swap out her spent magazine for a fresh one. Please, Maira, she thought. Not like this. Don't make us do it like this.

"Maira, we know you're here! It's Brenda! It's your cell! Please, you have to come out! You have to stop this!"

The silence stretched.

"Guys, call out to her," Brenda said on the comms.

There was a pause and then they all started up.

"Maira! Come out!" called Leo.

"Maira, if you're hurt, I can help you!" That was Colin.

"Maira, we came to bring you home! We came to help you!" said Yeong-Ja.

"Brenda?"

The voice on the comms sounded rusty with disuse, but Brenda knew it instantly regardless. Her heart leaped in her chest. It was Maira, there was no doubt about it. She didn't sound good, but it was definitely her.

"It's us, Maira. We're your friends. I don't know what's going on, but we're here to help."

"Brenda," Maira repeated. "Colin. Leo. Yeong-Ja. I... What are you doing here? You're not supposed to be here."

There was terror in her voice. Something about it set Brenda's skin to crawling. She sounded raw, like an exposed nerve. Unwillingly, Brenda thought of the fire in Rowan's eyes, the burning that would not be checked.

"We had to come, Maira," Brenda said. She tried to keep her voice soothing. "They think you've gone rogue. Anyone else isn't going to ask any questions. They'll just start shooting."

"You don't understand," Maira mumbled. "The damage I've done. The danger I've caused. The danger I've brought with me. You're not supposed to be here. You're not supposed to be caught up in it."

"Maira, I–"

"You were supposed to stay away!" Maira suddenly screamed. "You were supposed to stay safe."

The scream was audible even outside the comm network. Brenda turned toward the source. Maira was there, on the roof of one of the buildings. She had a rifle in her hands. It was hard to tell exactly what kind, because Brenda found herself staring directly down the barrel.

"Maira, you're right. I don't know what's going on. But I didn't come this far to hurt you." The dark mouth of Maira's gun held surprisingly little fear for Brenda. She realized with awed shock that she still trusted the younger woman, despite everything. "Please, you know us. Put the gun down. Let's talk. Tell us what's happening, and we'll figure it out together."

"It's too late," Maira whispered shakily. "You're in danger now."

She fired.

CHAPTER 11
July 17

Maira didn't want to believe the report of her own eyes. It was bad enough to see and finally understand that the Black Tusk assault she was taking part in was against a Division target. For it to be one of the three Cores was the worst possibility she could think of. It must be the Texas Core, she thought distantly. She would have recognized the blocky layout and locale in Kansas, even from this high-up distance at night, and they hadn't flown nearly far enough to have reached the one in North Dakota.

She darted a glance at the two Black Tusk soldiers sitting in front of her and guarding her. Both watched her silently through the eyeholes in their balaclavas. She hid a wince. Don't do anything to give yourself away, she remonstrated with herself. Not until she had to, at any rate. She realized her hands were shaking and clenched them into fists to try to hide it.

Her eyes went back to the screen. Her creation had no moral qualms, of course. The program was continuing its work with impressive efficiency. She was very good at what she did. The thought brought a bitter smile to her lips. This was not the first time the efficacy of her own programs had unforeseen side effects. At this rate, it would only be a few minutes tops before the program had reached the base directives of the Division server.

A server that used the exact same structure and coding as the one Black Tusk was using. The thought made her sit up straighter. That was the whole point of the program, really. They were two trunks of the same tree, so normally anything that crashed one crashed both. Her program was meant to isolate one before bringing it down. But if it worked so well against the Division, well...

Maira carefully schooled her face into unreadability. Or she tried to, anyway. She had never been much of a poker player. This didn't have to be perfect, she told herself. They didn't have any reason to think she was doing anything but exactly what they wanted. Instead, she forced calm into her mind and searched for the network signals the Black Tusk assault force were using.

It wasn't difficult. They really did work almost exactly the same as the Division tech she was used to. The level of similarity verged on comical. It was like someone had turned in the same paper to two different teachers and hoped that no one would notice. The only significant difference seemed to be that Diamond – the system Black Tusk used – didn't have the added interface level of an AI handler. No ISAC counterpart, in other words. Instead, it piped data directly to users.

Maira could see the advantages to that approach. ISAC was far from perfect, after all. Still, the AI provided a useful means of filtering a veritable torrent of data and making it user-friendly. Diamond had no training wheels. If someone didn't use it just right, they could drown in information they didn't want and never realize they were missing the information they actually needed.

If anything, the lack of artificial oversight made infiltrating the system even easier. Her isolation program set to work drilling down into that network exactly as it had the one the Division was using. She switched back and forth between the two of them nimbly, monitoring their progress. It wouldn't be long until...

"Maira, give me a status report," Natalya said on the radio.

Maira froze like a kid with her hand caught in the cookie jar, the screen from the computer balanced on her knees bathing her face in a blueish glow. She was sweating too much, she realized. She hoped her overseers took that as ordinary nerves. No one understood this program like she did, she told herself. That's the whole reason they needed her in the first place. Even if Black Tusk, Natalya, anyone with this mysterious organization, were watching, they wouldn't understand what was happening. Not until it was too late.

She hoped.

"Almost got them by the guts," Maira replied, a sensation

of hurt twisting her heart. She'd put her faith in Natalya and look what it got her. "Trust me, you'll know when the moment arrives. They'll never know what hit them."

Natalya gave a low laugh at that. "Now that's what I like to hear. It's a pleasure to see you work, Maira."

Maira glanced at the guards again and gave a nervous smile. "I'm glad you think so."

A low chime brought her head back down to study her computer. The first infiltration was complete. The program had accessed the prime directives of the Division's system. Hot on its heels, a second chime told her the same readiness applied to Diamond. All it took now was a simple broadcast command to initiate the final stage: the crash.

What Black Tusk would be expecting would be for all the SHD tech on the field to stop working while theirs continued to function. In this kind of fight, that would be an advantage that would see the Core crushed completely. The defenses of these installations leaned heavily on emplaced, AI-controlled armament. With that shut down, they would only have what weaponry the human defenders could bring to bear. It wouldn't be enough.

What would have been ideal, Maira mused, would be to have a way to flip the script. If she could have shut down Black Tusk's technology but left the Division standing, they could shred their assailants and drive them back much more easily. Unfortunately, that was no longer an option. Both iterations of the code were waiting for the same signal. She could activate both, or neither.

She had incredible power over the battlefield below, but

at the same time, her hands were tied. Still, she had seen what the Black Tusk was bringing to bear in this fight. All those combat chassis and hovering battle drones. They were counting on their steel soldiers. Without the autoguns, the Division fighters could still fall back into the bunker and defend it the old-fashioned way.

Maira watched her guards with her peripheral vision, too. She had to be ready for the fallout of whatever choice she made. One way or another, this wasn't going to go how Black Tusk had wanted. She'd make sure of that. Maira had been shot more than her fair share of times, she wasn't eager to repeat the experience. She had no weapons; she needed some kind of edge.

Her eyes fell on the drone the one guard carried. Her isolation program wasn't the only technological trick at her fingertips. One she still had was the code she had stolen from Rowan all those months ago. It had originally been created by Theo Parnell, a fire and forget program that let someone seize control of SHD tech. Now, this wasn't SHD tech… but there wasn't much difference, was there?

Maira brought up the code and offered a brief mental thanks to her old rogue enemies. Without the tool they had been kind enough to provide her way back then, she probably wouldn't have stood a chance. She located the control frequency of the drone and set that program to work as well.

"Here goes nothing," Maira said and braced herself for what was to come.

She sent the shutdown command. The effects were

gratifyingly immediate. In an instant the raging battle below simply stopped. Machine guns went silent. Drones dropped from the sky like dying birds. Combat robots stopped midstride as if turned to stone. A thousand acknowledgment bursts flooded her screen, letting her know as each piece of technology shut itself down in a wave.

The radio erupted into chaos. No calm reports here.

"Everything has stopped–"

"–can't connect with–"

"–gone nonresponsive–"

"–completely vulnerable out here!"

The command line cut through it all like a hot knife through butter.

"Maira, what have you done?"

It was Natalya. Maira had never heard her sound like this, though. The warm amusement that marked her tone had disappeared. Now, her voice was unutterably cold. The Black Tusk agent didn't even sound angry, Maira realized. That just made it more chilling. It was just ice, hard and matter of fact. Was this who she really was? Had Maira broken through whatever mask she had been wearing?

It didn't matter.

"That's the thing about control, Nat," Maira said, keeping her tone level. "The tighter you try to hold on to everything, the worse it is when something finally slips."

She didn't wait for a reply. Maira yanked the headset off and tossed it to the side. The two soldiers were obviously getting orders over their comms. Their eyes went wide and both of them went to stand and bring their weapons to bear.

"Get on the ground!" one of them shouted.

"Sorry," Maira said, and activated the last program, her finger swiping across the keyboard, with one command for the drone.

The drone came to life with a mechanical whirr, detaching itself from the man's harness and hovering up to head height. Both soldiers looked at it in surprise. Whatever confusion they were feeling, it was the last thing one of them felt. The gun on the drone opened fire. At point-blank range there was no chance it was going to miss. The spray of bullets shredded the cranium of the soldier who had brought it. Blood, bone, and brains splashed across his compatriot.

"What the hell–"

Maira attacked with a scream for a battle cry. She snatched the laptop up in both hands and swung with her whole body behind it. The second soldier turned from the gruesome sight beside him just in time for the device to smash directly into his face. There was a distinct crunching noise and the man fell to his knees.

His eyes looked glazed, and blood was already soaking through the fabric of his dark mask. Maira didn't give him a chance to recover. She raised the laptop and brought it down three more times, rapid hammer blows to his face and skull. He crumpled.

Maira dropped to one knee next to his body and retrieved the MK16 he was carrying. A quick check revealed a thirty-round magazine with one in the chamber. She headed for the front of the craft. The pilot looked back and saw her coming. The other woman's eyes went wide, and Maira could hear her talking into her headset.

"I have a problem here! She's turned on us! I think she's killed–"

"Are you going to be a problem?" Maira cut her off.

The woman stared. She had a sidearm, Maira could see. She wore it on her left side, opposite from where Maira was standing. As a pilot, had she ever used it in anger? Maira couldn't help but wonder. In the end, it didn't matter. She was staring down the barrel of a rifle. Still, Maira saw her hand twitch in that direction.

"You could be Annie Oakley, and I could still shoot you before that clears the holster," Maira said conversationally.

The woman froze again. "Look, I don't want to die."

"That's great. I have no particular urge to kill you. You fly me where I want to go, and I won't have to."

The pilot shook her head rapidly. "I can't. You realize she's not going to just let you get away, right? That's not how she works. She'll kill me just for not stopping you."

Maira frowned. "Then I'll ask you again: are you going to be a problem?"

The woman swallowed hard. Don't do it, Maira thought grimly. Don't–

She went for the gun. Maira shot her through the face. Just like with the drone, at distances like this it was hard to miss. Her face dissolved under the burst of fire. Her body spasmed and went limp. The hand hadn't gotten halfway to the holster.

Maira sighed. "I told you."

She grabbed the body by the shoulder and yanked it out of the seat. It collapsed to the ground in a heap. She stepped over it and settled into the pilot seat. The controls were vastly more complex than she had hoped. Lights and screens held a plethora of data she had no clue how to navigate. She frowned at them. Action heroes in the movies never had this problem; they could always fly whatever they needed to. But she wasn't going to be figuring this out by trial and error.

Still, if there was one thing that the Black Tusk loved, it was their automation. This craft wasn't a drone, obviously. Small blessings, for if it had been it would have powered down with all the others. But if she searched the controls very carefully then maybe…

There it was. An autopilot. She tapped the control and one of the screens in front of her changed. Maira had been hoping for a way to enter coordinates. A kind of aerial GPS as it were. Instead, what she found was a menu of what must have been Black Tusk installations. There were more of them on here than she had imagined. The organization, or whatever the hell Black Tusk was, must have been establishing bases all over the United States.

Maira glowered at the locations. The one thing they all had in common, of course, was they would be full of Black Tusk. Flying to any one of them might as well be turning herself in. OK, she thought, so what was the most advantageous of the options in front of her? On the list she saw the Albuquerque base. Her eyes narrowed.

At least she knew her way around that one. That was something like an edge. Besides, there were other considerations that were even now unfolding in the back of her mind. For one thing, tonight had proven one thing absolutely true: her program worked. She had created something capable of bringing the Division and ISAC to its knees – or for that matter, Black Tusk and Diamond. Even the rogue network, ANNA, should be vulnerable, though that had not been tested.

And the only thing between the Black Tusk and her creation was one hastily established firewall. It might buy time, but it would not hold them off forever. So, one way or another, she had to go back to Albuquerque. She had to destroy what she had created. Otherwise, the consequences would be on her, and she wasn't sure she could live with that.

She tapped the selection. The computer chimed acceptance, and she could feel the plane bank onto its new heading and accelerate. Maira took a deep breath. The die was cast. In the meantime, it seemed wise to scavenge what resources she could.

"It isn't too late, Maira."

Maira froze. The voice came from the aircraft console. Natalya. She swallowed hard. In all honesty, she had hoped they could forgo any extended exchanges. She was my captor, she told herself. She saw the potential in me and believed in it, her heart answered. Surely not all of that warmth had been faked. Surely Nat did value her to some extent.

Shakily, she reached out and touched the radio control. "Too late for what, Nat?"

"To come in from the cold. Nothing you've done can't be forgiven," Natalya replied.

"I trashed your battle plan," Maira pointed out. "And maybe you haven't picked up on it yet, but I killed three of your people."

"Oh, I'm aware," the Black Tusk leader replied with disconcerting calm. The ice in her tone from earlier had retreated. "I can replace any of them, Maira. As far as I know, you're one of a kind. As for the battle… your loyalties were divided. It was confusing. But the program worked, Maira."

"So it did," Maira replied sadly. "I wish it hadn't, honestly."

"You're still not thinking clearly. Come back, and we can talk things out. I understand all of this must be overwhelming. But if you take the time to hear me out, you'll realize everything I've done has been for the greater good."

"Whose greater good, Nat?" Maira couldn't keep a note of anguish from her voice. "You drugged me! You used me!"

"You're upset about that, I can tell. But the greater good we're talking about is bigger than any one of us or our feelings. Bigger than you, and bigger even than me. I told you I had a vision for the world, Maira. Not just to bring it back, but to make it better than it ever was. I meant that." There was a certain verve to her voice as she said this.

Maybe she really believes it, Maira thought. Maybe she really has sold herself on whatever crusade she's imagined up. What if she's right? an uncomfortable part of her asked. What if she really does know better? Certainly, she seemed to have more resources than anyone else that was left. Couldn't those be turned to good ends?

"A better world," Nat repeated into the silence. "And you can still be the means that secures that future. You can be right beside me as we bring it about."

Something about the way she'd said that stopped Maira. *The means.* Maybe Natalya meant every word she said, but even if she did, didn't that lay her worldview bare? Willing or not, Maira was always just going to be a tool in her hands. To join Black Tusk was to set aside her own hopes, her own vision of the future, her own conscience. She would never be more than an extension of Natalya.

"I'm sorry, Nat. I don't want to be the means to your ends, however glorious you think they are. I have my own judgment, and I have to trust it."

There was an extended pause, the quiet crackle of the radio seeming loud in the cockpit.

"I'm sorry, too," Natalya said finally. "Goodbye, Maira."

The radio went dead.

Maira's heart ached, but more than that her skin crawled. There had been something about the way Natalya said goodbye. Maira definitely couldn't claim to be an expert on the woman, especially if she was only just now figuring her out. But that note in her voice, to Maira it was more than just getting the last word. Natalya didn't expect to see

Maira again in this lifetime. By some means, she considered Maira already dead.

Maira's gaze scrambled across the control panel. Was there a clue here somewhere? That was a radar screen, wasn't it? Was there some other aircraft closing in to shoot her down? Certainly, Maira didn't have a lot she could do about that. She was not a fighter pilot by any stretch of the imagination. But no, if that was the radar screen it seemed empty. No jet-tailed avenger was closing in to eliminate her.

A small red light caught Maira's attention. It was blinking steadily. That hadn't been there a moment ago. Some of the controls were labeled. Maira leaned closer with a frown to try to make out the imprinted writing about the light. The word "loyalty" was all it said above it.

Maira took a moment to think that over. What exactly would Natalya consider a loyalty guarantee? Her throat felt very dry. The answer seemed painfully clear. She didn't trust anyone, and so she had some way to bring down any of her equipment lest it be turned against her.

"Well, hell," she finally rasped, "that's one way to go out." She hastily buckled the pilot seat's harness around her and waited for the inevitable.

The bomb detonated.

Maira came to slowly. Painfully. She was hanging upside down. Her brain felt like it had been wrapped in cotton and beaten with a hammer. The whole world was blurry. Her mouth felt as if it were stuffed with cotton, too. She tried to spit to the side. It didn't work. Her hands swiped around dumbly as she tried to touch her face.

Before she managed to make contact there, she found the buckle on the harness. Maira blinked at it and hit the release. The moment she did, regret spiked. She had no idea where she was, or what she might land on. She didn't even know if she was critically hurt.

It was too late. She dropped to the ground below and landed in a heap. The world threatened to tumble back into darkness. Stubbornly, Maira shook her head.

"No," she said thickly. "Gotta…"

"There's someone alive in here!" called a voice.

Metal creaked nearby. Maira tried to focus, but that remained beyond her capabilities. What did it mean that she'd been found? And by who? Rough hands grabbed her under her armpits and began to drag her. She opened her mouth to protest, but nothing came out except a dull groan.

"Easy does it," someone said. "We're not going to hurt you."

There was a night sky above. The stars were beautiful. Maira wasn't sure she could trust these people. But that orange glow was so comforting. She closed her eyes.

When Maira opened her eyes again, most of her bodily pain had receded. She sat up with a groan and touched a hand to her head. That part of her still ached. On the whole, though, she felt much more human. She was lying on a makeshift bedroll amidst Texas scrub. The stars shone overhead.

"Welcome back to the land of the living," someone said.

Recent memories flooded back. That was a familiar voice, if only barely. Maira turned in surprise and found herself facing a man in rough and tumble garb. He was sitting on the ground nearby. Vastly more interesting, he was wearing an orange-glowing watch and had a brick of a similar light on his shoulder.

"You're a Division agent," Maira breathed. Her heart soared.

"That's good," he replied amiably. "I was worried you'd have some permanent loss of your faculties, but that was pretty quick."

"And you saved me..."

She turned her head and there it was. The wreckage of the Black Tusk aircraft. It had cratered the desert. Parts of it were still burning. She could see the engine where the bomb had detonated. It must not have been a very big one. Just enough to cripple the vehicle and make sure it came crashing down.

"How charming of her," Maira muttered.

The man raised an eyebrow but didn't say anything about that cryptic comment. "Yeah, we pulled you out. As best we can tell, you're battered. You're gonna be a human bruise for the next week or two. But you'll be OK. Your brain was our last big concern."

"Thank you for not leaving me in there," Maira said. She turned her gaze back to him. "Wait, 'our'?"

"Me and my cellmate," the man said. He motioned. "Here she comes now."

There was a scraping noise, and someone came clambering up out of the crater the aircraft had left. She wore jeans and flannel, and had her long hair pulled into a ponytail. And of course, she, too, wore the telltale watch and brick. Maira could scarcely believe her eyes.

"Oh good, she's alive," the newcomer said cheerfully as she joined them.

"Yeah, I just got done thanking him for that. I guess I should thank you, too," Maira said. She couldn't believe her luck. Somehow, she'd leapt out of the arms of her enemies and back into the embrace of friends. Or maybe just an organization that wasn't hellbent on reshaping the world to their whim.

The woman smirked. "Well, I was the one who actually got you out, so probably."

"Details," the man averred with a chuckle. "So, seeing as we did save your life, and you are largely intact and capable of speech and reason, could we ask you a question?"

"Sure," Maira hazarded, suddenly uneasy.

The man leaned forward, eyes sharp in spite of his smile. "What is a dead Division agent doing in a crashed Black Tusk aircraft in the wake of an attack that nearly brought down one of the Cores?"

"Ah," Maira said. "That's a really good question."

"Thanks," he replied. "I thought it was."

"OK, for starters, I'm not dead. Thanks for tattling on me, ISAC," Maira said wryly.

"That's a good start. I imagine your cell will be glad to hear it as soon as we can reach them."

Maira frowned. "My cell? But they died in… they died at Houston."

The man frowned. "All the local agents heard what happened out there. It was a hell of a scene, and sure could have killed all of you had things gone even a little bit askew. But from what I heard – and ISAC confirms – the only agent reported dead that night was you, Maira Kanhai."

The world shrank to a point. Maira took a deep breath. The only other option was to hyperventilate. "They're alive?"

He tilted his head, and a kind note entered his voice. "They are. Seems like someone fed you a line, sister."

"Seems that way," she said dizzily.

"Rupert," the other Division agent said.

He held up a hand as if to forestall her. "So, we've established you're alive, which is great. Now why are you here? What happened to you?"

"That's a really long story," Maira said. "Look, place me under arrest, whatever. Take me back to the Core. Find Brenda Wells, she can vouch for me. I'll tell you everything. You have to help me. I made… I made a terrible mistake, and tonight could be just the beginning of the fallout from it."

Rupert frowned. "You seem sincere. Yeah, we can–"

"Rupert!" exclaimed his comrade.

He turned his head, annoyed. "What, Janice?"

"What's wrong with ISAC?"

"What?" Rupert asked. He tilted his head, confused. "ISAC?"

There was a pause. Maira watched with concern.

"Nothing for you, too?" asked Janice.

"I crashed the network," Maira began. "It should be recoverable, but maybe–"

"No." Rupert stood up, uneasy, stepping away from Maira. "No, we brought that back up an hour or two later. I wasn't aware you were behind the crash, mind you, but that's interesting. But still, something is ..."

A shape loomed out of the darkness. The moment etched itself, bitter and vibrant, into Maira's mind. A figure dressed in all-black combat harness, more extensive even than the gear worn by the Black Tusk troopers, came into view. From that harness hung watches. Red and orange, they flickered and flared. There must have been a dozen of them.

It wore a mask, too, but this was no mere balaclava. It was a ballistic mask, and even by the light of the moon and stars Maira could see it was stylized. Painted with interlocking gears down the middle, like some abstract representation of clockwork. Only the figure's eyes were visible, cold and measuring. Metal gleamed in this apparition's hand, a razor-sharp blade. An ax.

"Shit!" Rupert said and went for his gun. The figure moved. Fast. So fast.

The ax came sweeping around in a gleaming arc. How had this person gotten so close without ISAC warning the agents? Had he scrambled the AI somehow? Or was it the lingering effects of her own attack on the network after all? All these thoughts and more overwhelmed Maira as the blade sank into Rupert's forehead all the same. It stuck there with a meaty *thwock*, then wrenched free in a spray of blood. The agent collapsed.

Janice screamed. She came up with her shotgun and the weapon boomed. Maira could hear the shot impact on the figure's armor, but the figure didn't make a sound. Not so much as a grunt of discomfort. It just whirled and sprinted. The gap between them couldn't have been more than fifteen feet. Janice backpedaled desperately and fired again, but this shot went wide in her panic.

The ax swept around again. This time it thudded into Janice's abdomen. The figure twisted it and yanked the ax free. As it came loose, so did Janice's innards. The agent gave a choking scream that ended as the figure stepped forward and caught her by the throat and squeezed.

Terror howled in Maira's mind. This was not something she had been prepared for. She had no weapon, no ability to defend herself. This was something out of a nightmare. She lunged toward Rupert's body. The wound to his skull had left him alive, but he was in a grim state. Maira had no way to help him.

His gun lay there, but a firearm had done Janice little good. Instead, Maira grabbed at the grenades on his combat vest. She came away with one hot in her hand. A flashbang. Not what she'd hoped for. She turned–

The apparition stood just a short way away, staring at her. Maira froze. Had she ever seen anyone or anything take apart two Division agents so effortlessly? It had been a systematic demolishment. What chance did Maira stand if she stood and fought?

None. The figure came on in a rush, and Maira yelped and fell back. She hurled the grenade with all her might. The flashbang caught the nightmare right in the center of its mask. It went off, brilliant as the midday sun. Maira didn't have a chance to look away. The world dissolved into colorful splotches, her ears ringing under the onslaught.

The only thing that saved her was that, by cosmic grace, this thing was no more proof to the attack than she was. Instead of killing her instantly, its charging caught her in a blind bull's rush. As the figure slammed into her, they fell together. Momentum carried them further, tumbling along the ground. Something heavy and metallic scraped her hand. She seized it and yanked. It came free.

Maira hit the dirt. She was still somewhat blind and deaf. She didn't let that stop her. Though the world was nothing but swirling colors, she got her legs underneath her. Gasping and terrified, she ran.

There was no doubt in her mind that the merciless Hunter would pursue.

CHAPTER 12

August 21

"Maira, no!"

The shot rang out across the abandoned shopping center in time with Brenda's shout.

She froze. She knew Maira's capabilities well; if the rogue agent had wanted to kill her, she'd be dead. She turned her head in alarm, mouth open to ask the other agents of the cell if they were all right. It was only by the grace of that movement that she saw the actual target.

The apparition had erupted from the shadows inside a nearby building. It was a swathe of black under the noonday sun, a wraith. It sprinted toward them, a gleaming ax held low and ready in its hand. Maira's bullet caught it on the shoulder. It staggered. No blood showed… because of armor? But the impact threw it off just enough to buy seconds.

"Hostile incoming!" Brenda yelled.

Where the hell was ISAC? There should have been a warning. The HUD on her vision glitched as if in response. Orange lines scattered and fizzled.

"Unknown network detected," ISAC said. The machine voice slurred, hitched.

Brenda had no time to worry about that. The unknown person had recovered. It hurtled on toward her at high speed. She brought the Honey Badger to bear and held down the trigger, shooting from the hip. The weapon sprayed fire. It pinged on empty in less than a second.

The wraith was ready for Brenda's attack this time. It came on through a hail of bullets like it was nothing but heavy rain. The ax came up. Brenda hurled herself to the side in a last-second lunge. The blade sliced down through the space she'd occupied a heartbeat before. Brenda hit the dirt and rolled. She ejected the empty magazine and slammed a new one home as she came back to her feet.

Leo approached from the side. He had his MP5 at his shoulder and fired controlled bursts as he came. The dark shape whirled to confront this new threat. As it turned, it pulled a shotgun from its back. It wielded the weapon one-handed. A chattering burst of buckshot smashed Leo from his feet. He spun away, hitting the ground hard.

"Get clear!" Yeong-Ja yelled. She raised her TAC-50 to bring it to bear. A snap shot cracked out, the peal echoing off sand-grimed walls.

The wraith stumbled. Its masked face turned toward the sniper. A banshee's wail slammed into Brenda's senses through her comms. It was like having white-hot liquid metal poured into her ear. Her vision dissolved into a storm of static. She staggered and clutched at her head involuntarily, mouth open in a silent scream of pain.

Brenda snatched the comms earpiece out of her ear and threw it away; she could hear it shrilling as it tumbled across the ground. She squeezed her eye with the contact in it shut, trying to block out the assault ISAC was inflicting on her. She came up with her gun held ready. There was no sign of their enemy. Only a cloud of blue smoke where it had been standing.

The sensory assault had washed over the other agents as well, to judge by their reactions. Colin was dragging Leo by his shoulders, but his face was a mask of pain, tears streaming down his cheeks. Yeong-Ja had dropped to one knee, her head snapping back and forth like a blinded animal. Brenda strode to her and pulled the earpiece loose, sent it clattering to join her own.

"What the hell was that?" Yeong-Ja snapped, her customary reserve shattered.

"Information warfare," Brenda said grimly. "ISAC is a liability in this fight. Help Colin!"

She rid herself of the useless contact with a swipe of her hand. Brenda swiveled her head back and forth. The collection of abandoned buildings had been innocuous a little while ago. Now the darkness within each held terror. There was nothing to give away where their enemy had fallen back to. Maira had vanished from her roost as well.

There, near where the blue smoke billowed... a

splattering of vivid red against the ground. Blood. The .50
round from Yeong-Ja's rifle had actually gotten through. It
was the first sign that this thing was capable of being hurt,
that it was, in fact, a human underneath the brutality.

"Leo?" Brenda asked. She caught herself: no comms.
This time it was a yell. "Leo?"

"I'm here," the man himself answered. He sounded
annoyed. "Took it on the plates."

"Most of it," Colin corrected. "I'm going to be picking
shot out of his face and neck. I can't decide if you're blessed
or cursed."

The other three agents were sheltering in the lee of one
of the buildings. Brenda fell back toward them without
taking her eyes off their surroundings.

"Maira!" she called. "Maira, what is going on?"

There was no answer. Still, whatever this thing was, it
wasn't working with the rogue agent. Maira had shot it.
Brenda knew such an action had been an effort to protect
them, to warn them. Was the wraith here for them, or for
her? Brenda's gut told her it was the latter. They had to find
Maira and get out of this place. She had to understand
everything before she truly labeled Maira as their enemy.

Colin had an autosyringe out. He stabbed it into place
against Leo's chest. There was a hiss. Brenda didn't need
to watch to know what was happening. They were repair
nanites. They'd seek the damage already done to Leo's
armor plates and mend any weaknesses. Not exactly as
good as new, but a second place good enough for field
work.

A shadow swept across the group. That was the only warning. The wraith landed among them in a crouch, leaping from the top of the building above. The ax whistled in a butcher's arc. Yeong-Ja screamed and there was a crunch. She caught the edge on her rifle – it sank into the weapon's material before lodging. They wrestled briefly for control of the joined armament.

Yeong-Ja was a hundred pounds on a good day; the unknown was bigger. It whirled her clear off her feet and powered her into the side of the building. The sniper's cry was cut off midway by the thud of impact. She fell limp to the ground.

Colin snarled. It was the angriest Brenda had ever seen him. He had his Ka-Bar knife in hand and lunged into the masked attacker's side with heedless force. The unknown used that power against him and hefted Colin up in an expert throw, sending him tumbling away across the ground. He kicked up dust on impact and was left coughing. The knife had vanished from his hand.

Leo drew his sidearm and fired. One, two, three shots angled into the center mass of the wraith. He might as well have been shooting spitballs at an elephant. It bulled through and delivered a series of controlled blows that doubled Leo over and snapped his head around. Brenda took the chance to kick it in the back of the knee. The wraith went down.

She found herself looking down into that mask. Even now, in the heat of desperate fighting, its eyes were cold and calculating. Brenda smashed the stock of the Honey Badger into that armored face once, twice–

It yanked the Ka-Bar from its own side – ah, that's where that had gone, Brenda thought distantly – and slammed it down through the top of Brenda's boot. Twisted. She couldn't help but scream as blood welled and bone grated. It came up in a lunge, catching her under the chin with a rising headbutt. The world went white, then black.

Brenda came to, dizzily and moments later, in the midst of a thunderstorm. She tried to push herself up, but someone snatched her back down to the ground.

"Stay low!"

Brenda shook her head vigorously. Her mouth was full of salt and copper. She spat, and a tooth went with the blood, a splash of white amidst the red. She wiped her mouth and looked to the side. Leo had a grip on her. His eyes were wide, and his expression was even grimmer than usual.

Brenda's brain caught up with her. They were not, in fact, caught in a New Mexico thunderstorm. Instead, they found themselves in the center of a dizzying barrage. Half a dozen SHD turrets had activated in buildings all around and opened fire. A relentless hail of bullets tore through walls and windows, only a foot or two above their head. Standing would have seen her cut down in a heartbeat. Dust and debris surrounded them.

"Maira?" she asked.

"Maira," agreed Leo.

The turrets were tracking something. The wraith, sprinting just ahead of their onslaught. It fled into one of the nearby buildings, smashing through the door as though it were made of cardboard. Bullets stitched in its wake.

Wood splintered and glass shattered. Brenda watched, somewhere between awe and horror. It was like the guns couldn't quite lock on to their assailant, as if the deadly enemy really were just a ghost.

The lines of fire had tracked from over their heads. Boots crunched across the dirt nearby. Brenda blinked and turned to look. Maira stood over them, a bag slung across her back. Her face was gaunt and weathered. She had a battered tablet in her hand and a watch on her wrist, its ruby glow almost lost in the midday brilliance. She tapped a control on the tablet.

Something shrieked past overhead, a small aerial shape. It rained burning shots across the building their attacker had escaped into. Without pausing it then plowed into the structure and promptly detonated. An incendiary payload washed out, setting the structure ablaze. Within seconds the whole thing was burning merrily, a store-sized bonfire.

"I have no idea how long that's going to buy us," Maira said. "On your feet, agents. We have to move."

Maira could feel the eyes of the Division cell boring into her back. She studiously did not look back to meet their gazes. The earliest part of their flight from the unnamed shopping center had been hectic enough that no one had time to wonder. They just gathered up, helped each other along, and limped away as fast as they could. That had been two hours ago, and now they were starting to calm down. That gave them time to think, and to want answers.

Maira just wasn't sure what answers she was ready to give them.

They trekked on through the heat of the New Mexico day. None of them had come through that fight completely unscathed. Maira could hear their little pained grunts as they powered through the injuries rather than let them slow the group. That wasn't surprising; they were Division agents. Even so it was hard for her to listen to. Each sound made her guilt burn hotter.

"All right," Colin said finally. His tone had the firmness of a concerned father. "We've made it far enough. We have to deal with some of these wounds."

Maira glanced back south toward where they'd been. The smoke cloud of the burning building was still visible. It had probably spread to the other parts of the complex. There would be nothing but an ashen ruin for the next set of travelers to wonder over. She nodded slowly.

"All right," she said. "But try to hurry. The more ground we can gain, the better."

"Surely it's dead," Colin said uneasily.

"Maybe," Maira said without hope. "I don't plan to bet on it."

The group pulled up wearily. Colin swept his gaze over the group and released his little hovering drone to help him diagnose and treat their various wounds. Brenda's foot was where he started.

"Sit down and let's get the boot off," he said.

"I'm fine," Brenda protested. "Are you sure someone else isn't hurt worse?"

Her voice was a bit slurred; her jaw was swelling, too. Colin waved her off with irritation. "He put a knife through your foot, Brenda. Save me the self-sacrifice routine. This is my job, let me do it."

"All right, all right," Brenda said and moved to comply.

They made a makeshift chair for her with a couple of go bags pushed together. The boot came away to reveal a sight that made Maira wince. The blade had gouged clear through her foot. She could see bone and meat through the opening. Now that the pressure of the boot was gone, the wound was steadily bleeding, too. Colin set to work cleaning and bandaging it.

Brenda closed her eyes and took a deep breath. When she opened them again, she focused on Maira.

"So, I think it's time for some answers."

"Amen to that," Yeong-Ja said, sounding exhausted from where she'd collapsed to sit cross-legged on the ground nearby. Her gaze was locked on her damaged rifle. They had retrieved it, but it would likely never shoot again. She was obviously miserable at the sight.

Maira sighed. The reckoning had come. It was just as well. It could only be put off for so long. She sank to the ground herself. Her whole body was weary beyond all reckoning. It went beyond just being tired and became a dull throbbing ache that infested her entire skeleton. It was impossible to move without some bit of her complaining about the process.

"OK," she said. "Where do we start?"

"You're alive," Leo remarked.

Maira scratched her head. "Yeah, that's a good place, I guess, since it's where we left off. For what it's worth, I'm as surprised as anyone else. And I did die. My heart definitely stopped for a while, anyway."

"Someone saved you," Colin commented distractedly.

Maira nodded. "Correct. They retrieved me from the wreckage of the ship and flew me to their facility. Saving me took extensive surgeries with cutting edge technologies, and to my understanding it was still a touch-and-go matter."

"Who?" asked Brenda.

"At the time, I was told it was a Department of Homeland Security operation," Maira said. "The truth turned out to be more complicated."

"This isn't the time for eliding," Brenda said with clear frustration. "Full answers, Maira. Complicated how?"

"Right, OK," Maira muttered. She took a deep breath. "I think it was DHS assets involved at first, but they were acting on the request of someone else. I ended up in the hands of a different group: Black Tusk."

Brenda blanched and exchanged looks with Leo. "Black Tusk? Are you sure?"

"Pretty damn sure," Maira said with dry humor, thinking of the effort getting that information had taken. "I take it the name means something to you."

"Yeah," Brenda said. "They had attacked DC before we left on the mission where you met us. Easily one of the most dangerous foes the Division had encountered. They have technology that outstripped ours in a lot of ways, but also had more numbers, better training. I never quite understood what motivated them, though."

"Well, I didn't know anything about them," Maira said. "Never tangled with them. I had no idea how dangerous they were. Not at first. anyway. Not until it was too late."

"Too late?" asked Yeong-Ja worriedly.

Maira looked down at her hands and fidgeted. She knew she'd been manipulated and used, but everything that had happened as a result still felt like it rested solely on her shoulders. "They didn't snag me out of that river at random. They wanted my help with something specific. Something not just anyone could do. Something to do with the Network."

Brenda shrugged. "I'm not surprised. That's your area of expertise these days. It came up before we ever set out looking for you; nobody knows ISAC and the Network like Maira does. Makes sense that if someone was going to target you, that's why they'd do it."

"Well, you're right. They weren't after my charming looks or impeccable sense of fashion," Maira said with a tired laugh.

"You said it was too late," pointed out Yeong-Ja. "Are you saying you helped them sabotage the Division Network?"

Maira flinched. "Not exactly." She swept her gaze over the group, but couldn't meet their eyes. "I didn't know they were dangerous. And they drugged me. I didn't start to put things together until I'd been there for weeks and weeks."

Colin's head came around. "They drugged you?"

Maira nodded sadly. "In my food, in my drink. Kept me complacent. Kept me from questioning. And in the end, I did develop the means to do what they wanted."

"Which was?" asked Leo.

Maira hesitated.

"Don't clam up now," Brenda said.

"I'm not trying–" Maira sighed and swept a hand over her face. "Look. It gets technical. I'm not trying to hide anything, but I want to explain it right."

"Gotta dumb it down for us," quipped Yeong-Ja.

Colin had finished with Brenda's foot and moved over to the sniper.

"Your shoulder is dislocated," he told her. "This is going to suck."

"Do what you have to do, sawbones," Yeong-Ja said.

Maira looked away. She could still hear the crispy sound of the joint being resettled, and the low grunt of pain it dragged out of the sniper. She tried to just look at her hands. Bony and worn. Dirt under the nails. Lots of calluses and little scars. Life had not been easy these past years. She didn't want to say any of this out loud, but her cell – if she could even still call them that – deserved the truth.

"OK," she said finally. "What you need to understand is I learned a lot while I was there. Things they probably wish I hadn't, now. For one thing, their technology and ours? It comes from the same place."

"How do you know?" asked Brenda in surprise.

"Because we're using the same servers," Maira said softly.

"Our network and their network, they're not actually two separate entities. They're the same thing. Two trunks of the same tree."

"How?" asked Leo after a silence.

"I don't know that part," admitted Maira. "It must all track back to stuff that happened before the Poison ever came along. Which means, for one thing, these Black Tusk assholes? They've been planning something before the Green Poison ever happened, too."

"OK," Brenda said after processing that. "So, what did they want you to do?"

"Figure out how to isolate one of the trunks without killing the whole tree. As near as I can tell, there must have been some moment when they realized the commonality. I'm guessing they tried to crash the Network, only to discover it crashed them, too. They wanted that to go away, to be able to bring ISAC down but have their own tech keep working."

Colin moved over to sit next to Leo. He had medical tweezers in his hand. "Gotta get the shot out. Don't want it to get infected."

"Joy," remarked Leo, but he didn't resist.

"And you did it," Brenda said wonderingly. "You figured out how to make it work?"

"I did," Maira said. "The program was in a working state before I figured out what was going on, but that doesn't change the reality. If deployed, it can wipe out our support systems and leave them working just fine."

"That's impressive," Brenda said. "And awful. So every

Division site in the nation is fundamentally vulnerable now?"

Maira shook her head. "Almost, but not quite. The program is complete, but I did finally catch on to what was happening. They took me along to attack the Texas Core, and I shut down all the tech on the field rather than what they wanted me to do. That was when I tried to escape."

"That explains some things we heard about the Core attack," Yeong-Ja observed. "No one could figure out what happened to all the tech. Both sides just shut down at the same time. It worked out in the favor of our defense, but it was definitely a chaotic night."

"I hoped it would hit them harder," said Maira. "I couldn't be sure, but I hoped."

Silence settled over the little group again. The only sound was the repressed noises from Leo, and the occasional clink of a new bit of bloody shot being dropped into a little tray by Colin.

"Still, they have your code, don't they?" Brenda asked.

"They have it and they don't," Maira said. She held up a hand to forestall their frustrations. "I know! Look, it's in their servers, but I walled it off. They can't access it yet."

"Yet?" asked Brenda.

"No defense is perfect. They'll get through it eventually if I give them the chance."

Brenda stared at her. "That's what you're doing. This wild trek. You set out to try to stop them from accessing your creation. You came all this way to try to stop them alone."

Maira sighed. "When you put it like that it sounds stupid. But I had to do something. I created this problem, so I have to try to fix it. I can't just leave everyone else holding the bill, you know? Besides," Maira said and held up her wrist. The red light gleamed. "I couldn't exactly call out for help from the Division."

Brenda nodded slowly. "You're not wrong. They wouldn't have listened, most of them. And Maira, I have to know…"

Maira tilted her head. "What?"

"Did you kill those two agents?"

The silence was complete this time. Nobody was staring at Maira, but she was the absolute focus of the group's attention all the same.

"Kill…?" Maira frowned. She didn't kill anyone. Surely, they didn't mean to imply that she would do such butchery… her face twisted. "What? You mean the two who saved me? Of course I didn't kill them!"

"They saved you?" asked Colin.

Maira nodded. "They pulled me out of the plane I stole when Black Tusk brought it down."

"So who killed them?" asked Yeong-Ja.

Maira couldn't hide the guilt that welled up. The memories of that night were painful to relive. The sudden, horrifying violence. And in the end, maybe she had killed them. Their only crime had been finding her and trying to help her. If she hadn't been there, they would have lived.

She motioned back the way they had come. "You met him. My shadow."

"I'd believe it," admitted Colin. "It sure as hell attacked

us without hesitation. Whoever that was, they were a killer through and through."

Maira nodded sadly. "It ambushed and murdered Janice and Rupert that night. I only survived by dumb luck. If they hadn't found me, they'd still be alive – and it would have found me helpless in that crashed plane. And ... I guess that would have been the end of that."

"So that person – it bled, I saw it, it's a person," Brenda said. She exchanged a look with Leo before saying, "They were sent after you by Black Tusk?"

"As best I can figure," Maira agreed. "They've been hounding me ever since that night. Why else would they appear when they did? I've survived by running and hiding, and even then it's always been close. One step ahead at most. Then I found that SHD supply store, and I thought ... maybe this is my chance."

"Then it caught you there, too?" asked Brenda.

"Yeah," Maira said. Surprise furrowed her brow. "How did you know?"

"Saw the site," said Leo. He winced. Colin was back to picking the shrapnel from him. "Saw the aftermath."

"Yeah, it jumped me there. I got away with a bunch of tech, though. And I knew I couldn't run much longer. So I found that shopping center, and I got ready to make my stand."

"And then we stumbled right into the middle of it," Yeong-Ja said. "With impeccable timing and panache."

Maira laughed softly. "Something like that. I can tell you it was the last thing I expected, to see all of you there. I was still coming to terms with the idea you were all alive. Black Tusk and DHS lied to me. They told me you died in Houston."

"Oh, Maira," Brenda said quietly. There was a deep well of sympathy in her voice.

Colin turned and set the tweezers down. "It was hard for us just thinking we lost you – I can't imagine what it was like, thinking you'd lost the entire cell, and being in unfriendly hands at the same time."

"It wasn't my favorite time," Maira said. "I… Look. I'm just glad you guys are OK. And I'm sorry you're here now. I never meant to drag you into this mess."

Tears stung her eyes. She looked down, hoping they wouldn't see them. Instead, Brenda got up and limped over to her. She reached down and offered Maira a hand up to her feet. Reluctantly, Maira let herself get pulled back to her full height. Her body creaked and complained on the way up.

"Maira, you silly girl," the elder agent said, gripping Maira's shoulder and looking into Maira's eyes as if she could touch her soul. "You should have realized: the moment we found out you were alive, there was nothing in this world that was going to keep us away."

Brenda pulled her into a hug then. Maira tensed. The older agent stank of gunpowder and sweat, and she was too warm under the hot sun. But in all honesty, it didn't matter. Maira buried her face in the other woman's shoulder, and a sob tore its way out of her.

It was too much. She'd bottled it all up for too long. The

fear, the isolation, the guilt, and the pain. She let it out now, wrenching cries that racked her body. Quietly the rest of the agents gathered around her, resting hands on her back and shoulders. She wasn't alone any longer.

"How much farther do you have to go to get back to where your program is?" Brenda asked once she'd calmed again.

"Not far. It's in Albuquerque. They've set up some kind of base there," Maira managed to say.

"All right. Well, we've come this far. Might as well see this thing through, right?" Brenda looked around to the rest of the group. "Let's see what Black Tusk has waiting for us, at least."

They trekked on for the rest of that day and made camp that night. The next day they rose early and pushed on. ISAC was working again, and their connection was up and running thanks to the spare earpieces and contacts Maira had collected from the destroyed storehouse. By mid-morning they had reached the edges of the city of Albuquerque. Unlike their failed approach at El Paso, there was no smoke signal that anyone was on to them this time. However, she knew that Black Tusk wouldn't be so overt in announcing their presence.

Brenda led them through the quiet streets lined with buildings. Had people fled during the collapse of society, or was this something Black Tusk had done recently? Most cities had at least a few survivor enclaves, but this city felt emptied. The buildings became skyscrapers as they pressed

in toward the city center. Brenda noticed the tension
growing in Maira the further they pressed on, too. The
woman had been through so much. Brenda was in awe of
all that she'd endured.

They stayed tactical as they covered the last of the
distance. No one spoke. What communication they
required had to be accomplished with hand signals. They
crept from cover to cover, just in case. Brenda kept waiting
for the inevitable ambush to crystallize. Perhaps Black
Tusk didn't see the need for such methods, though. Maybe
they felt confident that they could handle any assault head-
on.

It was in turning the final corner that Brenda realized
where that confidence might have come from. There in the
center of the city was a tower. It might have been a hotel
once. Now it was a base of operations. Black Tusk had taken
over the entire structure and all the buildings surrounding
it. Brenda couldn't begin to imagine the kind of resources
they must have invested in this place, especially in terms of
the fallen world they all lived in now.

Nor had they left their investment defenseless. She
stopped and stared. The rest of the cell slowly accumulated
at her sides. No one said anything. No one had to. This
place was more than just a research laboratory or testing
ground. It was a fortress. Hovercrafts, soldiers, helicopters,
emplaced defenses and more.

Brenda looked at Maira and could see the despair written
on the younger woman's face. They had come all this way,
across hundreds of miles and through blood and fire. And

now at the end, they were in sight of what had started it all – and between them and their objective lay an army the likes of which Brenda hadn't seen since the onslaught that swept through DC when their enemy first revealed themselves.

Brenda rested a hand on Maira's shoulder.

"We have to fall back," she whispered. "We'll figure something out."

Maira nodded slowly, but there was no hope in her eyes.

CHAPTER 13
August 25

"You have her."

Brenda crossed her arms over her chest. The communication came in surprisingly clear. It was Agent Thaddeus Greene. The radio signal had come in through ISAC while Maira and Yeong-Ja were performing reconnaissance in the city. Colin was on watch for any threats to their temporary base. Only Leo remained, sitting nearby with a grim expression.

"We found her, and she came along willingly, yes. You seem remarkably up to date on our situation," Brenda said.

"You are not the only one who can keep an eye on tracking signals, Agent Wells. Anyone interested knows you caught up to her."

"I'm flattered by your concern, especially considering your distaste for the whole mission," Brenda said.

"I believed then – I still believe – that there are better uses for the resources you've spent in retrieving a single rogue agent. However, I am prepared to give credit where it is due. You set out to retrieve Maira Kanhai, and you succeeded. Congratulations," Greene said.

Brenda smiled tightly. "Thank you."

"When can we expect you to return her to the Texas Core?"

Brenda raised an eyebrow. "I beg your pardon?"

"You have detained a dangerous rogue agent. That it is to your credit. I assumed you would bring her to a secure site where she could be questioned safely," Greene said.

"I'm not convinced she did the things she's accused of, Greene," Brenda said. "For one thing, she says she didn't. For another, the ISAC recording of those events is missing."

There was a pause. "Missing?" Greene asked.

"As if it got carved out of the system completely," confirmed Brenda. "A giant blank spot where it was supposed to be."

"That is unusual," Greene admitted. "It would be even stranger if the accused were not a noted information technology specialist and expert on subverting ISAC-based systems."

"You're suggesting she deleted the information herself."

"I'm suggesting that we have two dead agents, and someone with a motive to want those events concealed," Greene said matter-of-factly.

"I agree with both of those things, but I'm not convinced Maira is the culprit."

"You have an alternate hypothesis?" Greene asked.

Brenda hesitated. She had a feeling how this was going

to go from here. "There was an encounter with a Hunter," she said.

The silence was even longer this time. "A Hunter."

"Yes," Brenda said. She tried to infuse the word with every ounce of certitude she could muster. "I saw them myself. They attacked Maira and the cell I brought with me."

"Perhaps you have similar explanations for other recent events. Network failures might be attributed to gremlins, missing supplies could be laid at the feet of sasquatch."

"I'm telling you, Greene, I saw them myself. This wasn't a scary story around the fire, this was a dangerous assailant with high-tech equipment," Brenda insisted.

"Do you have evidence to support this remarkable claim?" Greene asked.

"Of c–"

Brenda cut herself off. Did she have evidence? Normally, yes. ISAC would have kept a record of everything they experienced and easily been able to reconstruct that data into an ECHO to show other agents. She had not checked. What if she pinned her hopes on that, and there was nothing but blank tape, so to speak? That would only seem to damn Maira further.

"I'll take that as a no," Greene said flatly.

"You can take it however you like," Brenda snapped. "No matter how much you wish for it, I don't answer to you, Greene. I have the same unlimited operational authority that you do."

"True, of course," he said, calm. "But if there is one thing this world has taught me, Agent Wells, it's that even the unlimited finds its borders eventually. As far as most people know, we've been shut down. All we really have any more is each other. Think hard before you turn your back on the Division for the sake of one rogue agent. You may find the world a cold place once all those old bridges are burned."

"I don't take kindly to threats," Brenda said through gritted teeth.

"Not threats," Greene said coldly. "Concerns. I only want what's best for you and your cell, Agent Wells. This path you're choosing won't just cost you, after all. It will cost them, too."

"Maira has made mistakes, and she is more dedicated to seeing them corrected than anyone. In time, her status will be a subject for review. As it is, it is not my top priority, and when she does answer for her decisions, it will not be to a kangaroo court controlled by you."

"So be it," Greene replied. "You already must live with one terrible mistake which only compounds and worsens with the passage of time. We must hope your judgment has improved."

The connection broke to static.

"Transmission ended," ISAC said.

"Damn," Brenda said. She pounded her knuckles into the table in front of her, fury fading to weariness.

"Could have gone better," Leo observed.

"No kidding," Brenda said tiredly. "Greene wants someone to pin the Texas attack and the murder of those agents on, and he thinks he has the perfect candidate in Maira."

"I wondered at first," Leo admitted. "But he's wrong."

"Yeah, I don't think it was her anymore either. But how do we prove that?"

"One thing at a time," Leo said. "We have enough problems on our plate. Besides, if we all die out here, it won't matter anyway."

"I need to find someone else to talk to," muttered Brenda. "Your relentless optimism and upbeat nature are wearing me down."

Leo snorted. "Seriously, should we tell her?"

"No," Brenda said with a firm head shake. "Like you said, one thing at a time. Maira has enough on her mind. I'll talk to her once we've handled this program she created."

Maira crouched against the lip of the building's roof. She and Yeong-Ja had spent an arduous hour climbing up here. A task that would have once been simple thanks to elevators had been rendered exhausting by entropy. It wasn't just a matter of having to take the stairs; by this point ceilings were collapsing and footing could be treacherous. And this was in the dry climes of the American Southwest. It was significantly worse in the more humid climates, where many buildings were in the process of rotting themselves into collapse.

It was worth it, though. From here they could see the city laid out beneath them. The tower that Black Tusk had claimed as their headquarters lay off to the west, the tallest building in the city. Yeong-Ja kneeled next to her, her dark eyes focused on the distant streets and avenues like a hawk. She had a new rifle slung on her back. She had retrieved the TAC-50 on her way out of the shopping center where they'd clashed with their mystery assailant, but the ax blow had compromised the barrel. The weapon could no longer be safely fired.

Luckily, Maira had collected a small arsenal while she had the chance, before the nearby supply storehouse got destroyed. Not only had she obtained a CQB variant M1A for her own use, she had a Mk20 SSR. She had intended it as a backup weapon, or perhaps something she could break out for precision work. It worked even better in Yeong-Ja's practiced hands, though.

The sniper lifted said rifle around to her shoulder and peered through the scope. If the shoulder that had gotten battered out of its socket was still bothering her, she gave no sign of it. Instead, she swept the scope back and forth, obviously collecting as much information as she could. In all honesty, Maira trusted Yeong-Ja's eyes better than she trusted her own. She waited patiently.

At last, the sniper lowered her rifle and sighed. That didn't forecast good results.

Even so, Maira couldn't keep herself from asking, "Any changes?"

"Nothing good," Yeong-Ja said. "I think it's actually gotten worse. They must be bringing in reinforcements from other locations."

Maira's shoulders slumped. "I guess that explains the helos we've seen coming in."

"It does." Yeong-Ja shook her head. "I haven't seen a force concentration like this since the Green Poison, Maira. This is insanity. I know Brenda and Leo say that there were numbers like this gathered by some of the factions in the big cities out east, but they're not pulling from local populace here. We're talking about a group with force projection in regimental strength."

Maira winced. "Got a rough idea on that in numbers?"

Yeong-Ja sat down heavily and got out her canteen to swig from it. "It would not surprise me to learn they have more than two thousand soldiers on site."

"I didn't see anything like that while I was there," Maira said wearily.

"I'm not making…"

Maira waved a hand. "I know. I trust you. I'm just reeling. If I had known…"

"Partly a build-up after the failed attack and your escape. Partly, I imagine, they just kept you isolated from the main body of the soldiery. Tucked you away near the labs with the other pencil necks."

"The 'other' pencil necks?" Maira snorted. "Now you're out to hurt my feelings."

Yeong-Ja gave her a wry smile. "Perhaps to try to get you to laugh once, at least."

Maira patted her knee. "Thanks. I promise I'll be in more of a laughing mood once I'm not responsible for the imminent destruction of the Strategic Homeland Division anymore."

She had meant to say it lightly, but nearly choked on the last few words instead. Her eyes burned. Frustrated, she pounded her fist into the meat of her thigh. There had to be something she could do.

"You can't think of it that way," Yeong-Ja protested. "Maira, you were literally a drugged captive. And you still figured it out in the end and got away."

Maira looked off into the distance toward the Black Tusk base again. "Not fast enough."

"You need therapy, girlfriend," Yeong-Ja said firmly.

Maira cracked a grin at that. "Honestly? No argument from me. You find me a shrink once we're done here, and I'll lie down on the couch."

"I think they only do that on TV," the sniper said.

"I'm glad you're here to tell me these things," Maira said.

"All right," Yeong-Ja said. She rose to her feet and dusted her legs and hands off. "Shall we head back to camp? Maybe the others had better luck spotting a weakness than we did."

Maira nodded acquiescence and pushed herself to her feet as well. They set off back down through the abandoned skyscraper. Maira supposed it had been an office building once, at least in the main section. That was what it looked like when she stole an occasional glance through the doors leading off the stairwell. Just endless offices with nothing to indicate what kind of work had been done here.

It was all moldering now. Paper yellowed and ink faded. How many babies had been born since the Poison ravaged the world? Maira wondered. She knew there had at least been a few. For some people, of course, the idea was unthinkable. Who wanted to bring a child into a world that was this riven with conflict and fear?

But in a sense, the world always had been. Some people got lucky and lived lives of relative peace and comfort, but it had never been the majority. There were always warzones, always disasters, always refugees and the desperate. The crazy part was that no matter what, humanity adapted. They carried on. No matter what happened, eventually it was the new normal. Everyone just carried on.

And so it was nowadays. People survived. Where people survived, they had babies. These children, Maira guessed, would grow up in a world that bore no resemblance to the one she remembered. Would they even be able to understand when we describe it to them? What would the concept of an office building sound like? Jam as many people that might remain in a whole city these days into a single structure, and make them move bits of paper around. Just a different kind of insanity.

"You're making that face," Yeong-Ja commented.

"What face?" asked Maira with as little wheezing as she could manage.

Somehow the tiny sniper didn't even sound out of breath, despite all the stairs they had clambered down. Maira couldn't help but resent her for that a little bit. Yeong-Ja hadn't had to survive a trek across the desert alone, with only the supplies she could scrounge, she told herself. Not that she couldn't. But maybe if she'd had to, she wouldn't have the same energy reserves in her body either.

"The philosopher face," Yeong-Ja said. "Like you're trying to figure the whole world out. Solve all the big problems. Answer all the big questions."

Maira stuck her tongue out at the sniper. "Oh, so now I'm not even allowed to think in peace?"

Yeong-Ja grinned. "Nah. It's just that it's funny how you can be so different from Brenda, and then in other ways be just like her."

Maira raised an eyebrow at that and waited until they'd done another two loops of the staircase.

"OK, name a similarity."

"Well, there's the face I just mentioned. You're both Big Thinkers." The way she said it, Maira could hear the capital letters.

"Is that a bad thing?" asked Maira.

"Not at all. We gotta have the thinkers, because they're the ones who figure out what needs doing and why. Leave someone like me on my own, we'll just go sit in the sun. Maybe have a drink."

Maira laughed. "I see, so you're dividing us into thinkers and doers?"

"Not at all," the sniper said amiably. "All of us are doers. The Division doesn't recruit people who won't get their hands dirty."

"So what's the divide?" asked Maira.

"Worriers and relaxers," said Yeong-Ja.

Maira stewed on that for a couple of minutes. They had to leave the stairwell here; it had fallen through and jumping across risked even more of a collapse. Instead, they cut down a hallway and climbed down through a collapsed point in a nearby office, then returned to the staircase.

"You know, that just kind of makes me sad when you put it that way."

Yeong-Ja paused and clapped her on the shoulder. "Because you worry too much! Exactly my point."

"And thus you are proven beyond a shadow of a doubt to be the greater scholar of the two of us," Maira said with a chuckle.

They emerged onto the street level of Albuquerque. It was still early enough in the morning that the temperature had not gotten unpleasant yet. The sun was still climbing into the sky. Maira knew it wouldn't be long before it was hot enough to cook an egg on the asphalt. She sighed and reseated her rifle onto her other shoulder. They headed away from the city center.

"So you're saying you don't worry at all about why we do what we're doing, about where it all leads?" she asked.

Yeong-Ja shrugged. "What good would worrying about it do me?"

"I thought you just said we needed thinkers?"

Yeong-Ja grinned. "We do. I didn't say it does no good at all. I asked what good it would do me, personally. And the answer is nothing. In fact, it'd probably give me an ulcer."

"That's fair. The less I think about what's going on in my guts, the better. Probably looks like Swiss cheese in there at this point," Maira said.

Yeong-Ja made a face. "Could do without that visual, thanks."

"My tiny vengeance for your many misdeeds," Maira said smugly.

"Damn," Yeong-Ja said. "I hate having to deal with the consequences of my own actions."

Maira sighed. "I feel that in my bones."

"Ugh, and there she goes again! I was not referencing you! I already told you I think you're being too hard on yourself," Yeong-Ja insisted.

"Bang, bang, and you were both too busy talking to watch out, so now you're both dead," Colin called from above.

They had arrived at the place they had set up camp and had slept the night before. Maira thought it had been a cafe before the Green Poison, but it was getting harder and harder to tell as time passed. It had definitely been some kind of eatery or drink shop. That much was clear from the counter, the chairs, and the tables.

Colin sat in the broken window of the eatery's second floor. It made for a good vantage spot to see if anything was headed toward their camp. Maira wasn't sure what they would do if the enemy did detect them and set out to destroy them. There were so damn many of them. They could have rolled over this place with no problem. Hell, they had the firepower to literally bring the building down on them if that's what they wanted to do.

The threat of the Hunter remained in the back of everyone's minds.

Even so. Maira tilted her head back to look at him. "They don't even do patrols this far out from the center, Colin. That's why we set up camp here."

"Not yet," he said reprovingly. "They could start at any moment."

"And that's why I hacked their comms when we got here," Maira concluded and tapped her earpiece. "I get where you're coming from, but I refuse to walk around making hand signals for a week."

"As much fun as it is watching you two play mom and rebellious teenage daughter," Yeong-Ja said, "are Leo and Brenda back yet?"

Colin nodded. "They got back about fifteen minutes ago." He paused. "And I am not your mom!"

"You're right," Yeong-Ja said. "My mom never worried this much about me."

"Come on inside, Colin," Maira said. "Let's hash out any new information as a group."

Colin nodded. "All right. I'll meet you two there."

They continued into the building. The early morning sun slanted through onto the floor, the rays scattered by shards of broken windows. The refraction on the glass drizzled tiny rainbows all over the place. The air was clear and quiet. She saw Leo and Brenda sitting at one of the little green tables. Brenda even had a steaming cup of something sitting in front of her.

If it weren't for the circumstances, this wouldn't be so bad, Maira thought. Relative safety, relative comfort, and people she loved. Granted, the surroundings would have horrified her two years ago, but at this point she had lived in a lot worse situations. Too bad it was an illusion that could break at any moment.

Maira dropped into a seat opposite the two waiting agents. Yeong-Ja hopped up to sit cross-legged on the next table over. Boots on the stairs announced Colin's arrival from the floor above. He walked over and dropped into a seat at the table Yeong-Ja had claimed, stepping over a chair to sit backward in it. Yeong-Ja promptly leaned against his back.

"So what's the situation?" Brenda asked.

"No good news," Maira said reluctantly, and motioned to Yeong-Ja.

"I believe they're pulling in reinforcements from elsewhere. Standing strength north of two thousand by my guess," the sniper said.

Colin gave a low whistle.

"What about you two?" asked Maira.

Brenda sighed and shook her head. "The sewers aren't realistically human passable. To try to use them, we'd have to effectively low crawl for miles. And that would still assume they didn't consider the possibility and guard against it."

"Can't say I wanted to go mucking through sewers, but I think that was our last idea," Yeong-Ja said regretfully.

That unpleasant truth hung in the air. Maira ran her hands through her short hair frustratedly. It wasn't that she was a fool. She knew fairness didn't enter into it. But they'd come up against hard odds before, and yet never had they felt so stacked against them.

"They have the numbers, they have the firepower, they have the prepared positions," Leo said darkly. "Be a hard nut to crack with a thousand agents, and we have five."

"Four and a half," Maira said and waved her red watch. A laugh bubbled up in her. It felt dangerously close to hysterics, so she choked it down.

"Maira could crash their defense systems…" started Colin.

"...and in doing so lose all ability to access their databases as well once inside, negating the point of the effort. Not to mention, even without tech, they have the numbers to stone us to death." Brenda said it all without rancor.

They had been over this ground repeatedly now. It was like gum chewed to flavorlessness. The enemy wasn't perfect, but they were strong enough that exploiting every conceivable weakness still wouldn't level the playing field. There was a point at which no amount of clever ideas made up the difference. This Black Tusk base seemed to have such an overwhelming advantage.

Everyone sat in silence. Leo kept flipping some coin he'd found and catching it. Maira took the chance to consider each of them. Colin had a burned arm. Leo had a gunshot wound. Brenda had a bum foot. Yeong-Ja was the best off, and Maira had seen the bruises when they went to bathe. Her torso was a mass of slowly fading purple. None of them were letting it stop them, for her sake. It didn't change the fact that they had already suffered on this journey.

"All of you should go," Maira said.

"We've been over that, too," Brenda said. "We're not abandoning you."

Maira rubbed at her eyes. "I love all of you, and I mean that. I will not have you kill yourselves trying to salvage my mess. If I go in alone, then maybe they'll accept me back. And then I have a chance, maybe of... of..."

"She'll shoot you in the head," Leo said matter-of-factly.

"He's not wrong, Maira," Colin said softly. "You told us about this Natalya woman. The best-case scenario if you fall back into her hands? She tortures you to break you. She knows the game's up, and she's not gonna put you on a long leash ever again."

"Listen to me," Maira said desperately. "We are running out of time. ISAC, show them."

They all would see the same thing. The graphic representation of the firewall she had put up in between her creation and the Black Tusk. The organization had set to cracking it during her trek across the country, unsuccessfully so far, but it would only take time.

"Maybe none of them are a match for me one on one," Maira said. "But that's not how they're handling it. Same as everything else, they're bringing unmatchable resources to bear, and now they're close to succeeding."

This wasn't new information exactly, but she hadn't actually made them look at it before. Each of them sat contemplating the middle distance, the graphics only visible on their augmented reality view.

"How long?" asked Leo.

"Four days," Maira said. "I mean, I can't be sure, but that's my best bet. Besides, that's not the only problem."

"The Hunter," Brenda said softly. A name to put on the unknown, and in so doing rob it of some fear, at least.

Maira nodded. "The longer we sit here, trying to figure this out, the greater the chances it strikes again. Last time all five of us tried, and I had a bag full of tricks. Now those are all but gone, and I don't know if we can pull it off."

"I still maintain they're probably dead," Yeong-Ja said. "You burned the damn building down."

Maira shook her head slowly. "No. It was after me for weeks. Inexorable. I'm not lucky enough for it to have ended right there."

Brenda hesitated. "I have to say, I think she's right."

"What?" Yeong-Ja asked with surprise. "We can't leave–"

"Right that the Hunter is closing in," Brenda hastily clarified. "Leo and I were talking about it, and that's where I got the name from. This isn't the first time we've heard of someone like this."

Leo nodded. "Ghost stories."

"But apparently it's true," Brenda said. "Agents in DC have reported a lot of strange encounters. Figures in masks, people ISAC doesn't pick up on. Blue smoke and surprise attacks. Worse, I know we've had agents go missing. A lot of them. Too many. I mean, the world is dangerous enough, but..." She frowned.

"But something weird was going on, and now you have an answer," Maira said.

Brenda nodded. "The Hunters, people call them. I don't know who they are, mind. Foreign agents? Some kind of serial killer cult? Could be anything, honestly. But those watches on the harness... those were trophies. Killing people like us? That's what they do. That's what the stories agree on. And they're very good at what they do."

Colin cleared his throat. "I never really put two and two together, but yeah. I heard stories like that back in New York, too, as early as that first winter. Unstoppable agent-killers. I mean, it's the kind of thing people make up under stress, right? But... having seen one..." He shrugged uneasily.

"Whatever they are, that thing had equipment that makes SHD tech look like yesterday's news," Yeong-Ja said. "The armor alone took anti-material rounds to get through it."

"Something next generation," agreed Leo. "TSAM or carbon nanotubes, maybe."

"We'd need a sample to even try to start to figure the details out," Maira said, with a shrug. "And they didn't seem the kind to hand over a swatch in the spirit of fair play."

"No," Brenda noted wryly. "That does seem unlikely. My guess is beneath the armor they're also being treated to a steady flow of something similar to our own combat cocktail. That would explain the extreme endurance and complete disregard for pain."

"Wouldn't that also mess up your body something fierce?" asked Yeong-Ja.

"The version we have? Sure," Colin said grimly. "But carefully modulated and designed around an individual's metabolism? Maybe not. The difference between boilerplate and bespoke."

"In the end, this is all speculation. We are here," Maira said. "Caught between a Hunter and a Black Tusk base. But you don't have to be. None of you did what I did. You can walk away, and I wish you would."

"Stow that," Brenda said flatly. "We're not leaving you here to get yourself killed."

"There is one option we haven't considered," Colin said thoughtfully.

"I'm excited to hear this," Yeong-Ja said and turned around to face the medic with her eyebrow raised.

He gave the sniper a dry look. "Your faith in me is overwhelming. I'm not saying this is anything but a long shot. But we could try radioing for help."

Everyone stared at him. Maira wasn't certain what to think. It was true nobody had mentioned the possibility yet. Mostly because there were huge issues with it that were immediately obvious to any consideration.

"Like I said," he appended weakly. "It's a long shot."

"Count on mom to come up with that one," noted Yeong-Ja.

"We don't have the infrastructure to get any reach," noted Brenda.

"Yeah, I know," Colin said. "That's why we'd have to take some."

"Take some how?" asked Maira.

"Either find something salvageable in the city, or take what we need from Black Tusk," Colin said. "We don't have to hold it, we just need it long enough to send the signal."

"The moment we do that, they know we're here," Leo said.

"If Yeong-Ja is right, they're already bracing for a counterattack of some kind. And as we've already admitted, we don't have another way. Infiltrating the tower is already out of our reach, so we can't spoil our chances." Colin shrugged.

Maira found herself nodding. "OK. Who would even answer?"

Colin winced. "As far as that goes, I don't know. There might be some local agents who would hear the call – there have to be some of us all over the place, right? And if there's any JTF in the area, they might respond, too. The truth is we just don't know enough about this region."

"So we do this, and in the end we have a big question mark on what good it does?" asked Yeong-Ja.

"It's something we can actually do, though. That's the point. We can take action on it," Colin said. "It's better than sitting here being miserable and waiting for the Hunter to murder us."

Maira looked to Brenda. The senior agent shrugged.

"The man had a point when he said we can't make the situation any worse. In a weird sense, even if it amounts to nothing, if it kicks them in the ass that could be a good thing unto itself. Even if all we manage to do is make Black Tusk sit on their heels and pull troops from everywhere they can, that's time they don't spend ruining someone else's day."

"All right," Maira said. "ISAC, show me strong radio signals in our vicinity."

The whole group settled in to peruse the data. Maira couldn't deny that Colin had already been extremely correct about one thing: it felt good to have something they could actually do.

CHAPTER 14

August 26

"Eyes on target," Brenda murmured on the comms.

She stood at the end of an alleyway. There were scraps of paper and plastic underfoot. trash that must have accumulated here before society went the way of the dodo. Of course, the end of the greater part of the human species had kept the problem from worsening. No one was coming along to do any cleanup, but nobody was adding more litter either, especially in Albuquerque where the community had been eradicated.

Around the corner from her was the target. Leo had called it a "heavy duty tactical communications trailer." To Brenda's eyes, it looked like a big truck with a trailer that had a satellite dish on top. The whole thing was impressive to look at, of course. It was shiny black and embossed with the blue diamond logo of the Black Tusk. Even so, it wasn't as big as she'd been expecting.

"The trick isn't to find the world's biggest radio transmitter," Maira had explained. "We played that game at the Gulf Coast, but options there were a lot more limited. Here, we have an enemy with an extant nationwide comms network. We don't need to build our own. We need to steal theirs for just long enough to get the word out."

Thus, this support vehicle. If the cell could get hold of it, they could piggyback their way onto the Black Tusk comms. In theory that would let them reach almost anywhere in the country. Black Tusk was one of the few groups who still seemed to be able to communicate across such distances with ease. They had to, to be able to coordinate operations of the scale they regularly enacted.

There was a certain ballsiness to the idea that appealed to Brenda. Sure, the enemy would realize pretty quickly what they were up to. But that was the problem with radio; they were never going to have been able to make contact unobtrusively. A big enough comms burst was going to draw attention no matter how they did it. Turning the enemy's own comms against them had the side benefit of being satisfying to her, as if they were the creators of their own demise.

"The first trick will be keeping them from alerting anyone to the fact that they're under attack," Maira had said.

Six Black Tusk soldiers guarded the trailer. Brenda would not have described them as on high alert. Mostly they were shooting the breeze with each other and complaining about how hot the day was going to be. Still, they had their angles covered. These weren't propped up conscripts, they were bored professionals. She eyed the one closest to her. It was a woman in full black combat gear, carrying an ACR in a casual slope across her arms.

"That one," Brenda mouthed.

ISAC tagged the trooper, highlighting her in orange for Brenda. That information would be shared with the rest of the cell, letting them know which target Brenda had picked. Within seconds information was flowing back toward her from the others. One each, except for Yeong-Ja claiming two. Nobody was likely to contest that. She was easily the best shot in the group.

A five-count pinged on Brenda's vision. It counted backward smoothly. Brenda raised the Honey Badger to her shoulder and leaned out around the wall just enough to line up the shot. Three... two... one. She squeezed the trigger. Every Division agent fired in unison. A burst of fire scythed across center mass on Brenda's target.

Then, Brenda was off and running. She sprinted across the distance toward the trailer, the alternation of her boot and racing blade clattering against the ground as she went. Thud, clang, thud, clang, in perfect rhythm. The woman she'd shot had fallen, but she was getting back up. Armored or tough. The Black Tusk soldier yanked off her balaclava and coughed up blood.

She looked up just in time to see Brenda closing. Her eyes went wide. Brenda threw her whole weight behind a kick. Her boot smashed into the woman's temple with a resounding crunch. The soldier went down like a sack of potatoes. Brenda scarcely glanced at her, moving on toward the back of the trailer. There were no cameras, so anyone inside would only have heard the gunshots.

She got there just as the doors swung open to reveal a surprised technician.

"What's going on out – oh my god!"

Behind the technician, Brenda could see that this person was one of two in the vehicle. They were surrounded by consoles, presumably the controls for their little corner of the Black Tusk comms network. The other one looked up at the exclamation and lunged toward a nearby headset. Not a bad reflex, but too slow.

The first technician's leg was in the way. Brenda shot the second through him, bullets punching through his knee and thigh. The first guy screamed and collapsed, clutching at his wounded appendage. The quick thinker lunging for the headset slumped against the console and then slid to the ground, motionless, the headset dangling uselessly.

"Trailer secured," Brenda said. "No alarm."

She grabbed the first guy by the collar and yanked him out of the vehicle. Blood pulsed straight between his fingers. Brenda diagnosed it in an instant as she laid him on the ground. She'd blown out his femoral artery. He wasn't long for this world. She put him and his suffering out of her mind and stepped up into the trailer. She had a mission to accomplish.

The rest of her cell arrived. Brenda gave Maira a hand up into the trailer.

"Time to do your thing."

"I'm on it," Maira said. She sat down at one of the consoles and pulled her necklace off.

Good luck charm, maybe? Brenda put that out of her mind, too, and turned to the others. "Set up a perimeter. Sometimes people going quiet is enough to arouse suspicion. We don't know what Black Tusk's protocols are. I don't want to be surprised by a rescue party or some do-gooder checking things out."

Leo and Yeong-Ja nodded and turned to set out. Colin dropped to one knee next to the wounded man. Brenda hopped down and touched him on the shoulder.

"Come on. You can't help him."

The mortally wounded technician was already sobbing, but it redoubled at the sound of her words. He was trying to say something, but it was hard to make out. Colin shook his head and got something out of his kit.

"Easy does it, pal. Here, this will take the edge off, OK? Nothing like a little Circle K to smooth things over."

Colin inserted the nasal spray into the man's nose and gave two quick squeezes. The man coughed and tried to grab at Colin's wrist, but his strength was already draining out of him. All he managed to do was smear blood up and down Colin's forearm. The medic scarcely seemed to notice. He paused and squeezed the man's hand between both of his own, gentle as a lamb, before getting to his feet.

"Does it help you?" Brenda asked him softly.

"Help me what?" the medic asked.

"Sleep at night. After doing all the things we have to do,

to try so hard to hang on to your humanity, and help people like him. Does it help you?"

She sincerely wanted to know. She had enough terrible memories and bad acts on her conscience. For Brenda, it was easier to push it to the side as quickly as possible. Add it to the pile, worry about it later.

Colin looked down at the man. He was fading fast now, his eyes rolling back into his head. The analgesic did seem to have calmed him, though. Taken some of the pain and the fear away. The medic sighed and shook his head.

"No, it doesn't help me. I still see the faces every night when I try to sleep. But I have to hope it helps them some. I guess I just figure if it was me on the ground, counting out my last seconds, I'd hope the last person I saw would spare five seconds and a painkiller." Colin looked at Brenda and gave a sad smile. "Or maybe it's just a waste, and I'll wish I'd held on to it before this mission is over."

Brenda clapped him on the shoulder. "Don't change, Colin. Whatever you do, stay who you are. The world needs more people like you."

"We have a problem," Leo said over the comms.

All the other concerns fell away from Brenda and Colin alike. She could see in the medic's face, too, the snap back to ready and alert. Prepared for the shit to hit the fan.

"What's up?" Brenda asked.

"Transport bird just took off at the Black Tusk base and is headed this way. ETA three minutes."

Brenda cursed and leaned back into the trailer. "Maira, we've got company inbound. What's the situation?"

Maira held up a hand without even looking at her. "I heard. Be quiet. I'm working."

"Right," Brenda said and dropped back out onto the asphalt. "Best case scenario is we're cutting it close, people. Get ready to engage hostiles. Remember that there's no bonus points for kill count. If we do end up in a firefight, our only objective is to hold until the message is sent then effect a withdrawal."

"Got it," Yeong-Ja said.

"Copy," said Leo.

Colin gave her a quick nod as he swapped out for a fresh mag on his rifle.

"ISAC, can you show me the transport's approach?" Brenda asked.

A map of the city expanded into her augmented reality. A blinking dot showed the bird's location. It was already more than a third of the way to them. Brenda sighed quietly. It would have been nice to have their own air support to swoop in and save the day. As long as she was wishing, though, she might as well just ask for a miracle win on the whole ordeal.

"If wishes were fishes..." Brenda muttered.

"All right, I'm in!" Maira called. "Setting up the broadcast to send now."

"Got it. Faster is better, for the record," Brenda replied.

Brenda could hear the rotors of the approaching heli now.

"Find cover," she told Colin.

"What about you?" he asked.

"I'm staying here to guard Maira until she's done. Don't worry, we'll get out."

Colin nodded and sprinted off into one of the nearby alleyways to avoid being too much of a target. Brenda crouched in the doorway to the trailer, her weapon pressed into her shoulder and ready to raise in an instant. Her breathing seemed too loud in her own ears, one of those curious bits of hypersensitivity that came before a fight. She focused on making it even and steady.

The helicopter swept into view. It was a black swath against the brilliant sky, its primary rotor a thrumming blur above it. Brenda squinted to see it clearly. It hovered over the little intersection where the Division agents were conducting their heist like an avenging angel. The roar of a heavy gun opening up dashed any remnants of hope Brenda harbored that the helicopter was after some other threat.

She clocked the assault coming from the side gun, sweeping back and forth. Bullets pounded the area like a summer rain turned lethal. Whatever had set this bird into motion, their assumption was their people were already dead. Brenda could see stray rounds impact the Black Tusk corpses where they lay exposed. Nothing came close to the trailer itself, though – forget the meat, save the metal was apparently the policy of the day.

A rope spilled out of each side. Within seconds black-garbed troopers were hurtling along them toward the ground below. They came on fast, separated by only a couple of feet between each descending soldier.

"That side gun has me pinned, I can't get a good shot!" called Leo.

A thundercrack rang out in time with his last words. The side gun went silent, and a flailing figure tumbled out of the helicopter. They hit the ground with a resounding crunch audible even over where Brenda sheltered in the trailer. She hazarded a glance. They weren't moving anymore.

"Three," Yeong-Ja said calmly.

The gun had served its purpose, though, and the cargo of soldiers had deployed unchallenged. There were eleven of them total, and the troopers spread out from the helicopter in all directions. Brenda leaned out and was the first to set off a warning burst, her lips curling into a fierce grin. No joy; her shots must have gone wild. It did make them scuttle faster seeking cover, though.

Unfortunately, it also drew a hail of return fire in her direction. Whatever injunction had kept the helicopter gun from risking damage to the trailer either didn't apply now or was being ignored. Brenda ducked back with a curse as bullets spanged off the metal all around her. She scrambled further back into the trailer and covered the door. Behind her, Maira hadn't budged from her post.

"Guys, keep them off us!" she cried.

The comforting chatter of friendly weapons confirmed their efforts to do just that. Another shot rang out. Brenda wasn't able to get a clear view of what was happening beyond the doors of the trailer, but Yeong-Ja's lethality was not up for question. Brenda had no reason to doubt it when the inevitable...

"Four."

…came around.

"Maira!" barked Brenda.

"Close! Close… OK, I've got it! Transmission is going out!"

Finally. "All right, let's move! Everyone, head for the fallback position!" called Brenda.

It was time to get her and Maira out of here, too. She stepped toward the door only for a black-garbed soldier to throw the doors wide. Behind his mask there was no doubt his eyes went wide, too, right before Brenda walked a line of shots down from his face along his sternum. He fell back to the asphalt, his mouth reduced to ruin by a pair of .300 BLK rounds.

Brenda knew it was grim, but she had to protect Maira and her cell.

Brenda jumped out of the trailer and almost crashed into another of the Black Tusk soldiers moving to support their fallen comrade. They lunged into her with no hesitation, and Brenda was driven back into the door of the trailer with a metallic impact that set dazzling sparks alight in her eyes. She retaliated with a boot to the knee; it hit perfectly and the joint reversed with a sickening snap. The soldier started to scream, muffled by their mask, and Brenda smashed them with the stock of her gun, sending them spinning to lie amongst the other fallen enforcers.

She looked up in time to see another one bringing their assault rifle to bear. Brenda ducked and spun to the side just in time, bullets peppering the place she'd been standing a half second before. Before the hostile could correct their aim, a trio of shots blew through their chest and stomach. Maira emerged with her own rifle held ready, smoke trailing from the barrel.

"What would you do without me?" she commented lightly.

"I was very sad!" Brenda replied as Maira came to stand beside her. "Run now, snark later!" She gave Maira a shove toward their escape alley.

They set off at a pelt for the side street. One of the remaining hostiles must have spotted them once they were close. A spray of fire shattered brick and splintered wood all around the turn. Brenda ducked and picked up her pace. Fragments of paper and plastic scattered as the pair sprinted down the alley. They turned, sprinted to another side street, and ran farther. What pursuit was after them quickly fell away; the enemy must have been more interested in reclaiming the trailer than in trying to hunt them down.

They skidded to a halt in the lee of one building. Brenda paused at the edge and looked back to make sure there was indeed no one chasing in their wake.

"Looks to be all clear," she said with relief.

"Everyone all right?" Maira asked on the radio.

"I don't think anyone got shot for once," Colin replied wryly, though he sounded out of breath. "Not even Leo."

"Where's the fun in that?" Yeong-Ja asked.

"More than enough blood and mayhem for one day, thank you very much," was all he said in response.

"I think he's getting tired of patching us up," Maira commented.

"Tired of being patched," groused Leo.

"Maybe I'll be more careful for a few days then," Yeong-Ja said. "You know, as an early Christmas present or something."

"All right, you creatures of chaos," Brenda said. "Head for the fallback position. I'll see you there."

They gathered anew in the shop-turned-camp that served as their home base in the city. Maira sat in one of the faded green chairs and sipped a bad rendition of green tea. She couldn't even remember where she'd picked up the drink packets at this point. Eventually you got tired of the rubber-and-metal taste of canteen water and became willing to try almost anything, though. Even instant tea.

She was exhausted. Maybe that made a certain amount of sense; certainly, if she told someone she'd been through a life or death gun battle, a little weariness afterward would seem only reasonable. Regardless, it felt weird considering the whole thing couldn't have taken more than a matter of minutes. They had set out to seize the trailer in the early morning, and by the time they'd regathered here it still wasn't even noon yet.

"So the signal went out?" asked Yeong-Ja.

"For the umpteenth time," Maira said with a yawn. "It went out. I promise you it went out. I watched it upload, I watched it send. The only question now is if anyone was actually listening."

"Well, there's one more question," Brenda said dryly. "And that's even if someone did hear, are they going to do something about it?"

"Cynical but fair enough," Maira said with a wince. "I made the message as compelling as I could without giving away the farm."

"What did you tell them?" Colin asked curiously. "I guess that whole side of things didn't even occur to me."

"I identified myself as an escaped Black Tusk captive, and said they were nearing a technological breakthrough that was going to tip the balance of power permanently in their favor. I said we had only a couple of days, and if we didn't band together to stop them by then, further resistance might become hopeless."

"Hell, the way you described her, Natalya probably loved that once she got a chance to listen. Breakthroughs, permanent power, and hopeless resistance. Everything she wants for her twisted organization," Brenda said.

Maira looked down. She hadn't exactly told them everything. Almost, of course, everything that mattered. But she hadn't told them about the feelings she'd developed for Natalya Sokolova, much less the fact that she still wasn't sure if those feelings had ever been returned. Of course, mutual or not, Natalya had tried to kill her. That was definitely closure of a sort. Maira wasn't in the habit of going back to exes who had tried to murder her.

Brenda looked awkward. "I'm sorry, Maira, I didn't mean… look, none of us actually consider this all your fault the way you do. I'm not saying you gave her the keys to the castle, I'm just pointing out she's the kind of psycho to celebrate our desperation."

Maira managed a smile for the elder agent. "You don't have to say those things, because I will. Sokolova… Nat… she was dangerous enough before I came along to give her a helping hand. I've seen the best and the worst of that woman, and trust me when I say she does not need to obtain unchallenged primacy. That would be bad for everyone."

"Then it's a good thing we got that message out," Yeong-Ja said. "I know I started off the most skeptical of this whole idea, not least because it was Colin's idea…"

Colin rolled his eyes expressively. "You know it makes it really obvious that you're baiting me when you pause for a response after you say something like that."

Yeong-Ja smiled beatifically. "Of course. What would be the fun in being sneaky about it? Regardless, I do mean it. I feel good about this. Allies will show up before you know it, and we'll bring this whole thing crashing down."

"It doesn't even have to be that grand," noted Brenda. "All we need is enough of a force to draw Black Tusk's attention. If we can get Maira inside, she can destroy the code and we'll be ready to ride off into the sunset once again." She looked at Maira. "Right?"

"Something like that," Maira replied dryly. "I mean, I'm not a miracle worker. But yeah, if you can get me direct access with their on-site servers before my firewall comes down, I should be able to wipe it."

"Is that the smartest thing to do?" Leo asked.

Maira raised an eyebrow at him. "What do you mean?"

The taciturn agent frowned. "Well, by your own description, this program you've created isn't picky about who it targets."

"That's not exactly…" Maira sighed and shook her head. "I just mean, it's not that it isn't picky. It's that us and them? Our network backbones? We're fundamentally the same, so we're both vulnerable to it. It's like having a genetic tendency toward a certain illness."

"What about ANNA?" Leo asked.

Maira tilted her head and shrugged. "I've thought about that a little. As far as I know, it's pretty much the same substrate as well. Something that works on one of them should work on any of them."

Leo nodded. "So what you've created could also give the Division the advantage against Black Tusk and Keener's rogues both?"

Maira blinked. "You're saying that what you want is for us to take the program and, instead of deleting it, use it ourselves?"

Leo nodded. "Why not?"

Maira pulled her legs up and wrapped her arms around her knees. "I have to admit, now that I'm thinking clearly and not a drugged-up mess anymore, part of me is worried about unintended consequences."

"Like what?" Colin asked. "Wouldn't it be worth it to have the advantage?"

"We still don't know a lot about how all these things interconnect, and we don't know all the ways that Black Tusk use their system. What if they have people on life support, and the ventilators are run by Diamond? You bring that down, and suddenly a bunch of civilians are choking out their last minutes."

Leo winced. "Grim."

"But possible," Maira emphasized. "And it worries me even more with our own network. ISAC was a government operation. There's no telling what odd interlinks and dependencies might exist. Nuclear launches? Failures of biological containment at the CDC? You kick away one piece, and sometimes the tower stays standing. But sometimes you yank something innocuous and the whole thing comes crashing down."

Silence hung over the group. Every face at the table was long now, contemplating such awful outcomes from the program being used. Maira felt a bit uncomfortable and looked down at her tea, taking a sip.

"Have I mentioned that she's a remarkable worrier?" Yeong-Ja asked, sounding bright.

Maira snorted and threw a drink packet at her, which the sniper nimbly ducked.

"These are valid concerns," Leo finally allowed. "Serious ones. Even so, once it is deleted, we have given up any choice. There could be a dark day in the near future when we would need to take risks like these. I merely ask that you consider your options thoroughly."

Maira blinked. "That was quite a speech coming from you."

"Yeong-Ja, if you would," Leo said with a serious mien. *Wha-ACK!*

Yeong-Ja pegged Maira in the face with the same packet the sniper had just dodged. Maira's reflexes, it turned out, weren't quite so well honed. She laughed and rubbed her cheek before sticking her tongue out at both of them.

"Nyah. But yes," she said, serious again. "I promise you, Leo. I will think about every angle of this, whether I want to or not."

It had been three days since they sent the signal.

Brenda woke early that morning. First, she checked the bandage on her injured foot. It was healing pretty well, considering how nasty the wound had been. For one thing, that was a testament to Colin's skills as a medic. For another, the healing made it itch like crazy. She had to fight the urge to dig her nails into the new skin. That would have ended poorly.

She attached her prosthetic next. There was a risk, she supposed, to taking it off at night. If they had come under attack, being the one-legged wonder wasn't going to help their situation. Even so, she had to get quality sleep sometime, and her skin had to breathe. So she gave herself the nights after she did watch.

Once her feet were both as functional as they could be, she rose and geared up. Armor plates. Holsters. Grenades. The Honey Badger and her side arm. Brenda had been an operator long before the Division had recruited her, ever since her days in Marine Force Recon. All of these little tasks were so familiar to her they might as well have been a ritual. Each action had earned a comforting sense.

The others were starting to stir. Brenda was usually the first to wake, but being a deep sleeper was not a survival trait in this world. Once one of them was up and moving, everyone else wasn't far behind, just because there was no way to block out the feeling of insecurity. Colin had had the last watch shift the night previous. He saw her as she stepped out of the building and took a deep breath of the morning air. They exchanged small waves.

The unspoken question hung in the air. Brenda let it. This one time, what was the point of rushing? Let everyone get ready at their own pace. Let them make sludgy cups of instant coffee or mix processed orange-tasting powder into their canteens. One way or another, this was going to be a day of days. Better to start it with as much peace as possible.

At last, they all made their way out in front of the building. They stood in companionable silence for a last minute or two.

"Any signals?" Maira asked finally.

Colin looked down. That said all that needed to be said. By luck of the draw, he was the final bearer of bad news. For three days they had waited, their electronic ears peeled. Every day hoping against hope they'd get some kind of response. Some proof their cry for help hadn't gone completely ignored. And every single day they had been disappointed. There was only the silence, and the throb of the enemy base close by.

"What's the status of your protective firewall?" asked Brenda.

Maira turned her head, consulting something ISAC only

showed to her this time. Her lips pressed into a thin, grim line. "It won't survive another day. By this time tomorrow, no doubt they'll have gained access to the program."

"So it comes down to it in the end," said Yeong-Ja quietly.

Brenda nodded in remorse. "The only question left for us is this: do we fall back, knowing that we'll always be on the run after this? Or do we say damn the torpedoes, and try just the five of us?"

"One last time..." Maira started.

"No," Leo said flatly, cutting her off.

He stepped up to her and looked her dead in the eyes, then rested his hands on her shoulders.

"No," he repeated gently. "All or none."

Tears shone in the young woman's eyes. "I didn't ever want any of you to get hurt. I'm so sorry. But I can't walk away knowing it will all be my fault."

"There's your answer, then," Brenda said and swept her gaze over the group.

None of them looked their best. They were battered and bruised, lower on ammunition than they liked, with no clever technological tricks to fall back on. Nevertheless, at that moment, Brenda couldn't have been surer that she was looking at the fulfillment of everything the Division was supposed to be.

None of them were perfect, but none of them had an ounce of quit in them. They had seen the world crumble and fought every day since to keep the fire alive. To pass it on one more day, even as everything fell apart. And now when the only choices were to run and hide or die trying, none of them had flinched. She took a deep breath. There was a lump in her throat. She was getting soft in her old age. The thought made her chuckle.

"All right, agents. You hope a day like this will never come, but if it does, you hope to face it next to people like all of you. I am proud of all of you. So, one last time, gather your gear and ready yourselves. We fight to save what remains."

They stood straight-backed facing her. Yeong-Ja pulled Colin into an arm draped hug. Leo crossed his arms over his chest. Maira stepped forward and took Brenda's hand between both of hers.

"One last time," Maira repeated. "Extremis malis…"

"Extrema remedia," the rest of them chorused.

CHAPTER 15
August 29

"Excuse me! I'm hoping you wonderful people could help me out," Maira called.

She walked slowly down the broad street toward the central plaza. There was a stiff breeze this morning whistling through the city. It kicked up dust and little bits of paper and sent them tumbling along the cracked asphalt and crumbling cement. The skin between her shoulder blades itched, a bodily sensation indicating she felt painfully exposed.

That was the point, of course, but that didn't necessarily make it easier.

Maira wore her full kit, but it was arranged as nonthreateningly as possible. Her M1A was slung on her shoulder. The only thing she was actually carrying was a battered computer tablet. It had been white at one point early in its life. By now it was at best a grimy gray. The portable computer was held in her left hand, but she kept her right hand extended out in front of her, palm up, in the classic "please don't shoot me" gesture. She made no effort to hide the glowing red watch on her left wrist.

Up ahead of her the layered defenses of the Black Tusk base began. Surrounding buildings had been turned into security checkpoints. Barricades blocked the road. Soldiers in black combat gear were everywhere. Maira could count a dozen in plain sight out in the street. Who knew how many more were tucked into nearby strongpoints and makeshift bunkers?

Her appearance had kicked off a predictable flurry of activity among the Black Tusk troopers. For a solid second most of them just stared at her in surprise. A heartbeat later Maira was the focus of a rapidly growing quantity of lethal firepower. She found herself staring down the barrel of rifles, machine guns, and more.

"Who are you? What are you doing here?" demanded one of the closest of the troopers.

Maira put on her best winning smile. "I'm almost offended. I figured I merited at least an APB or something by this point. That's all right, though. My name's Maira Kanhai. If you don't know the name, you might want to run it up the chain."

They were wearing their customary balaclavas – those must get itchy and stifling in the heat of the day, Maira thought. Even so, she could read the consternation in their body language. Whatever they had been told to prepare for, it probably wasn't a lone woman with a beaten-up tablet. The spokesman turned and shouted something back to the rest that Maira didn't catch. A pair of warhound robots came trotting forward to join him. The creepy four-legged robots had the appearance of a hound, and their weapons raised up from their back and trained on her with mechanical precision. He came back around with his eyes narrowed.

"Keep your hands where we can see them!"

"Not a problem," Maira said amiably as she slowly continued to walk forward. She knew she was sweating. Hopefully they couldn't see that. "Do you want me to spell the name for you? People get it wrong all the time. Oh, man, and the mispronunciations! Don't get me started. Moira, Mara, Mira. Lovely names, but that's not me."

Who was this man up front? Was he just the unlucky sod who happened to be closest, or was he actually in charge of any of this? Maira wasn't sure, but she mumbled a quick note to ISAC, nonetheless.

"Tag him."

"Never heard of you," he said coldly.

"Well, that's disappointing, too," she admitted. "I'm pretty famous in certain circles."

"Stop where you are!" he demanded.

"Hey, of course. No problem. We're all friends here." Maira pulled up her approach. "Maybe this is one of those things where I'm better known for my works. You ever heard of a little ditty called the Countermeasure?"

"The what now?" he asked, perplexed.

"Oh, it's an old trick of mine at this point. But there's nothing wrong with the oldies, right? 'An oldy but a goody,' that's what my dad always said. And I've taken the time to bring this one up to date with all the latest bells and whistles." Maira unobtrusively shifted her grip on her tablet and tapped a control.

"What are you talking about?" he demanded, obviously annoyed. "Is there something wrong with you?"

"Honestly, I get that a lot. Often enough that there's probably something to it," Maira mused.

New data was piped into her augmented reality. It was the two robots closest to her first. They took on a ruby halo in her vision. It spread quickly from there. This was not a full network attack, of course. It was a much more localized effect. She couldn't risk bringing the whole thing down. But that didn't mean this couldn't be used to good effect.

"Even one of my good buddies told me recently I need therapy," Maira added. "Not that there's anything wrong with that. I'm a big supporter of people getting the help they need. Sometimes the world just doesn't make sense, and nobody should have to navigate that alone, right?"

The man paused, his head tilted. A radio comm, unless Maira missed her guess. The news of her arrival must have worked its way up the chain. Was that Nat herself, Maira wondered, shouting in this guy's ear? If it was, did it include any warnings?

"All right, on your knees, hands behind your head. I've got orders to bring you in."

Maira ignored him completely this time. "Hey, if you make it through this, remember what I said, OK? Nothing shameful about getting help. Because your world is going to stop making sense right about… now." She raised her voice. "Subvert."

"I said–"

The Black Tusk trooper didn't get a chance to repeat himself. As Maira had noticed previously, his faction had a love affair with drones and robots of all kinds. There must have been several dozen just within a block or two. Her passcode activated the second stage of the program she'd disseminated from her tablet. In a rippling wave the glowing blue lights on all those deadly machines flickered and went out. A heartbeat later they came back in red.

Within the space of a second, chaos came to this sector of the Black Tusk defenses. The sound of gunfire echoed in from every direction. Drones and robots turned on their masters. The two warhounds facing Maira whirled back toward the assembled troopers. There was no display of hesitation. Loyalty did not linger in a robot's CPU. New directives had been issued, and they were obeyed without question.

The Black Tusk spokesman turned back and forth in horrified surprise. "What the hell – you! How did you do this?" He brought his gun to bear on Maira.

"Same way I do everything," she said amiably. "With skill and aplomb, and a little help from my friends. Yeong-Ja?"

The spokesman's head dissolved into red mist. The sound of the shot echoed hot on the heels of the bullet's arrival. His body twisted to the side from the impact. The strings had already been cut. He spun to the ground, dead before he hit.

Maira broke into a run. She stowed her tablet as she went and brought her rifle around into her arms. Most of the Black Tusk soldiery were occupied battling their own rebellious mechanical servants. One of them noticed her coming and turned with eyes wide. Maira shot him as she ran, silencing him mid-shout. She slid in behind one of their barricades, putting her shoulder against it and keeping her head below the top.

"Now would be the time!" she said on the comms.

The street-turned-battlefield was already painfully loud, but the rattle and thunder of more guns joined the pandemonium. Preoccupied Black Tusk soldiers, turned to face their surprise internal threat, were cut down from the rear. Fire swept across them in controlled, precision bursts. Professional and deadly.

One of them began to bring an emplaced machine gun around to bear in Maira's direction again. She pulled a frag grenade from her harness and arced it up and over. The gunner didn't see it coming. They opened fire blithely, hosing down Maira's position. She crouched as bullets pinged and spanged off the reinforced metal of the barricade. The grenade clattered into the emplacement. The gunner just had time to look down. The gun nest dissolved into fire and shrapnel.

Maira vaulted her cover and advanced into the bedlam. The distraction was wearing off. Maira saw a red-lit drone sweep past, then suddenly tumble to the ground inanimate. Others followed suit. She glowered, but it was unsurprising. Black Tusk had their own tech-heads after all. They might not be able to just undo what she did, but they could shut down their subverted weaponry.

A pair of Black Tusks were headed toward her. Gunfire rang out. Maira fired off a wild burst to get them to duck, but she was forced to seek cover herself. She scrambled behind a parked APC, the angry hornet sound of passing bullets making her jaw clench.

Maira came around the other end of the vehicle to try to return fire, but they'd anticipated that move. A near miss blasted out a window and sprayed her face with glass. She dropped down with a repressed scream. Her eyes were squeezed shut, and she was afraid to open them. Terror pounded in her chest. Desperately sweeping hands came away with sharp bits and wetness.

Nearby gunfire echoed, and the suppressive fire pinning her stopped. The next second, as if by magic, someone friendly was there. She couldn't see him, but something about his gangly presence was unmistakable. Colin had her by the wrists, grip firm but gentle.

"Be cool, Maira! I've got you!"

Tepid water washed over her face in a flood. It smelled like the inside of a canteen. Startled, Maira inhaled and coughed.

"How bad is it?" she asked. "How bad?"

"You're OK," Colin said soothingly. "Open your eyes. Your eyes are fine."

Maira blinked them open. Colin's concerned face swam into view. She forced herself to take a deep breath and nodded to him.

"Thank you. I just..."

"I know," he said. "No sweat. You're good. Your face is a little cut up, but you'll heal."

He turned his head at the sound of an explosion. As if that were the signal, the greater sounds of the battle poured back into her senses. It still raged in all directions, unchecked mayhem. She shook her head vigorously, scattering water droplets.

"All right. Help me up. Let's get back into it," Maira said.

"That's the way," Colin said.

He rose partway and pulled her back to her feet, dusting her off. Maira picked her rifle up and leaned out to get a look. If any of the rebellious robots remained, they couldn't be seen. Instead, Leo and Brenda were both committed to the fight. Leo stood in the lee of a building, trading fire with a squad trying to advance up an alley. Brenda knelt behind a barricade, popping up every few seconds to take pot shots at bunkered Black Tusk soldiers closer to the base.

As Maira watched, Brenda hurled a grenade with the pinpoint accuracy that was her trademark. The explosive zipped straight through the fire slot on a reinforced checkpoint. Geysers of fire and smoke vented through every opening. No more hostile fire came from that location.

"Yeong-Ja, you there?" asked Maira.

"Angel on your shoulder, always," came the reply.

"You and Colin help Brenda. I'm going to try to help Leo."

"Got it," Yeong-Ja replied.

Colin nodded. "Good luck."

Maira set off at a sprint across the street. It had only been minutes since things had touched off, but this stretch of road was already littered with corpses and burning wreckage. The wind burned in Maira's cuts as she ran. A shut down warhound stood in her path. She leapt up and caromed off him, hitting the ground still running.

"Leo, keep their attention on you!" Maira said on the comms.

"Will do," was the simple response.

Maira could hear his sporadic fire become more concentrated. He'd burn through ammo supplies faster that way, but it would definitely focus the enemy on his position. She resolved to make the most of the opportunity, sprinting down a side alley parallel to the one he was trying to hold. Debris crunched underfoot as she hurtled along.

If this goes wrong… some part of her pointed out. *It won't,* she reassured herself. *I just have to be fast.*

Maira completed the maneuver, turning the corner on an L shape. It brought her in along the side of the cluster of Black Tusk soldiers that Leo was trying to hold his own against. He'd done his part perfectly – not one of them was watching in case they were outflanked.

Maira skidded to a halt and dropped to one knee. Her rifle braced against her shoulder, she unleashed a deadly enfilade of fire into the Black Tusk rank. The first two died without even knowing what killed them. Her bullets tore them to the ground, and she was on to the third. That one was a woman, who turned in surprise at the butchery of her comrades, just to let her meet the bullet with her name on it. The last two turned to face her, guns strobing with return fire.

Maira gritted her teeth and held her ground. A precision burst caught the fourth in the groin, hip, and stomach. Blood sprayed and they fell clutching at themselves. The action on her rifle locked open with a click. Magazine expended. She ejected it. It fell to the ground in what felt like slow motion.

Her last mag was on her harness. Maira's hand felt three times its usual size, swollen and numb. She grasped for it, fumbled. It slipped through sweaty fingers once. The last Black Tusk soldier had her dead to rights. All he had to do was calm down enough for a controlled shot and she was dead. They both knew it. Even at this distance, she could see the triumph in his eyes.

A bullet took him in the side of the head. He had forgotten the original threat in his haste to meet the new one Maira posed. The triumph was gone from those eyes, and so was all the light. His body hit the ground, which was already slick with the blood of his comrades. Maira reloaded her gun and rose. She jogged toward the fallen hostiles, pausing only to retrieve her spent magazine on the way.

"Goddamn, Leo. That was a hell of a shot," Maira said.

"I was aiming for his arm," admitted the other Division agent.

Maira barked a laugh at that. Surely one of these guys had the right ammunition. Sure enough, there were the same rounds her rifle was chambered for. She pulled their magazine and ejected the bullets into her hand. A quick scan of the battlefield made sure she still had time to reload hers. Once that was done, she tucked the mag back into her pouch on her harness.

Leo had already departed to help the others. Maira loped along in his wake. Weariness tugged at her. Fighting like this ate into the body's reserves quickly. She shoved the feeling aside. They weren't even halfway to the enemy facility. Things would get harder before–

Bullets shattered concrete as she started to emerge back into the main road, driving her down and away out of self-preservation. She glanced out and cursed. When she'd left, Brenda had been dealing with a few hardpoints. Now those same places were joined by ten more Black Tusk soldiers fresh to the fight.

The grown volume of fire was forcing the rest of the cell to keep their heads down. At least her arrival was forcing the hostiles to divide their attention more, Maira thought. She fired hasty pot shots in opportunistic retaliation. If any of them hit home she couldn't tell; however, the range and the pressure made it unlikely.

"Bad news," Yeong-Ja said in her ear.

"No, thank you," Maira grated.

"What's up?" Brenda asked.

"More Tuskies on the way… must be twenty headed specifically for your location. I've got another ten of them headed for the alleys again to try to flank you, too."

The sheer weight of numbers the enemy was able to bring to bear tugged at Maira's heart with despair. If this had been the limit, then maybe. Unfortunately, they all knew this was only the beginning. The longer the fight went on, the more people Black Tusk could bring down on them. Their advantage would only grow as the Division agents became exhausted from continuous fighting.

"Maira, you're the only one in the alleys right now. Can you disengage and pivot to fight the flankers?" asked Brenda.

"You got it," Maira said.

Frustrated, she gave up on her back and forth with the main line of Black Tusk defenses. Retreating back up the alley she maneuvered quietly and carefully to figure out where the hostile detachment was. By luck, she spotted them first; they were moving low and tactical themselves, clearly eager to get in a position where they could hit the Division agents in the side and turn this back in their favor.

Maira got their attention by gunning down their vanguard. Spent brass skittered off down the alley with each shot she squeezed off. With pinpoint accuracy the frontmost Black Tusk soldier took a bullet through their side. They fell writhing and clutching at their chest, still alive but obviously in hideous agony. Two punctured lungs, unless Maira missed her guess. A bad way to go.

The second took the bullet through the side of their knee. The leg folded instantly, and their momentum carried them forward and tumbling. Her element of surprise was spent. The attention of the rest of them came down like a hammer. Bullets pinged and popped all around her as she yanked back behind a concealing wall. Plaster rained from above as bullets went straight through thin spots.

Maira took that as her cue and fled further up the alley. A grenade pinged around the corner after her, and the place she'd been standing dissolved into smoke and fire. Narrowly escaping being turned to raspberry jelly, the blast still hit Maira in the back like a bowling ball. She landed on her stomach, coughing and wheezing.

The world had gone silent except for a painful ringing. There was no time to worry about that. Maira levered herself over onto her back with the butt of her gun. The first of the troopers came around the corner after her. They were looking for someone standing and missed her for a half second. That was enough to put a bullet through their throat.

They collapsed, clutching at the wound. Arterial spray washed down their front and hit Maira's boots. The void of sound made the whole thing an awful pantomime. Maira wrenched her gaze away, trying to scramble back to her feet. She was only on her knees when the second one came on. She dropped her M1A and lunged for their weapon instead.

Maira found herself eye to eye with the Black Tusk trooper as they wrestled for control of the weapon. Their eyes were wild, frightened. She spat into them and followed it up with a headbutt that sent the trooper reeling. Maira used the chance to grab at the grenades on her foe's harness. She pulled the pins on all of them and kicked the man backward into the street beyond.

She fled.

The detonations behind her covered her escape. Those eyes lingered in her mind. Human. She shoved it away.

Another log on the fire, another scar on the soul. It didn't matter anymore. What mattered was seeing this through to the end.

She dodged into a doorway alcove and pulled up, breathing hard. A glance down revealed she was covered in plaster dust and pulverized building. Blood spatters had turned it into a hideous paste in places. She grimaced and shook her head hard, touching her ear. There was blood there, too. Hers? If her eardrums had burst, then...

"Maira!"

No. The ringing was receding, and her hearing was coming back, just a little.

"I'm here," she managed. It was like she was hearing herself underwater, and she could still tell she sounded like the creature from the Black Lagoon. "ISAC, give me subtitles."

"Thank god!" It was Brenda. The AI spelled that out for her in orange letters. "We lost contact with you."

"Yeah. Hard fighting, sorry. I couldn't stop them. There's just too many. Had to retreat."

"Common feeling. We'd give ground, but..."

"When we tried, I got shot in the back," Colin interjected.

"Are you OK?" Maira asked.

"Fractured rib, maybe. Plate held, but it hurts to breathe," the medic said.

"It's going to get worse," Yeong-Ja said. "Another full company of Black Tusk soldiers are moving up in support of their push. I'm also seeing four birds taking off."

"Transports?" asked Leo.

"No, it looks like they're configured for CAS," Yeong-Ja said.

Close Air Support, Maira translated mentally. She leaned her head back against the door behind her. They would be coming with rocket pods, miniguns, air-to-ground missiles. It was the feeling of a fly watching a person grab a swatter. They had no good counter. Yeong-Ja had lost her TAC-50 anti-matériel rifle, and even if…

She squeezed her eyes shut for a second and forced herself to take a few deep breaths. The only thing that really forced her to open them again was knowing the remaining flankers were out there somewhere, with more following behind. Her hearing still wasn't quite there, but she thought she heard boots on debris approaching.

"Taking this all a bit personally, aren't they?" Maira said.

"Does seem like an overreaction," Yeong-Ja replied.

"We knew what we were getting into," Brenda said.

No one could say anything to that for a few minutes. It was true. They had known what their words would be this morning before they set out. They were saying goodbye. They had kicked the anthill knowing full well what the consequences would be. All that was left was to play it out to the bitter end.

"Let's give them something to remember," Maira said.

"Give 'em hell, agents," Brenda agreed.

Maira flexed her fingers around her rifle. On three, she told herself, and come out shooting.

"Helicopters are beginning their attack run now," Yeong-Ja reported.

Maira could hear that, even now. More than that, she could feel it. It was like an avalanche coming down the mountain. It was a tornado shredding its way down the street toward your house. The rumble came up through her boots and shook her whole body to jelly. Dust rained. It was like the finger of God coming down to wipe her off the chalkboard of life.

A different sound. An explosion, yes, but of a different timbre.

"What the–" Yeong-Ja said.

Maira saw a helicopter come down. It was partly obscured from her vantage point, but also hard to miss. It slammed down into the main street nearby, a blur of screaming metal. That impact shook the buildings around her, too, and Maira dropped to one knee, startled.

"What the hell?" she demanded on the radio.

Someone shouted, a Black Tusk trooper just nearby. Maira stepped out instantly. It was a woman, and she was right there, fifteen feet away. She stared at the destroyed heli open-mouthed, shocked. Maira shot her with her stolen gun.

"AA missiles! I'm getting AA missiles from somewhere!" Yeong-Ja reported with clear astonishment.

"So, is this a private party or what?"

The voice was familiar. The name that ISAC provided was not. Ryan Vall? Still, that voice… but it was impossible. There was simply no way. Maira stood in the dusty street with her own mouth hanging open now.

"Dixie?"

"You're goddamn right!" the truck driver replied. "And I brought a couple of friends. I hope you don't mind."

Maira sprinted out toward the main street. Was this some kind of nervous breakdown? Was she coming unglued from reality? But new vibrations under her feet certainly felt familiar. This time, they felt good. Because if she was right, what it meant was...

She burst from the alleys in time to see them coming. Semitrucks, militarized. Equipped with guns and armor for battle. It wasn't just one, either. There must have been a dozen of them that she could see. They came tearing up the road toward where the battle was happening. The vanguard were equipped with heavy-duty plow blades, and they didn't give a damn if old rusty cars got in their way. They were smashed aside like so much trash.

The Black Tusk barricades did nothing to slow them down either. Brakes only howled as they closed in on the battle, and mounted guns opened up. Maira stared as mortars, cannons, machine guns, and more opened fire. Black Tusk hardpoints and bunkers vanished under a wave of explosions.

The lead truck showed no sense of self-preservation. It careened on into the heart of the fighting and turned, a lumbering behemoth forced to dance. For a second, Maira was sure it couldn't take the physics of its own maneuver and would tip over. It righted itself at the last second, placing the trailer between the Black Tusk soldiers and Maira's pinned down cell.

"Don't you worry, daddy's got ya," Dixie Dog said. And

if he was suppressing terror in his voice, well, Maira could overlook that completely.

She ran forward to where the others were coming out of cover. Their expressions of pure astonishment told Maira exactly what her face must look like. The passenger side of the truck slammed open, and a man scrambled out carrying a shotgun. He was the picture of physical mediocrity, from his bald man's baseball cap to his beginnings of a beer gut. Maira didn't even slow down as she ran to him and threw her arms around his neck.

"Dixie! My god, my god, you beautiful bastard!"

He grinned at her. "Maira! Hell, you are a sight for…" He pulled back and looked her over, wincing. "Well, if I'm honest, you kind of look like the slasher from a horror movie right now. But we thought you were dead, hon! I can't believe you're here in the flesh."

"It's her all right," Brenda confirmed as she limped up. "If I told you we had to go into hell to snatch her back, would you believe me?"

Dixie chuckled. "I'd call that just another day for the Division. But I'm pretty sure hell is up ahead, and that's what we're here to do something about."

"We couldn't be happier to see you," said Colin. "But the defenses only get heavier from here. I'm not sure your trucks can punch in much further without getting chewed to bits. They're big targets."

"That is a problem we foresaw," Dixie agreed. "That's why we didn't come alone."

The truck driver touched a comms headset in his ear.

"Forward position is secured, the agents are alive. Unload the cargo."

Cargo? Maira turned her head in surprise. Sure enough, the trailers further back were opening up. People came spilling out. Ten, fifty, a hundred, more. It was an astonishing collection of fighters. They came in two main groups, as far as Maira could tell. One set wore all black. They didn't actually look all that different from the people Maira had spent the morning fighting, except that their cut had a distinctly more military vibe. The others were dressed in simple homespun clothes mixed incongruously with combat apparel.

Once more, Maira saw what was in front of her, but her brain was left yammering to catch up like a dog chasing the mailman's truck. It wasn't until two particular people approached through the gathering forces that everything really clicked into place.

"May I present Colonel Marcus Georgio and Guardian Raffiel Fourte?" Dixie said.

The colonel snapped off a crisp salute in greeting, which Maira returned reflexively. Raffiel tipped his head graciously.

"Agent Kanhai. I see the rumors of your death were greatly exaggerated."

Leo stepped forward. He swept his gaze over Raffiel. "New title?"

Raffiel smiled slightly. "I liked this one better than the old one."

Leo nodded. "It's better."

They embraced, firmly, slapping each other's backs.

Maira grinned. The brothers' renewed connection was one of the kindest things she'd seen come from the chaos of the last few years. The fact that she'd been able to play any part in bringing it about was a fact she was always going to be grateful for. She turned her attention to the colonel.

"The Molossi and the Reborn taking the field together?"

"The Reborn volunteered first. In fact, they got in touch with us while we were still putting together our own response," Dixie noted dryly.

Colonel Georgio cleared his throat with a clear flicker of irritation. "It was merely a matter of ensuring our other security commitments would still be met and discerning what forces we could spare. I had no intention of letting the Reborn mishandle this little skirmish. We're here to make sure it's done right."

"Well, we're glad you came," Maira said wholeheartedly.

"I told you from the beginning, Agent Kanhai, the Molossi are dedicated to the security of this region. Anyone who threatens that will learn to regret it. Black Tusk appears unaware of that fact. We're here to set them straight."

"What are we dealing with?" asked Raffiel, approaching with his brother in tow.

"Regimental strength oppositions. Hovercraft. Military aircraft. Emplaced defenses and fortifications," Brenda listed off.

Raffiel nodded. "We will move to engage the Black Tusk infantry immediately."

Maira reached out and caught him by the shoulder. "These people…"

The Reborn leader made eye contact with her, and his face softened slightly. "Are volunteers trained and equipped to fight. You will find that not everything is as you left it, Agent Kanhai."

Maira nodded and let him go with a smile. "I'm glad to hear it. And I'm so glad to see you again."

"As for their various other accoutrements," Colonel Georgio said. "I am providing something more than a half-trained rabble. We brought Stinger missiles for their birds, as you already may have noticed…"

"Much appreciated," Maira said. She glanced at the smoldering wreckage of the dropped helicopter nearby.

"And for their fixed defenses, I've brought an answer for that, too."

It growled into view. A low shape of angled armor on treads. A mighty barrel preceded it, swiveling back and forth slowly on the integral turret. It was painted in Molossi black and silver, abandoning any pretense of stealth for the impact of its presence. Maira stared. Leo stepped forward, cleared his throat.

"Excuse me," Leo began. "Is that…?"

"An M1A1 Abrams Main Battle Tank? Why yes, yes, it is," Colonel Georgio said smugly. "Fuel provided by the Roughnecks and transport to the battlefield contributed by our Freighty friends, of course."

The gathered infantry were separating off into squads and fireteams and moving to engage. Maira could hear the contact they made with the Black Tusk, a rising din from the direction of the base. It was like the groaning of a dam as pressure slowly increased. If Maira had never expected this, neither had their foes.

"They'll swivel, commit everything, as the scale of the threat becomes clear," Brenda said. "This is an impressive showing, but they're far from done. This is going to get ugly."

"Leave this side of things to us," Raffiel said. "It will fall to you and your team to use the distraction we provide and infiltrate their facility. This technological advantage you warned us of? We have come together to stop it, but the deed itself falls to you. We will help however we can."

Georgio nodded and turned his head toward the tank. He lifted a handheld radio. "Captain? I am told there are emplaced defenses between us and the Black Tusk facility."

"Yes, sir."

"I want them gone."

"Acknowledged."

"We have a chance now," Maira said, so overwhelmed her voice seemed bled of emotion even in her own ears. She thought she was going to go out in a blaze of glory but ten minutes ago, and now a shred of hope meant maybe she might just get to see more sunrises. "I can't believe it. We could actually do this."

"I just wish we had a few drones to provide us with intel on the approach," Yeong-Ja noted. "My vantage point is great and all, but I have to come down to join you."

"Perhaps we could assist with that," a new voice said on the comms.

"Rogue agent detected," ISAC reported.

Maira blinked. "What?"

Dixie Dog winced. "Yeah. There was... one more thing. One more group who showed up to offer help. Rather unexpectedly, I admit, but this kinda felt like a 'beggars can't be choosers' situation if I'm honest."

Maira saw them now. Her back straightened in response. She saw the reaction in her cellmates too, a rising tension. They came down the street at an arrogant saunter, that casual rolling walk that made Maira's teeth itch. Somehow, they all seemed to have that down pat. It was like they got together to practice it in their off time.

There were four of them. Each was dressed differently, if all under the same basic umbrella of rugged outdoor wear. They were heavily armed, carrying rifles, shotguns, sidearms, and more. That wasn't the most interesting part, of course. No, ISAC had warned them, but the truth was still surprising to see. They each wore the same watch and brick as the Division agents, but instead of orange all four glowed the same ruby red as Maira's own.

The one in the lead wore mirror shades and an insouciant grin. "Hey, everyone. Name's Gold. Here today to help out, just like the rest of these people. Pleasure's all yours, I'm sure."

Brenda's jaw was clenched so tight Maira was worried she was going to start splintering teeth. "You're rogues."

"You're observant," Gold replied.

"Why, exactly, do we not draw down on you here and now, and make the world a better place?"

"What, you have a problem working with rogue agents?" he asked with a pretense of wounded feelings. He motioned to Maira. "Doesn't seem that way."

Brenda took a step forward, prosthetic clicking against the ground. "I have a problem, very specifically, with Keener's merry band of terrorists. Which you are a part of."

His grin only widened. "Then it will please you to learn that most of my compatriots aren't happy I'm here. 'Fuck them' was the consensus, I believe, along with a hearty spoonful of 'let them kill each other off.' But me? I'm a softy." His grin faded. "And in all honesty, if this is about what I think it is? I'll be damned if I let them get a leg over us that way."

"What do you think is happening?" Maira asked uneasily.

He turned his gaze on her. It was impossible to read behind the sunglasses. "Well, you're involved. The woman who stopped Rowan and David both. And not only that, word is you hacked ANNA. You know, there are a lot of my friends who would love to talk to you about how you managed that."

"They're welcome to come and find me," Maira said coldly. "It's funny, the ones who do never seem to come around for a second chat."

"You've definitely got the fire everyone talks about. That's good. We'll probably need that today. Putting a stop to what you created, hm?"

Brenda glowered. "We still haven't agreed to work with you at all."

"Are you going to turn us away?" Gold asked. "Like your friend said, beggars can't be choosers, Agent Wells. You need people who can keep pace with your group, and help you get inside that building. Besides, I brought toys, and I'm OK with sharing."

He motioned, and one of his comrades released a drone

that hovered forward and between them. Maira had to admit, it was nice to imagine having more SHD tech available for use. She'd blown through her own supplies trying to catch the Hunter in a trap, and she knew Brenda and the others didn't have much with them either.

"This is a bad idea," Leo said darkly.

"Say the word and we're gone," Gold said with a shrug.

"No," Maira spoke up. Everyone turned to look at her. "They're right. We need help. If they want to bleed and die with us to see my mistakes undone, so be it. I'll swallow my pride today. It's on me."

Brenda nodded slowly. "All right then. But we'll be watching you, asshole."

"Fine by me," Gold said. The rest of his cell gathered closer around him. "Make sure to watch extra close. I'm always happy to show you good little boys and girls how to get results."

The Abrams spoke as if to punctuate the point. The cannon's thunder washed over the group and sent everyone there stumbling a step away. Something in the distance detonated massively. An entire building sagged and caved in on itself in a gray rain and a spreading cloud of dust.

"Well, like you said, Brenda, we're operating on borrowed time. The longer we give them, the more forces BT is going to bring to this fight." Maira took a deep breath. "Let's not waste the sacrifice our allies are making. Let's get in there and get the job done."

CHAPTER 16

August 29

Brenda stepped forward to take point as the group of Division agents, loyal and rogue alike, moved toward the plaza and the Black Tusk facility situated there. There was no hiding the fact that the presence of the rogues made her skin crawl. She also had no illusion that she had failed Rowan O'Shea. The agent had been one of the most promising recruits she had ever seen, and Brenda's guidance and lies had set her down the wrong path.

Even so, it was Keener's faction who had taken her dangerous abilities to the next level. Brenda had wounded Rowan, but the rogues had weaponized her. They had taken her pain and turned it into a gun to hold against the Division's head. They had encouraged the worst in her, and so destroyed any chance of Rowan finding redemption. That was something Brenda could never forgive.

She did her best to force the matter out of her mind. The

here and now demanded all her attention. For one thing, this was her chance to do better by Maira. For another, they were in an active warzone, and a lapse of attention was liable to get her killed. She gritted her teeth and checked the Honey Badger one last time to make sure it was fully loaded.

Warzone was no exaggeration. The arrival of the allied forces had turned pest control into a pitched battle. All around them, squads of Reborn and Molossi engaged their Black Tusk counterparts in desperate firefights. Great clouds of acrid smoke flooded the streets, both from discharged weapons and burning buildings. The screams of the wounded echoed from the walls.

A pair of helicopters thrummed past overhead. Brenda and the others dodged into the shadow of nearby buildings to avoid their attention. Luckily, they seemed to have a target already. They disappeared beyond the rooftops in the direction of the allied bridgehead. Explosions resounded in that direction. Neither helicopter returned. Successful or not, they had not survived their assault.

Thunder clapped. A shell screamed overhead into the depths of the Black Tusk defenses. Its detonation shook the ground beneath their feet. That was no mere mortar. It was the gun of the main battle tank that the Molossi had brought. Brenda wondered how long they could keep it moving, much less firing. Depleted uranium shells and jet fuel did not grow on trees.

Someone advanced out of the smoke. They were wearing a uniform much like the rest of the Black Tusk, only the negative image: all white instead of all black. The obscuring smog left Brenda and her foe surprised.

"Contact, contact!" shouted the Black Tusk soldier.

They raised their weapons at the same time. Brenda's burst of fire neatly clustered on the hostile's chest. Their return shot went wide; she heard it hiss past. The trooper staggered but did not fall. Brenda didn't give them time to recover. She crossed the gap between them in an instant. A closing burst as she ran blew out their knee. They fell to the ground, and she shot them in the back of the head, the shattered bricks now blood-soaked.

More of them emerged from the smoke, shouting battle cries as they came. Brenda pulled a flashbang and hurled it into the midst of their advance. The stun grenade caught several of them midstride.

"I'm blind! I'm blind!" one screamed as they staggered away.

Brenda cut them down with another burst of fire. That center mass armor was impressive, she noted. She targeted extremities instead. A few rounds to the arm or leg could still take a lot of fight out of someone and leave them vulnerable to a killing shot. She kneecapped another of the Black Tusk defenders, then shot them where they lay. It was brutal, but she had to ensure victory. Anyone left might put her cell and their allies in danger.

The rest of the Division agents were getting involved. Unfortunately, Brenda's attacks had already drawn attention. She retreated into a nearby building to escape a hail of return fire. Her flight took her headlong into one of their number using the building to flank. They crashed into each other and reeled away.

The White Tusk carried an automatic shotgun. Brenda knew she couldn't afford to let them bring that to bear in the tight confines. She sidestepped the first blast, the thunder in the confined space like a spike in her ear. From there she lunged and pushed the soldier back into the wall. They hit hard enough that plaster crumbled down in a dusty rain.

"Looks like it's just you and me," the hostile snarled.

"No," Brenda gritted out.

They wouldn't give up their hold on the shotgun, so Brenda used her leverage to smash them back against the wall. One, two, three times in rapid succession. They were dizzied, off balance. She pulled a knife and jammed it straight up through the base of their jaw. A vile crunching sound announced the catastrophic damage the blade had done to them. Their eyes were empty as they slid to the ground.

"It's just me," Brenda finished. She switched to her comms. "Status?"

"Broke them," Leo said. "They're all dead or what's left of them have scattered."

"Last Man Battalion," snarled Colin with raw contempt. Such disgust was rare coming from him.

Brenda raised an eyebrow. "You know them?"

"Yeah. They were murderers and slavers who decided murdering and enslavement wasn't bad enough. So, when things went bad for them, they threw their lot in with Black Tusk just to be thorough."

"Murderers?" Gold laughed as he approached. He exchanged an amused look with his rogue comrades. "That's precious. How many people have you killed, agent?"

"I only kill if I have to," Colin said coldly.

"That's what everyone tells themselves," Gold replied.

Brenda paused to wrench her knife free from the corpse and wiped the blade on her pants leg. "Shut it, Gold. No one is here to listen to your mouth."

"No, of course. You brought us along to help you kill people. It's just you do it for all the right reasons."

"I..." Colin started.

"Enough," Maira snapped. "This isn't helping. Push on. The only interesting thing here is that it proves Yeong-Ja was right."

"I usually am," said Yeong-Ja benignly. "How in particular this time, though?"

"They were pulling in troops from all over to guard this place. Even their resources aren't infinite – they're really bleeding to try to hold this site," Maira said.

"Proof of the value Natalya places on the program," Brenda said. "Let's make sure she doesn't get what she wants. Come on."

They pressed on. Within minutes they were within reach of the tower. This area was desolate. The artillery that the various groups in the allied force had brought had swept what remained of the city center with fire multiple times now. Most of the Black Tusk troops were moving into the thick of the fighting anyway, leaving relatively few to hang back and guard the tower. Despite the desolation around it, the tower seemed to pierce the bright sky and loomed above them all.

"Two on the door," Gold said, consulting the feed of one of the recon drones he had released and announcing it to the cell.

"Yeong-Ja, would you be so kind?" Maira asked.

"Sure," the sniper answered.

She jogged up a nearby pile of rubble and then crouched on top. She was practically lying flat against the shattered bricks and splintered wood. There was a breathless pause, and then the first shot rang out. A second followed fast on its heels. With a rushing clatter Yeong-Ja came skidding back down the debris heap.

"One and two," she said steadily.

"Huh," Gold said, sounding interested and a little awed. "She's right, they're both dead. You looking for work?"

"Not in a million years," Yeong-Ja said. "But don't worry. I'm sure I'll see you again when this is all over."

The rogue grinned broadly. "I like her."

Maira had hurried on ahead of the group to the door. Brenda jogged to catch up with her. By the time she got there, the hacker had her tablet out and was frowning at the door controls. She tapped away at the little computer screen.

"Everything all right?"

"Yeah, it's peachy," Maira muttered. "They changed the passcode. I might wish they were slightly more complacent. All the same..." She hit one more control and the door into the building slid open. "It all ends the same."

"Hold up," Gold said from behind the two of them. "Got something interesting."

"What do you want?" Brenda asked, not bothering to try to sound friendly.

"Stow the hostility, you'll want to hear this." He tapped his watch. "Here, I'll let you see."

The drone feed slid into their AR vision as well. Brenda studied it. The little machine was doing a quick orbit of the skyscraper they were about to go into. Most of it looked as expected; it was a hotel converted into the base of operations of a militant group. At the top, however, there was a small helipad with a single vehicle parked. A white helicopter.

"The White Tusk transport?" asked Brenda.

"No," Maira said. She sounded shaken. "This is a personal craft. I only ever saw one person use it."

"Sounds like a high value target," Gold commented.

"You could say that," Maira whispered.

"Is it who I think it is?" asked Brenda.

Maira nodded unhappily. "It's Natalya. She must be here."

"Wait," Gold said. "Natalya Sokolova? The leader of Black Tusk? The person in charge of their entire operation? She's here?"

"You've obviously heard of her," Brenda commented dryly.

"We keep tabs on them just like you do. That's beyond a high value target. Some intel estimates think she's the glue that holds this thing together. You take out Sokolova, you might be setting her entire army on the course to dissolve."

"I'd believe it," Maira said. "She has a certain force of personality. You have to meet her to really understand, I think."

Brenda rested a comforting hand on the younger woman's shoulder. Maira flashed her a grateful smile. She wasn't sure exactly what had happened between her protege and the Black Tusk leader, but she could tell Maira was still working it all out in her head. People could be dizzyingly complicated.

"This changes everything," said one of the other rogues next to Gold.

"I'm sorry, I didn't get your name," Brenda said drily.

"You can call me Brave," he replied flatly.

Brenda rubbed her face and shook her head. "You people and your code names. This isn't a spy movie."

"The easiest way to understand who hasn't caught on to the situation is to take note of who thinks nothing shady is going on," rejoined Brave.

"Please stop," Maira said exasperatedly. "Why does this change anything? We're here now, for Pete's sake. I can take you straight to where we need to go to complete this mission. I need direct access to their servers."

"You're talking about taking one toy out of Black Tusk's toy box," Gold observed. "We're talking about putting them completely out of business."

"Nice mixed metaphor," Yeong-Ja said in a snide tone.

"We came here to destroy the program," said Brenda. "We do that, then we can worry about trying to capture Sokolova."

"That's stupid," Gold said with exasperation. "You said yourselves the only reason they're even putting up this fight is to try to keep whatever stupid thing you should never have created. What's going to happen when it's gone? You really think she's going to hang around? She'll be gone within a minute. We have to get her now."

"ISAC, firewall status," Maira said quietly. Her gaze focused on the middle distance before returning. "We can't. This is coming down to the minute. You try to snatch her, she slips away, they'll get the program, too. That can't be allowed to happen."

"There are nine of us," Colin observed.

"Another display of remarkable observational skills from our ISAC-loving friends," said Gold.

Colin snorted. "My point is, we got here with almost twice as many agents as we thought we would." He paused. "Well, for a certain value of agent."

"So?" asked Leo.

"So, we split up. Half of us go destroy the program, half of us go bring Natalya in. Even if she gets away, we'll keep the code out of her hands. And if we can take out both, all the better."

"We're going after Sokolova," Gold said firmly. "You can do whatever you want."

"You're not getting out of my sight," Brenda said. "Leo, Colin, Yeong-Ja, please go with Maira and make sure she gets the chance she needs to finish her task."

"You're not going with these assholes alone," Maira said with a frown.

"Hurtful," remarked Gold.

"I'll go with her," Yeong-Ja said. "Can you boys take care of Maira?"

Colin smiled. "She won't get a scratch on her."

Leo just stepped next to Maira as his answer.

"There we go," Gold said. "See? We resolved it so amicably. Everyone is one big happy family."

"Either of them have so much as a hair out of place because of you," Colin said pleasantly, "and I'll cut your liver out and feed it to you."

Gold locked eyes with the medic and seemed about to make another sardonic remark. It died on his lips. He frowned instead and stepped back. "I'm pretty sure he meant that."

"Never doubt it," Colin said flatly. "C'mon, Maira. Let's get this done before it's too late."

"Right," Maira said.

They all went inside. It looked like nothing more than a standard hotel lobby, perhaps a fancy one. Perhaps the most unusual thing was that the lights were on. Brenda tried to remember the last time she'd seen electric lighting. Had it been all the way back at the Kansas Core? Surely not, but she couldn't think of a more recent time.

"Take the elevator," Maira said. "It'll get you to the penthouse. If Nat is anywhere, that's where she'll be. We'll take the stairs down."

"Be careful, Maira. We'll see you on the other side," Brenda said and clasped hands with her friend briefly.

Maira held on to her for a second longer. "Please… take

her alive if you can. Don't risk anyone, but... just if you can."

Brenda nodded. "Of course. Be safe."

She piled into the elevator with Yeong-Ja and the group of rogue agents. There was a single button for the penthouse itself. Brenda hit it and they started off. She kept her eyes forward and tried to calm her breathing. Today had already been quite a day. She had to admit, Gold had a point about the value of this unexpected opportunity. It would make this all worthwhile if they could put the nail in Black Tusk's coffin here and now.

"I..." Gold started.

"Better to be silent and thought a fool," Yeong-Ja remarked, "than to open one's mouth and remove all doubt."

One of the other rogues snickered. Gold glared at him, and he gave an embarrassed shrug.

Brenda's HUD flickered. She frowned. "Hey, anyone–"

"Unknown network detected," the AI warned.

Maira hurried down the stairs with Leo and Colin falling in behind her. She took it two or three steps at a time. In the corner of her vision the readout on the firewall protecting her project was still there. It frayed by the second. Any moment now Black Tusk would break through, decrypt her work, and be able to move it somewhere she'd never find it again. They could disseminate a thousand copies at that point, if they chose to. There would be no way to unspill that milk.

Her thoughts distracted her at the wrong moment. She came around the last of the staircases and ended up face to face with a gun barrel. It stared her down like a black eye. Maira blinked and looked past it and her surprise only grew. She felt the motion of Leo raising his own weapon and shook her head.

"Wait."

"Hello, Maira," Keith said unhappily.

The weapon he held was nothing but a handgun, if a powerful one. It would still kill Maira stone cold dead if he shot her in the face with it. His hands visibly shook. He's not a soldier, not a killer, she thought. He's a physical therapist, for Pete's sake. What is this?

"Keith, what are you doing?" Maira asked gently.

"Flex," Keith corrected automatically. "She said you'd be coming. She said I had to stop you, or else."

Maira didn't have to ask who. She could tell by the fear in Keith's voice. She wondered about that. Most of the people here gave the impression of adoring their dear leader. But then she remembered the pilot manning the aircraft during the attack on the Texas Core. A woman who would rather go for her sidearm and risk certain death than face Natalya with failure. What had given Keith a glimpse of the cruel ice beneath her winning mask of a personality?

"Just because she says something doesn't mean you have to do it," Maira said gently. "You can just walk away."

"No, I can't," he whispered. Tears filled his eyes. "You don't understand. The people who don't do what she wants? They just vanish. You never hear from them again.

Didn't you wonder what happened to your doctor after he saved you? Why you only saw me after that?"

"I suppose I figured his part was done, and I was in your capable hands."

Keith shook his head violently. The gun shifted aim for a second. Maira almost lunged for it, but she held herself back. "She told us the plan to drug you. He refused. Said he'd taken an oath to do no harm, and that he wasn't about to break that for her. The next day, he was gone. Just gone. And she told me to do it instead. To make sure it happened."

"So that's how that came to pass," Maira said sadly.

"I…" He lifted one hand from the gun to wipe at his face. "I'm sorry. I didn't want to. I hated it. I kept hoping she'd change her mind. But I don't want to die. I don't want to disappear."

"Look, Keith—"

"Flex."

"No, Keith," Maira said with emphasis. "I don't want you to die either. And I'm going to be a hundred percent honest with you. You pull that trigger right now and shoot me, and one of these two guys with me is going to kill you. That is one way to guarantee you don't live through this."

Keith shivered at that. He looked like he just wanted to burst into tears and curl up on the ground. It was incongruous on such a massive slab of muscle, but Maira understood completely.

"I don't know what to do," he whispered.

"You walk away, that's what you do. Lower that gun.

Go up the stairs to the ground floor and walk out. Find the nearest unit of Molossi or Reborn, and you surrender to them. You have useful skills that anyone in this world will see the value in. Leave this place and start a new life. Please."

Keith stood shaking, his trembling finger on the trigger. He's going to shoot me by accident, Maira thought. Just another tragic absurdity in a cruel world. Then he nodded, and slowly the weapon came down. Maira reached forward and took it from his hands. He didn't resist.

"Thank you," he said. "And I'm sorry. I really am."

"Good luck, Keith. Remember what I said." Maira tried to smile. "Now hurry."

The physical therapist nodded and fled up the stairs. Colin reached forward and squeezed Maira's shoulder.

"That was well handled."

"It makes me wonder how many of her soldiers feel trapped, too. No good choices, just the ones she gives them. Brainwashed and absolutely terrified. Maybe it's only a few, but I'm sorry to kill any of them who wish they could be anywhere but here," Maira said tiredly. "I wish we could just talk to them."

"The program," Leo reminded her.

"Right," Maira said. Time was running out. The best way she could help those people was to make sure Natalya didn't destroy the world.

They hurried on farther down into the facility. There was no armed resistance. Black Tusk really must have diverted everything they had to fighting the invading force. Any of the technicians and workers they saw fled in haste. Maira couldn't help but wonder what they knew about Division agents. How much propaganda had they been fed, painting her and those like her as bloodthirsty monsters?

At last, they reached the server farm she'd been seeking. This was really only a part of the overall Black Tusk network, of course. Merely the local storage so to speak. But it was the part that contained all her work. For a moment she eyed it all and considered simply destroying it. An EMP grenade launched into the middle of the room would have done the trick. But for fear of unknown consequences, she followed her original plan instead.

The tablet came out and she connected it directly to one of the servers. It was a simple matter to find her work amongst the many files. She had worked here for months, and she knew her way around their systems like the back of her hand. It was a sixteen-digit hexadecimal code to access the files behind her firewall. That was burned into her head. She entered it.

There it all was. Her creation. More successful than she'd ever dreamed of. A weapon composed of ones and zeros that would change the balance of power in this new post-Green Poison world permanently. In a sense it didn't matter who used it, because the moment someone did everything would change.

She looked to Leo at her side. She had promised him she would consider every angle before destroying it. And in truth, part of her was reluctant. She had worked hard on this. It was the product of manipulation and mistreatment, but it was also the product of her labor and her mind. How many hours had she pored over it, refining it? Now she was effectively one click from burning all that hard work away to nothing.

But if she didn't, even if she just took it with her, this would never end. It was true what she'd said that night, that they could never be sure what side effects the deletion would have. Consequences would spiral in ways she never imagined. That was the nature of them. But as long as the program existed, it was also a target. Everywhere she carried it with her, it would be a crosshair on the back of her head. And she would never be able to trust anyone else to take care of it in her stead.

Maira assumed her most dramatic maestro stance, the position of a great master about to play a concerto that would change lives. Then with a small smile on her face she hit a single key.

In this case, delete.

A little countdown clock appeared. Within seconds, the files were gone. With a few more keystrokes, Maira unleashed a cleaning program just to be sure, to scrub it down to nothing. No one would be able to retrieve this work, or piece it back together from the scraps.

It was gone for good.

"I'm sorry," she said, turning to Leo.

"Don't be." He shook his head and gave her a small smile. "I trust your judgment."

"Let's get out of here," Colin said.

Maira nodded and they turned to walk out. She queued her comms. "Brenda, what's your situation?"

There was no response. Not so much as a burst of static. The three Division agents exchanged surprised looks. Maira's brow furrowed with concern.

"ISAC, what's the status on Agent Wells?"

"No status record on Agent Wells," the AI replied.

The concern deepened sharply into fear. "What's her location?"

"No location record for Agent Wells," ISAC said.

"What the hell does that mean?" Colin said with a frown.

"It can only mean one thing," Maira said. She could see the same conclusion dawning in the eyes of the others. "Someone has cut them off from ISAC completely."

And they had only encountered one person who could do that.

The trio sprinted for the stairs. They had to get to the penthouse before it was too late.

The elevator door opened on the penthouse. The lights were on here, too. Brenda emerged into it cautiously with her weapon held ready. The rest of the agents flowed after her, spreading out into the surrounding rooms of the suite to search for threats. ISAC continued to flicker unsteadily, as if ready to crash at any second. Brenda watched that nervously. She was afraid she knew what it meant.

Then, the hotel lights went out all at once, plunging them into instant darkness broken only by the sunlight cascading from the windows.

"ANNA?" said Gold. He touched his earpiece. "ANNA, what's wrong with you?"

A scream. It was cut short within an instant of starting. One of the rogues came tumbling around the corner into view. A giant gouge had been taken out of their chest. That was all the confirmation Brenda needed. She snatched out her earpiece.

"What the hell–" Gold said with real alarm and no sarcasm.

The dark figure stepped around the corner in the wake of that first corpse. Blood dripped from the silvered ax in its hand.

The Hunter.

The wraith was worse for wear than the first time Brenda had seen them. The armor and gear were melted and scorched. Even the mask seemed deformed now, the decorations and watches burnt to a black nothing.

"She's not even here, asshole," Brenda said, relieved Maira was as far from this monster as possible. "And the moment she realizes you're around? She's gone. She's in the wind. You'll never catch her."

The Hunter pointed directly at her. That was it. No words. Then, they took a step forward.

With a battle cry howl, the rogue agent Brave didn't wait. He opened fire, shotgun spitting a storm of shots at the Hunter in an automatic flood. Brenda darted to the side as the Hunter's own shotgun came out and around. If any of the blasts Brave launched even stung them, it didn't react. Instead, the Hunter returned fire with surgical accuracy.

The rogue fell away with his face reduced to a flayed ruin, all blood and stripped skull.

As if that was the signal, everyone else opened fire. Rounds ricocheted from the Hunter's armor with alarming frequency. Brenda couldn't help but wonder where such wearable technology had come from. The network hacking, the armor, the weaponry, the training. Whoever this thing was, wherever they came from, someone had spared no expense in turning them into the ultimate killer. The perfect means to kill agents.

The Hunter swept the third rogue's leg from beneath them. The ax came away in a bloody gush. The rogue fell screaming and tried to crawl away. Gold hit the Hunter with the butt of his weapon, which then spiraled out of his hands when one of the hits went wrong. Desperate and needing something, Gold reached to grab anything he could find and proceeded to hammer the Hunter in the back with a chair, trying to draw its attention from his wounded comrade. The wraith came around with a bladed backhand. Gold spun away into the penthouse's incorporated bar, trailing blood. Glasses and bottles shattered on impact, and he was lost to view.

"R-rogue agents d-d-down," ISAC blurted.

Yeong-Ja had been aiming carefully the entire time, standing back from the chaos. "Go to hell, you monster," she said coldly and squeezed the trigger.

Her rifle barked, and the Hunter's head snapped back. It turned out it felt pain after all, because it let loose a distorted howl. One hand was clapped to its face over the left eye hole. Even wounded, its presence of mind was sufficient to reward Yeong-Ja for her efforts with a series of blasts from its shotgun. She fell down, her rifle tumbling from her hands.

"W-warning," ISAC glitched out. "Agent d-down. Assistance r-required."

Brenda emptied the Honey Badger's full magazine into the foe. The Hunter staggered under the onslaught, and its hand fell from the mask. Blood dribbled from a hole where its eyes had been. The edge of the mask's eyehole must have taken the brunt of the shot, or the bullet would be loose in its skull right now. Yeong-Ja, that was a hell of a shot, Brenda thought. You tried.

She threw the Honey Badger off to the side, completely out of bullets. Brenda drew her sidearm with one hand and her knife with the other. She spread her arms challengingly.

"Come on. Let's find all the places that make you bleed."

The Hunter studied her briefly, then threw aside its own shotgun. It raised the ax in its other hand and motioned to her. Brenda took a deep breath.

The door on the elevator pinged open. Brenda and the Hunter turned at the same time as Maira burst into the room.

"Brenda!" yelled Maira.

The Hunter's primary target had arrived. It lunged toward her, ax-blade raised. Time seemed to slow. Brenda saw that blood-drenched razor tip. Maira was only just recognizing the danger she was in. Her head turned from the elder agent to her foe. Her mouth fell open. There was no way she was going to get out of there in time.

Maira, who had been through so much, and deserved to see a better world.

Brenda threw herself forward with all her might.

Maira burst into the penthouse without hesitation. The lights were out. The whole area stank like a charnel pit. Her worst fears surged to the fore.

"Brenda!" Maira called.

A thud. Maira turned. There was a flash in the semi-darkness. Maira's eyes were only just adjusting. It was a shadow a head or more taller than her, and the gleam of metal held high above it. The ax, some part of her whispered into a mind howling with fear. She was too slow.

Something slammed into her and pushed her into the wall. She hit hard enough that drywall caved in behind her back. Maira found herself eye to eye with Brenda, the elder agent holding her against the wall at arm's reach. She had tackled Maira out of the way.

There was a meaty thud, and Brenda's eyes went wide. She fell into Maira's chest, and blood gushed from her mouth.

The ax protruded from her back.

"No!" Maira screamed. "Brenda, no!"

The elder agent slid toward the floor. Maira struggled to hold her up, but she was too heavy. All she could do was slow her descent. Her hands grabbed desperately at Maira's harness, at her shirt.

"No, no, no," Maira repeated.

"Agent d-d-down," stuttered ISAC. "Imm-mm-mmediate medical attention re-required."

Someone blurred past her in the semi-darkness. Colin. The Hunter had lost their ax. He seized the moment by grappling with them full force. Together, the two of them stumbled back and forth, trying to get the advantage on each other. Colin was roughly the same height, but the Hunter was stronger. They slammed the medic's back into the bar, sliding him along fragments of shattered glass.

Leo came in from the rear and leaped onto the Hunter's back. He had his arms around their enemy's neck in a flash. The Hunter staggered backward and slammed the smaller agent into a column. There was a sound of cracking wood. Leo's expression never changed. He just hung on for dear life, digging his grip in as tight as he could.

"Hang on," Maira begged Brenda, easing her to the ground. "Please hold on. I have to help them. Hold on."

She scrambled to her feet and lunged to join the fight. There was a broken chair nearby. Maira grabbed one of the splintered legs. It had been left with a jagged point. She put her weight behind it and slammed it forward. It speared into the Hunter's midsection with a wet squelch. A mechanical screech emerged, like something from a horror movie.

The Hunter booted her with a lash of a powerful leg. She hit the wall and bounced off. Her head rang as she fell to the floor. Her body had already been through a great deal of abuse, and it begged her now to just stay down. She snarled and spat aside at that idea. Her legs back under her, she grabbed the makeshift stake again. If this thing didn't want to die the easy way, she'd kill them like a goddamn vampire.

Leo was still hanging on like grim death, despite the bludgeoning punishment the Hunter was dispensing for his stubbornness. With a robotic groan the bulky assassin fell to one knee. It shook its head dizzily. The hold was telling.

Colin was back on his feet. He pulled his Ka-Bar with a growl. Maira saw his intention and let the stake drop from her hands. Instead, she darted forward to be next to Leo and pulled the Hunter's head back with all her strength. There was blood all over the mask. The Hunter stank of blood and burned skin, of sweat and fear. She refused to let her hold slip.

Colin took one step forward on shaky legs and swept the knife across its exposed throat, deep enough that the blade could be heard scraping against bone.

Blood sprayed. The Hunter thrashed viciously one more time. Battered, Leo finally came loose and tumbled away toward the windows. Maira was flung in the other direction, smashing into the side of a couch. She slid to the ground with a grunt. With a desperate wheeze the Hunter tried to rise. Colin stood his ground, eyes blazing defiance, knife in hand.

The Hunter froze. Slowly it sank back to the ground. Its legs slid out from under it, and it hit the blood-soaked carpet with a wet thud.

"Brenda," coughed Maira.

She reached up and grabbed hold of the arm of the couch to lever herself back to her feet. Her legs carried her unsteadily to Brenda's side before she collapsed. She ended up kneeling next to the other woman.

Brenda's eyes rolled to look at Maira. She was still alive. She tried to smile. It showed red-stained teeth in the shadowy darkness. Maira stifled a sob and grabbed her hand.

"Colin, do something! Please! Please!"

The medic stood over her. His hands hung limply at his side. Maira looked up at him and saw his face. The expression tore at her.

"No! No, please, Colin! Help her!"

The tears came now, hot and bitter, flooding down her cheeks. She pressed Brenda's bloody hand to her cheek. The wounded woman spread her fingers and touched Maira's face ever so gently. Almost a caress. Colin sank to his knees on Brenda's other side and got something from his kit.

"Here we go, hon. Nothing like a little Circle K to take the edge off, huh?"

Brenda gave him a thankful nod and inhaled the nasal mist. Her pupils dilated, and she turned her gaze back to Maira. With the painkiller helping her, she managed to speak, if barely. It came out with bubbles of blood. In ghastly unison Maira could hear them popping in the wound in her back as well.

"You're OK... So glad you're OK."

"You're going to be OK, too," Maira said.

There was no reassurance in the words. To the contrary,

it came out as her begging, and she knew it. She lowered her head, pressing her forehead to Brenda's. The elder woman's skin was colder than it should have been, clammy to the touch.

"Maira," Brenda said. Each word clearly hurt, a struggle to get out. "Do... better... than... I..."

She was gone. The light in her eyes faded. Maira kept holding onto her hand, desperate for something. Anything. A returned grip. A flash of that old Brenda smile. Instead, there was nothing.

Maira pressed her cheek to the cold hand once more and wept.

"They're retreating," Leo said. "The Black Tusk troops are evacuating the region."

He was watching through the penthouse windows. The other four Division agents sat in various stages of disarray. Colin was treating Yeong-Ja's injuries. Her armor had taken the bulk of the shot, thankfully. According to Colin, some had only missed Yeong-Ja's carotid by millimeters. She was lucky to be alive.

"Someone must have done the cost-benefit analysis and realized this place wasn't worth dying for anymore," commented Colin sardonically.

Maira stood suddenly. She had sat numb since Brenda passed, lost in her own misery. Now anger surged hot in her chest. She strode over to the dead Hunter and booted the body in the side to flip the corpse over.

"C'mon, you bastard. Let's see your face. I'm gonna make

you famous. You're going down in history right next to Judas and Benedict Arnold."

She grabbed the mask and yanked. It was attached pretty firmly. Maira didn't care. She put everything she had into it and the mask eventually popped and came away.

Maira didn't know what she had expected to see, but the relatively ordinary face of a man of Asian descent was not it. She stared down. There were burn scars on his face. Her inferno must have inflicted those. Unwillingly she reached up to touch her own marks.

"I don't know who this is," she admitted wearily.

"Identification confirmed: Agent Thaddeus Greene," ISAC remarked.

Everyone in the room turned and looked.

"What?" Maira said. "ISAC, double check that identification."

"Identification confirmed: Agent Thaddeus Greene. Status: Classified."

"Thaddeus…" Leo said, coming over to her. There was a dark expression on his face. "He was at the Texas Core when you and Black Tusk attacked. Brenda mentioned it. Said he tried to insist she not come after you."

"The Hunter is a Division agent?" Maira said disbelievingly. Her hand gripped the mask tightly.

"This one certainly appears to be," said Colin.

"Not just any agent," noted Yeong-Ja. "I've heard of Thaddeus Greene. He's one of the senior agents. The first recruits. The one who helped put the whole organization together. You know, like…"

Like Brenda, she didn't say.

"He recruited people?" Maira asked. "What does that mean? Was he working for Black Tusk? Or if he was a Hunter, and he was an agent, and he was involved in selecting new agents, I mean…"

"It could mean nothing. A lone gunman situation," offered Colin. He sounded desperate to believe his own words.

"Or it could mean the rot goes deep," replied Leo.

Maira slowly sank into a seat on the couch. She held the burned mask in her hands and slowly turned it over. She felt stunned.

"Anyone we know. Anyone we interact with. Anyone we count on to watch our back. They could all secretly be…"

"One of them," Yeong-Ja finished for her.

Maira took a deep breath. "We're going to have to be very careful from now on. This opens a whole new can of worms. We can't trust anyone."

"We can trust each other," Leo said firmly.

Maira looked up. The weight of it all receded just a tiny bit. It wasn't much, but sometimes even a little relief could be everything. She managed an exhausted smile.

"We can trust each other."

Leo came over and sat across from her. "It's good to have you back, Maira."

"It's good to be back," Maira said.

She swept her gaze over the little group. Just four people now, but four people she would trust to the end of the world and back. A family in a world where few were lucky enough to have anything of the sort.

"There's a storm on the horizon," Maira continued. "I can feel it. Black Tusk, these Hunters... it all adds up to something, and it's going to be a problem. But no matter what happens, I know this with absolute faith.

"Come what may, we'll face it together."

EPILOGUE

August 29

Natalya Sokolova sat on board the private jet.

In one hand, she held a glass of champagne. A crate sat beside her, surprisingly utilitarian appearing in the luxury surroundings. She looked out the window. The clouds drifted along below them. At this height, people were invisible. They weren't even ants. They were microbes. They were nothing.

"You must be disappointed," Calvin McManus said.

The Secretary of Homeland Security sat across from her. He straightened his watch, a habitual gesture.

"Why ever would I be disappointed?" asked Natalya mildly.

"You suffered quite the defeat in New Mexico. Your project was destroyed. Many of your soldiers are dead. You even had to abandon the base there, to my understanding. I've never known you to like losing."

Natalya smiled and gestured with her champagne. "Just

one base, Cal. Just one project. There are others. Oh, for certain, it could have been a cheaper experiment. But all the same, the results were very gratifying. In the end, it is a trade I am more than happy to have made."

"Is that so?" Secretary McManus asked skeptically.

"It's a surety. Oh, and I do have one small correction for your assessment of the situation."

McManus raised an eyebrow. "Do tell. What did I get wrong?"

"You have no idea what I'd do if I lost, Cal, because you've never seen it happen."

The Secretary narrowed his eyes. She could almost read his thoughts. What delusion, he was thinking. She got her ass handed to her and has nothing to show for it, and she just can't deal with that fact.

Natalya smiled and traced her fingernails across the crate beside her. Inside was a mobile SHD server. Not just any one of them, either. This one had been captured months ago, and put to a very important use. In fact, it had been the subject of the first test of Maira Kanhai's particularly devastating little code package.

An older form, certainly. Cruder, in need of refinement. And it was a pity Maira would not handle that part herself. She had a certain pleasant wit. Natalya had found her company almost bearable. She sipped her champagne. It was going to be a particular pity when she would have to watch Maira be dragged out into the street and shot like a dog.

At any rate, what mattered now was she had the

foundation. The work would continue. Perhaps not as quickly, perhaps not as smoothly, but the program would be finished. In the end, she would get what she wanted. In the end, no matter how this world struggled and fretted, she was going to save it from itself.

Natalya Sokolova never lost.

ACKNOWLEDGMENTS

Lauren, your attention to detail makes me sharper, and your grand writing accomplishments always inspire me. Thank you for letting me play in your world.

Gwendolyn, you have been the best editor I could have asked for. Beyond "just" making my writing better, you have been the picture of grace, patience, and kindness. Thank you for everything.

ABOUT THE AUTHOR

THOMAS PARROTT is what happens when a witch accidentally turns a frog into a prince, instead. When not uncomfortably trying to rule the swamp, he plays a lot of games and even writes, sometimes. He is accompanied by his dark and terrible familiar, Kitiara the Cat, who is the real charm, brains, and muscle of the operation. He is the author of *Tom Clancy's The Division: Operation: Crossroads* trilogy, along with a variety of short stories across many universes.

ASSASSIN'S CREED

THE WAR BETWEEN ASSASSINS AND TEMPLARS WREAKS HAVOC IN THE VICTORIAN ERA, IN NEW ADVENTURES FROM ASSASSIN'S CREED®.

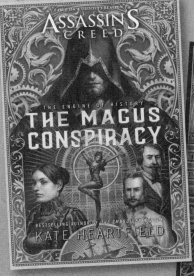

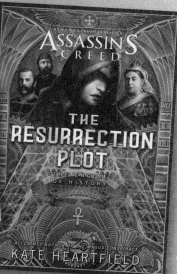

UBISOFT

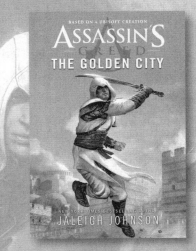